BLUE MOON

By Marilinne Cooper

CHAPTER ONE

"Hey, didn't I used to know you back in college?"

Sarah glanced up from the payroll time sheets she had been studying and looked around the room. Other than two elderly women sharing a pitcher of dry martinis in front of the fireplace, there was no one else the stranger could be addressing.

"I'm sorry. Were you talking to me?"

"You look familiar. I'm guessing that you probably went to the college twenty years ago. Am I right?"

The man had swiveled around on his bar stool to look at her more closely. Sarah had been too busy to pay much attention to him when he came into the inn. The bartender had called in sick at the last minute and there was no one else available to fill in. She had absentmindedly given the newcomer an imported beer and gone back to her bookkeeping.

Now she was very aware of the intense gaze of his pale blue eyes. Like most of the local patrons of the West Jordan Inn, he was dressed in clean but faded blue jeans and a plaid flannel shirt. His curly blond hair was cropped close to his head; his red beard was full and bushy in a neatly trimmed way. Still, there was something different about him that she could not put her finger on.

"What college?" she asked politely, not really interested in conversation but feeling it was her duty as innkeeper.

"How many colleges could there be around here?" He laughed. "Carlisle College, of course."

"Oh, you mean the old, uh, alternative school over in Carlisle that closed down back in the seventies? Sorry, that was before my time. I didn't live around here then." Sarah had heard innumerable wild stories of what life had been like during the "golden years" of the hippy college and how it was too bad she had missed out. She was not really in the mood to hear any more this evening.

"Hell, I figured anyone of our vintage who still lives in this neck of the woods in the 1990s must have gone to Carlisle at one time or another." He took another sip of his beer.

"I'm not sure I'm quite of your 'vintage'." It was hard to tell his age, but Sarah guessed he was in his early forties. "Most of the folks I've met who went to Carlisle are a bit older than me."

"So what are they doing with the old place now? Boy, it was quite a lay–out, all those chandeliers and mirrors and fireplaces left over from when it was a grand hotel... You ever been in the building?"

"No, actually it burned down about ten years ago. From what I've heard, you wouldn't recognize Carlisle now. Nearly all those abandoned grand hotels have caught fire or been torn down. It's kind of depressing." Sarah resumed her temporary station behind the bar again. The outside door swung open to let in two couples who were young enough to be carded before she could serve them. She left the Carlisle alumnus alone with his drink for a few minutes and let him contemplate the fate of his old alma mater.

"What a waste," he commented when she returned to her seat. She noticed that half of his beer was already gone. "There was so much fabulous turn–of–the–century architecture in that town. But it still must be pretty, with the lake there and the mountains."

She nodded her agreement. It was not a remark that required an answer.

Through a western window, a shaft of sunlight suddenly fell across the polished wood of the bar, temporarily blinding the stranger. Sarah got up and adjusted the shade to the appropriate level for a sunny evening in early May.

6

"Actually, I'm supposed to be meeting an old friend from the college here tonight. Someone I haven't seen in close to twenty years." Sarah noticed now that the fingers clutching his beer were quite tanned.

At the other end of the bar, one of the girls from the pair of young couples turned to stare at him in disbelief. Twenty years was nearly her whole life.

"Really? That's a long time." Sarah's lips tightened and her cheeks flushed as she tried not to laugh at the younger woman's reaction.

"Yeah, she's flying in from Hawaii, if you can imagine that."

Sarah smiled. From Hawaii to a small village in northern Vermont was a stretch for the imagination. "In mud season, no less. You should have gone there instead."

"Well, she sent me a letter that said she was coming up here and that she needed to meet with me about something." He upended his beer and then pushed the empty glass across the bar, indicating that he wanted another. "Can't imagine it's too urgent if it's waited twenty years. But I thought, what the hell. I only live about forty–five minutes from here. Something different to do for an evening."

"Why here? I mean, why are you meeting in West Jordan instead of Carlisle?" Sarah's large gray eyes searched his face and he knew his story had caught her interest now. She leaned towards him, resting her chin on her unusually long, almost aristocratic fingers; the other hand absentmindedly stroked the end of the sleek black braid that kept her waist–length hair away from a strikingly angular face.

"Oh, we used to hang out here all the time back then. Everybody liked the homey atmosphere with the fireplace and all. And the guy who ran this place was a cool, long–haired dude named Woody. Who owns the place now?"

Sarah laughed loudly. "Oh, a cool, long–haired dude named Woody." She stretched her graceful yet muscular arms above her head and stood up, displaying for a brief

7

second just how well–proportioned and toned the rest of her slim body was.

"You're kidding me! Woody still owns this place? Is he around?" His eyes darted quickly right and left, as though he were expecting Woody to appear.

"No, he's on a sort of permanent honeymoon. Spends part of the year in the Caribbean with his girlfriend and lives the rest of the time at her place down in Emporia. I just keep the place running for him." A group of hefty-looking men came through the door and Sarah tucked her ledgers away on a shelf behind the bar. It was going to be too busy to get any bookwork done for the next few hours.

"Is that right?" He shook his head and peered down the mouth of his beer bottle as though it held the answers to life's mysteries. "Some guys just have all the luck."

Sarah grimaced. "Not really. Woody had a bad bout with cancer a couple of years ago. He's okay now, but he's paid his dues. He deserves the life he's living." She looked up at the clock over the bar. "What time is your friend expected?"

"About fifteen minutes ago. I hope she shows. I've been looking forward to this all week." He slouched back on his stool.

Before Sarah could respond, a pair of regular customers entered the bar carrying on a loud, animated conversation. Red Higgins and Jake Morelli had frequented the West Jordan Inn on their way home from work long before Sarah had come into the picture. She pulled a couple of draft Budweisers and slid them across the bar.

"What's all the excitement, guys?" she asked.

"Oh, old Kerm Robichaux hit a moose over on the Dillard Road. We was coming the other way, first to come upon the scene. Old Kerm's okay, but his car is totaled. And the moose is a mess."

Out of the corner of her eye, she saw the Carlisle College alumnus getting ready to depart. "Giving up on her?"

8

"Well, I thought I'd like to run over and check out the remains of the old campus before the sun goes down. If my friend shows up while I'm gone, tell her I'll be back by sunset. My name's Reed Anderson, by the way. And hers is Mimi..." He pulled an envelope out of his shirt pocket and checked the return address. "Mimi Farrell is her married name. And you are...?"

"Sarah Scupper. Be careful going over the back road this time of year. It can be pretty mucky after all the snow melts off the mountain."

He grinned. "I've got four–wheel drive, I'll be okay. Will you still be serving dinner when I get back?"

"Sure." As he headed for the door, she called after him. "Hey! What's she look like?"

He shrugged. "After twenty years? Hell, if I know."

It was nearly dark when Reed Anderson returned. It had been a fairly quiet night, but that was to be expected in the first week of May. A few couples were eating by candlelight in the cozy dining room and the bar patrons had been replaced by others. Billie Holiday was softly singing the blues over the sound system.

Reed looked at Sarah expectantly but she shook her head. "You sure you got the date right?" she asked.

He consulted the letter in his shirt pocket again. "This is the fifth, isn't it? Damn, I was hoping she'd show."

"So how did you find Carlisle after all these years?" Sarah put a place setting and a menu in front of him.

"Kind of sad and different. Still beautiful though. The lake brought back lots of memories. You know, late night swims with my crazy girlfriend and wild boat parties, stuff I hadn't thought about in ages."

A high pitched bleeping noise went off a few seats away and a short dark–haired man stood up, apologizing as he turned off the beeper on his belt. "Mind if I use the phone?" he asked Sarah.

"Volunteer fireman," she explained to Reed as she let the fellow behind the bar.

His call took only a few seconds. "Centennial House over in Carlisle's on fire. Run me a tab, Sarah. I'll pay you tomorrow."

"No problem," she assured him as he flew out the door.

"The Centennial House! That's the place right next to the old college grounds. But I just drove by there a little while ago!" Reed protested. "It wasn't on fire then."

"Well, let's hope it hasn't progressed very far and they can stop it. It's a shame to see all those elegant old wooden buildings disappear. Seems like one burns down every few years now."

"Always a mystery too," spoke up a woman at the other end of the bar. "They never seem to catch whoever sets the fires. It's either some slick arsonist or the police don't try very hard."

Reed shook his head. "Back in college we thought the police in Carlisle always knew when to look the other way. Maybe they were just really never looking at all."

"My grandfather used to be the groundskeeper at the Centennial," an older man volunteered. "That was back in the twenties. During Prohibition. He had a whole repertoire of great stories about bootleggers and ballroom dances and..."

The increased excitement in the room was making everybody talk a little louder and drink a little faster. Sarah expected she wouldn't be getting to bed early tonight. But by eleven o'clock the place had cleared out except for Reed, who had definitely had more than his fair share of liquor. He alternated between periods of morose silence and long–winded monologues of how things used to be back when. He was in no condition to drive and Sarah knew that, as bartender and manager, she was responsible if anything happened.

"I hate to say it, but my life has settled into a rather predictable routine the last few years." Reed obviously had no intentions of leaving just yet.

"Why do you hate to say it?" She probably shouldn't encourage him but she could hear him out for a little while longer while she broke down the bar.

"Well, I know it might be hard to believe, but I used to run with a lot of wild and crazy, artsy types when I was younger. I'm always curious to see how they turned out twenty years later or whether I'm the only one who settled down into a ho–hum, workaday existence."

His words touched a sore spot in Sarah and, as she put away the juices and the garnishes, she thought about her own world. Her life had been a series of predictable routines that were broken on a regular basis by Tyler Mackenzie, an unpredictable investigative journalist from New York. Tyler's existence was never the same from one day to the next. He was always following his instincts and interests and stirring up trouble with his timely discoveries. Sometimes it seemed to Sarah that she was just a mooring for his boat; as soon as the wind changed, he sailed away again.

More than once she'd called their relationship off and gone in search of something more stable and secure. And more than once she had to swallow her pride and give in to the fact that there was no one else she felt as much passion for, or who made her feel as special as Tyler did. It had been at least two months since she'd last seen him. He'd taken off for Burma, or Myanmar as he had reminded her it was now called, to do a story on the turbulent government there. Each time he left for the scene of an earthquake or an uprising, she tried to make herself believe she didn't care about him so that she didn't worry herself sick. It was hard to be the one left behind for weeks at a time with only an occasional postcard for consolation. Just thinking about it made her anger begin to surface again.

"Are you okay?"

Sarah blinked. "Yes, I'm fine." She realized she had been staring into space for the last few minutes. "So what's so bad about having a stable, boring existence? At least your wife and kids know when you'll be home for dinner."

"Don't have a wife. Don't have any kids. That I know of, anyway. I share a hundred and fifty year old farmhouse with another guy. We bought it fifteen years ago with the idealistic notion that we'd be self–sufficient farmers. Now we're two old bachelors who work as carpenters just to keep the tax collector from breaking down the door." He finished the last of his beer and then smacked the empty bottle down on the bar just a little too loudly with a hand that was decidedly unsteady.

"You know, you're welcome to spend the night here if you'd rather drive back in the morning." She tried the soft approach, hoping she wouldn't have to advance to anything trickier.

Reed raised an eyebrow at her provocatively and she realized he had misinterpreted her invitation. To her surprise, she felt her cheeks grow crimson. Perhaps it was because, earlier in the evening, when he had not been so drunk, she had felt a stirring of physical attraction for him. She had dismissed it for what it was – physical attraction. She was old enough to know better. But with Tyler gone for months at a time, it was hard not to get, well, just plain horny.

She turned away abruptly, her long black braid whiplashing over her shoulder, and began to scrub down the bar. "I mean, we have three guest rooms upstairs. They're not much but it's the only show in town."

"Oh, damn. And I thought I was getting a personal invitation to come upstairs with the lady of the house." He grinned. "Well, actually I was planning to crash in the back of my truck. You don't have to be so polite about it. I know I'm in no shape to drive. But a bed sounds much nicer if it's not too expensive."

"It's not." Sarah could sense his eyes were following her body as she broke down the bar. She tried not to think about how tight her black leggings must look as she bent over to scoop some loose change off the floor.

"I've been admiring that stained glass over the bar." Reed changed the subject smoothly. "I'd forgotten what a work of art it is."

"Thanks. My mother did it actually, back in the early fifties. It was payment for an outstanding dinner check. It was the main reason I started working here." Sarah stopped for a moment to gaze lovingly at the long–legged night herons walking in tall grass that Winnie Scupper had crafted so long ago.

"Is that right? I thought you weren't from around here."

"My mother died when I was three months old. After that I lived with my grandmother in White Plains, New York, until I was out of high school. But since I was born here," Sarah affected a Vermont accent, "I guess I can say I'm a native."

"Hell, I've lived in Vermont over twenty years and I'll never be considered a native."

When Sarah was finished cleaning up, they sat in front of the dying fire for another hour or so, chatting idly. It was after one when Sarah finally showed him up to his room.

"Come down to the kitchen for coffee in the morning. If I'm not around, just help yourself. The pot will be on."She left him quickly, trying not to admit to herself that she was subconsciously counting how many weeks it had been since she had shared her bed with anyone but the cat.

"Looks like a good one, doesn't it?"

Sarah was sitting in the porch swing on the sunny side of the long, wraparound porch of the inn, drinking her morning coffee and thinking about cleaning up the perennial gardens, when Reed made his appearance.

"Good morning. I see you found the coffee. There's some muffins too if you'd like."

"Thanks. So what are you up to this fine morning?"

"Some early spring gardening, I think. Are you taking right off?"

Reed sat down next to her on the swing and took another sip of his coffee before answering. "On the

13

contrary, actually. I figure as long as I'm still here I might as well spend the day checking out my old favorite haunts, look up a few people. Maybe come back and take you out to dinner." He looked at her sideways. "If you're free."

Sarah smiled. "It could probably be arranged."

"After all, who knows when I may get back over here? I only live forty miles away but it might as well be four thousand for how often I head in this direction." He relaxed back against the wooden slats. "I'm putting off starting a job but, hey – life is short, you only live once, and a dozen other cliché expressions."

When he left a half hour later, Sarah found that she was looking forward to his return. He seemed a bit eccentric and slightly too talkative, but she hadn't met anybody who was perfect in a long time.

Ever, she corrected herself as she headed out to the old barn where the gardening tools were kept. She'd better make sure Peter, the bartender, was coming in to work tonight and Clive, the cook, had no thoughts of taking the night off. It was a rare occasion that she got to have any social life of her own.

As she worked the dirt around the plants, her mind even strayed to what she might wear.

What began as a cozy dinner for two in a quiet country inn was not destined to end that way. The restaurant they picked was not so different from the West Jordan Inn, but that didn't matter to Sarah. At least it was someplace other than home.

As the waitress brought the menus, Reed was describing how the smoking ruins of the Centennial had looked when he'd driven by that morning.

"They managed to save about half of it but I'm sure they'll probably end up taking it down. Nobody could get anywhere near the place, there were police cars and fire trucks around it all day."

"Are you guys talking about the body they found over in the Centennial fire? Not very pleasant dinner conversation, but pretty big news for around here."

"Body?" Sarah looked up. "What body?"

"You mean you haven't heard?" The young waitress's cheeks turned rosy as she held their rapt attention. "They found somebody in the hotel this morning, but they're not saying who it is until the family is informed."

Sarah shivered. "That gives me the creeps. Nobody's ever died in any of these fires before. I wonder what the person was doing there."

"Have you heard how it started?" Reed asked.

"Somebody said a stray cigarette butt but that might just be a rumor." She pulled out her pad, as though enough had been said. "Would you like a drink before you eat?"

"Probably some homeless tramp spending the night. He'll be sorry he fell asleep smoking in bed, so to speak." Reed shook his head at his own grim joke and straightened his silverware with a nervous gesture Sarah had not seen before.

"I'll have a margarita," she said loudly, in an attempt to close the subject. "No salt."

"They're saying it was a woman."

"A woman? Really? Well, there are plenty of homeless women smokers too. I'll have a Bourbon on the rocks."

"Well, that certainly adds another wrinkle to the story," Sarah commented when they were alone. "I bet there's a lot more to it that nobody's hearing about." Tyler would be fascinated by the hotel fires in Carlisle, she thought, and then hated herself for thinking of him right now.

"Did I tell you how beautiful you look with your hair down?"

Not only a steady homebody, but a charmer.

"Thanks. It's a pain in the butt, though. Always getting in the way. I haven't had it this long in years and I've almost had enough of it."

"Well, don't cut it yet. I haven't had a chance to run my hands through it."

15

Sarah was saved from having to respond to that leading remark by the arrival of their drinks.

"Here's to Mimi." Reed lifted his glass to hers. "Thank goodness, she never showed up."

Halfway through her blackened swordfish, Sarah looked up to see the hostess heading for her. "I'm sorry to disturb you, Ms. Scupper," she apologized. "But you have a phone call."

"A phone call?" Reed seemed to momentarily seethe with anger. "Can't you tell whoever it is that she'll call back when she's finished her dinner?"

"I'm sorry, but they insisted it was urgent." The older woman twisted her hands together nervously.

"It's all right. Probably something went wrong at the inn. I'll be back in a minute." Sarah placed her napkin on the table and stood up.

"You can take the call at the front desk." As soon as they stepped out of the dining room, the woman turned and whispered to Sarah, "It's the police."

"What?"

Now Sarah was worried and she moved swiftly to the telephone. "Sarah Scupper here."

"Sorry to bother you during your meal, Ms. Scupper, but we're looking for a man who was seen at the West Jordan Inn last night."

"I'm afraid you'll have to be more specific."

"A couple of people have mentioned to us that a blond, bearded stranger appeared in the bar just about the time the alarm was sounded for the fire last night. Someone heard him mention he'd just come from Carlisle. Do you remember him?"

"Yes, I do. Why? Is he a possible suspect?" Her tone was more sarcastic than she intended it to be.

"Ms. Scupper, everyone is a possible suspect at this point. He may be slightly more possible than others. Had he ever been in before?"

"No." Sarah glanced anxiously over her shoulder back into the dining room.

16

"Well, anything you can remember would be a great help to us. Any idea what his name is or where I could find him?"

With a burst of nervous laughter, she replied, "His name is Reed Anderson and I'm having dinner with him right now."

"You're what? I thought you just said you'd never met him before last night." The cop on the other end was sputtering with confusion. "Are you sure we're talking about the same person?"

"If we're talking about a possible arsonist, I doubt we're talking about the same person." But as she spoke, she realized how little she knew about Reed. He had disappeared for over an hour the night before. "Look, I'm sure he'd be happy to answer any of your questions. Why don't you meet us back at the inn in an hour or so?"

"Ms. Scupper, I'd advise you not to get in a car with this man or go anywhere at all with him. We're not just talking arson here, we're talking potential murderer."

"What?"

"You just keep him right there until we arrive. Go back and finish your dinner and order desert and coffee. Tell him the power went off at the inn and your bartender couldn't find the circuit box. And please – don't do anything foolish! You don't have any idea what kind of nutcase you might be dealing with."

"Okay! Okay! But I've got to say that I think you're out of your mind." She hung up the phone and leaned on the desk to steady herself. Her palms were clammy and beads of sweat were trickling down her forehead.

She wasn't sure which was more upsetting – the fact that the police suspected Reed or the idea that he might have set the Centennial fire. And murdered somebody as well? She couldn't believe her intuition was that poor. Part of her success as a bartender in past years had been the fact that she was a good judge of character.

Right now she hated the idea of going back in there and lying to him. But if she told him the truth and he bolted...

Well, she didn't have to tell him anything. Composing herself, she walked boldly back into the dining room and resumed her seat at the candle lit table for two.

"Everything okay?"

Reed looked so honest and trustworthy, sitting there waiting patiently for her. At the table behind him, a fat man in a shiny black suit with three gold chains around his neck bellowed loudly with raucous laughter. He looked far more like an arsonist than Reed.

"Fine." She flashed him a warm smile and immediately shoved a forkful of wild rice into her mouth.

Reed gave her a quizzical look and then shrugged. "If you say so. Your fish must be pretty cold by now."

She shook her head. "It's fine," she lied with her mouth full. Across the room, a sullen teenager dumped his full water glass into his astonished mother's lap and then stalked out of the room. A much more likely candidate for arson than Reed.

"Red is a great color on you," Reed commented, indicating the deep shade of her sweater. "It brings out the rosiness in your complexion."

Sarah smiled with her mouth full and continued eating. The room resounded loudly with the clatter of silverware on china against a background of idle conversation between unsuspecting diners.

The police were there in less than five minutes. Sarah had not even had time to finish the food on her plate, but it hardly mattered now. Her appetite was gone.

"Mr. Anderson?"

Startled, Reed looked up at the two overweight cops hovering near the table. "What's this all about?" he asked.

"We'd like to ask you a few questions if you don't mind coming down to the station with us."

Reed appeared rather defensive, but Sarah reasoned anybody would in this particular situation. "Wait a minute. What have I done? I know my rights—"

"As in 'You have the right to remain silent. Anything you say, can and will be held against you'? Come on, pal. Let's go."

"Well, I'd rather not stiff this fine establishment if you don't mind. Sarah, here's my credit card to pay the bill. Add twenty percent for the tip. And here are the keys to my truck. Oh, wait a minute." A fleeting look of relief crossed his face. "Is this about the registration on my truck? I thought I had a ten day grace period after the end of the month to get it registered."

"It's not about your truck, pal. Sarah, actually we'd like to ask you a few questions also, if you don't mind. Maybe you better come down to the Carlisle station too. You can follow us in the truck after you pay up."

And then they were gone, leaving a roomful of astonished customers staring at Sarah who, in turn, stared at the credit card and keys on the white tablecloth in front of her. What kind of criminal would trust someone he'd only known for a day with his Visa card and pick–up truck?

Maybe one who'd stolen both.

Sarah hated herself for thinking like that. Her instincts told her that anybody who worried about stiffing a waitress as they were being taken away for questioning by the police had to have an honest nature.

Unless it was a front, of course.

Angry with herself and the whole situation, Sarah paid the bill and headed for the police station.

From the narrow waiting room where she sat on a molded plastic chair, Sarah could not see where they had taken Reed. Eventually she was ushered down the hall to the town clerk's office which was not used at this time of the evening. In a small town like Carlisle, there was probably only one room used for questioning, if that.

Sarah described to the best of her ability what she remembered of the events the night before.

"Did you actually get a look at the letter he took out of his pocket?" The cop, who looked as though he were half

19

her own age, was scribbling notes on a clipboard as she talked.

"Not close enough to read it, no."

"So you don't know if it really was from this friend he was supposed to meet." The cop chewed on the end of a pen that apparently had been gnawed on through several other interviews.

"Look, I'm sure he still has it. Why don't you ask him if you can see it?" Sarah tried to not to appear impatient for fear it might look as if she was concealing the truth.

"And do you remember the name of the woman he was supposed to meet?"

Sarah hoped she seemed thoughtful and serious as she pondered his question. "Mimi something. I can't remember her last name."

His youthful freckled face registered first astonishment and then delight. He would be a joy to play poker with, Sarah thought glumly. "Mimi? You said Mimi?"

Sarah nodded.

"If you'd just stay right there, I'll be right back." He stepped excitedly into the hall and shouted. "Hey! Dwayne! Come here a sec!"

After an urgent whispered conversation in the hall, Dwayne, who turned out to be one of the overweight cops from the restaurant, came into the room. "Sarah, are you aware that a woman's body was found inside the remains of the Centennial this morning?"

Sarah had a sinking feeling about the direction this was headed. "I heard about it for the first time this evening. Why?"

"The identity of that woman has not been revealed to the public yet because we are still waiting for an immediate family member to positively identify the body. But from the rental agreement papers in a car we found nearby and from the description of the manager of the Brookside Cabins where she had taken a cottage for the night, we are fairly certain the woman's name is Mimi Farrell."

20

He paused for effect and to watch Sarah's reaction. Having already guessed what he had been leading up to, she merely frowned and waited for him to continue.

"Is that the name of the friend Mr. Anderson said he was supposed to meet at the West Jordan Inn?"

"Yes, I believe it is." Sarah tried to conceal how horrified she was by the thought of the vibrant woman Reed had described had now burned to death in an abandoned hotel.

Dwayne turned to the younger cop. "Fingerprint him and hold him overnight without bail. Oh, and ask him if he still has that letter."

"Wait a minute!" Sarah stood up indignantly. "Do you really have any hard evidence to prove he's guilty?"

"We'll know better after we fingerprint him. Besides, we'll have some of the state's experts up to question him in the morning. In the meantime, I think everyone in this community will feel safer knowing he's locked up until we're sure he's innocent."

"Doesn't sound very American to me," she muttered loudly as she swung her purse over her shoulder and headed for the door.

"Ms. Scupper! I'd watch what you say and to whom over the next few days. If it turns out Mr. Anderson does have to go to trial, I'm sure you'll be called to testify."

Once outside, Sarah sat for several minutes in Reed's truck feeling frustrated and helpless. Her need to know the truth forced her to open the glove compartment and rummage around in it for proof of Reed's identity. The truck was indeed registered to a Frederick Reed Anderson who lived on Rural Route 1 in Montgomery, Vermont. An old postcard from Mom and Dad vacationing in the Virgin Islands had come to the same address as had an envelope from a chiropractor in Burlington that was covered in figures that seemed to be lumber calculations and costs.

"Ms. Scupper?"

She jumped up startled. Dwayne was peering into the truck, indicating that she should roll down the window.

Shoving the papers back into the glove compartment, she complied.

"I'd like to go over this vehicle for any signs of evidence. So if you don't mind, I'll have Mike give you a ride back over to West Jordan."

Sliding out of the seat, she handed Dwayne the keys. But she'd be damned if she was going to turn over the credit card as well.

Sarah tiptoed up the back stairs at the inn, hoping none of the staff or customers would realize she was home. She would have liked a stiff drink from the bar to settle her nerves but she would have to make do with an old bottle of stock Chablis that had been in the refrigerator for a couple of months. As she poured herself a glass full, she remembered that Tyler had brought it up to cook with on his last visit before leaving for Burma.

Tyler. Suddenly she wanted him so badly she felt like a volcano about to erupt. It was being sexually flirted with (and the imminent danger she might or might not have been in), combined with the mysterious questions surrounding the fire and murder. If Tyler was here, it would all be interesting, not scary.

Kicking off her shoes, she sat down on the couch with the phone in her lap, composing the message she would leave on his answering machine. He should have been back a few days ago but you never knew with Tyler. She waited for the familiar sound of his taped voice and the inevitable beep.

"Tyler, it's Sarah. I don't know if you're even back yet. I'm just calling to say that....I guess I'm calling to say that I need you. Give me a–"

"Sarah? Hi, just let me turn off the machine." Although it was not late, Tyler's voice was thick with sleep. Sarah felt suddenly embarrassed for admitting her weakness while Tyler was listening. Sometimes it was easier to say what you really felt to a machine. "Sorry, I fell asleep a few hours ago. I've been having trouble getting back to an

Eastern Standard time schedule – I'm so incredibly jetlagged."

"Oh, well, that's all right. You can call me in the morning if you want." Sarah suddenly felt overcome with emotion at the sound of his voice. The idea that she had been entertaining thoughts of getting involved with someone else seemed crude and unfaithful.

"No, I'm up now." Through the receiver she could hear the click of his bedroom lamp being switched on and the thud of a pillow against his headboard. "What did you say before? That you needed me? What happened? Did your cook quit again?"

Just as suddenly as she had felt overwhelmed with love, she became angry at his sarcastic joke. Instinctively, her whole body stiffened. "Very funny, Tyler. We haven't spoken in almost two months and all you–

"Hey, hold on! I'm sorry, you were being serious, weren't you?" The immediate concern in his voice made Sarah realize she had flown off the handle at nothing and that she was much more on edge than she was admitting. She relaxed back into the cushions of the couch.

"Tyler, I don't want to seem self–centered, I mean, I do want to hear all about your trip as soon as possible, but there's some stuff going on here that I need your help with." Sarah cleared her throat and went on a little more confidently. "And, besides, I think you might find it really interesting. You might even want to come up here –"

"Of course, I want to come up there! As though I haven't thought about you every night for the last–"

"Tyler! Shut up for a minute and listen!"

This was not the first time they'd had this same kind of exchange. After a brief silence on the other end of the line, she began. "Last night this guy came into the inn..."

CHAPTER TWO

Sarah flung a long, slim leg over one of Tyler's equally lean lower limbs and kissed the back of his neck, sighing with contentment. Rivulets of sweat on their naked bodies glistened in the afternoon sun.

They had been in bed since Tyler had arrived shortly before noon. Months of pent–up sexual energy had superseded lunch and small talk. Each time they reunited after a lengthy separation, Sarah never failed to be stunned by Tyler's appearance. Even a ten pound weight loss due to a mild bout of dysentery looked good on him. It put a few angular hollows in his naturally boyish face and added some hard–earned maturity. His thick, wavy hair was shot through with streaks of gold from the sun and curled nearly to his shoulders; his mustache was almost blond. The bronze color of his skin made the amber brown of his eyes even more tiger–like than usual.

"Tell the truth. Were you really working in the mountains of Burma all this time? How did you get such a fine sun tan?" She ran a finger across the top of his buttocks where the waistband of his bathing suit had created the most dramatic contrast between his darkest skin and his whitest.

Tyler rolled over on his back and laughed. "I can't pull anything over on you, can I? All right, I admit I spent a week in Bali on the way home. I was so wiped out from this intestinal parasite thing that I needed some time to lay around and recuperate."

He held up his hand before Sarah could respond. "I know, I should have invited you to join me. After all, it's only a short, thirty hour plane ride away. But I didn't have enough energy to make love to a fly and it only takes flies

24

about three seconds to consummate their sex life. Somehow I didn't think it would be worth your time."

"Well, if you think all I want from you is sex —"

He slapped the back of his hand against his forehead in mock distress. "And now, if you're finished with me, I'm starving."

"I'll never be finished with you." Sarah straddled him with her lean, muscular legs and held his wrists up against the carved oak headboard of the huge old bed. "But if you're too hungry to perform—" she shrugged her shoulders and let his arms drop. "I guess I'll have to feed you."

He grabbed a handful of her waist–length sleek hair and tugged it playfully. "You better treat me right. Your hair is so long now I could drag you around caveman style. When I get my strength back, that is." He let her hair slide from his grasp and she climbed off him. "I've never seen your hair so long before. It really does something for you.

"Yeah, like drive me crazy. All right now, enough is enough. Tell me what is in this big box you hauled here from the airport." She slid off the bed and knelt down beside the large carton. Her dark hair tumbled over her shoulders like a finely fringed curtain, coyly covering her small round breasts.

Tyler grinned. "It's my liberation from you. I mean, from having to depend on the use of your car," he added hastily as she frowned. "It's a mountain bike. I thought it would be a great way for me to get around and keep in shape now that it's springtime."

"A mountain bike! Only one? You mean we'll have to share? Shit, this is one of those times I wish I kept some food up here." Sarah was now standing naked in front of the open refrigerator. "I guess I'll have to put some clothes on and go downstairs. Clive might be down there already prepping dinner."

"Oh, take a chance. I dare you."

"I dare you." She slipped on a blue silk robe and loosely tied the sash. As he watched her retreating figure, Tyler marveled how everything looked good on Sarah. From a sweater that was a size too small to an old barn jacket, any piece of clothing she put on looked right and stylish. And it was a good thing, because most of the time she didn't think twice about what she wore.

Over homemade soup, spinach salad, garlic bread, and a California chardonnay, Tyler delicately brought up the subject of Sarah's phone call two nights before.

"Well, they let Reed go yesterday afternoon. I guess there wasn't enough concrete evidence to hold him. His fingerprints didn't match anything that they found. But he's under police surveillance and they made it pretty clear that they are going to continue working hard to pin something on him." In the afterglow of sex, it was hard for Sarah to remember how important the situation had seemed to her a few hours before.

"What do you think? Did he do it?" Tyler was sitting cross–legged on the couch, bare–chested, the Balinese sarong he had brought for Sarah wrapped around the lower half of his body. She could not keep from admiring how relaxed and exotic he looked.

She shook her head to stay focused. "No! But I have to admit, he certainly was in the wrong place at the wrong time with no alibi. I think they're just really anxious to solve one of these hotel fires. You know in the last twenty years they haven't been able to make any arrests for all those hotels that burned down."

"So tell me about this town, Carlisle." Tyler started on his second glass of wine. "If it's so close, how is it that I've never been there?"

"Because eight months of the year the road between here and there is closed down and considered impassable. It's just an old dirt logging road over the back side of Darby Mountain that can really only be traversed in the summer and fall. The rest of the time you have to go around on the highway and it takes a good half hour. Besides, there's nothing over there but a bunch of boarded–up hotels and burnt–out ruins."

26

"But you know how I love groping around in old historic places." He flashed her a charming grin, the one that could still wrap itself around her heart after all these years.

"Yeah, more than you love me sometimes." Sarah took a large bite of bread and looked at him defiantly.

"Oh, someday you'll be old and historic and then I'll love groping you too." He grabbed her bare thigh under the table and squeezed it. "Anyway, what about the dead woman? Does anyone have any theories on what she was doing in an empty old hotel?"

"Yeah, the theory is she met Reed the way she had been planning and they went into the hotel together to reminisce about college days at which time he knocked her out, put a half smoked cigarette in her hand and then proceeded to burn down the building." Sarah shook her head and emptied her wine glass.

"Well, unfortunately for Reed, it makes a lot of sense. Did he have any idea why she wanted him to meet her here?"

"Nothing he admitted to." Sarah poured the last inch of wine into her glass and added the bottle to the debris on the floor. Tyler had only been here a few hours and already the apartment was becoming cluttered and disorganized.

"So it's possible she had some old dirt on him that she wanted to blackmail him with and maybe that made him mad."

"Of course, it's possible – if he really met her over there! But I don't believe he did. Besides, he's a really laidback, rational kind of guy. Not hyper and impulsive." Sarah's gaze drifted away from Tyler and towards the window where the branches of an old sugar maple were just beginning to sprout red buds.

"Like me, you mean." Tyler stood up and stretched.

"I didn't say that."

"So when do I get to meet this guy?" As Sarah watched, he began pushing furniture aside, clearing a space on the floor beneath the window.

"He's coming over for dinner tomorrow. He's pretty desperate – he says he's willing to pay you to find out what happened. What are you doing?"

"Unpacking the mountain bike." Tyler was using a kitchen knife to cut through the packing tape on the carton. "There's plenty of daylight left. I might as well put this thing together and get started. A mountain bike is perfect for an impassable logging road. How long do you think it will take me to get to Carlisle?"

Sarah shook her head again and laughed in disbelief. "It depends how many times you get stuck."

"Well, how many miles is it then?"

"Five or six. Up one side of the mountain and then down the other. I can't believe you're going to race over there now. Why don't you relax today and start tomorrow?" She didn't want him to be so busy; she had been enjoying their lazy afternoon.

"I feel like I need to get a handle on this story. I'll be able to talk about it better if I can see the remains of the hotel and talk to a few people over there about what's her name, Mamie?"

"Mimi. Then let's drive over together. I'm not planning to work tonight and you can ride over again in the morning when you have all day. Besides, now that I've fed you..." She knelt down beside him and undid her robe, letting the luxurious fabric slide sensuously off her shoulders to the floor. "...You owe me."

"I own you, did you say?" Tyler put down the front wheel of the bike and put his arms around her waist. "I'm sorry, I guess I am being too impulsive again. But you know how I am once I get started on something."

"Well, you better get started then." She laughed, pushing him down on the thick oriental carpet that covered the floor.

It was nearly five when they awoke, still entwined in each other's arms on the living room floor.

28

"Woody's heavy old oak furniture looks even more imposing from this angle," Sarah remarked half to herself. "And the room is so crowded; I wish there was some place to move some of it, but it's so big and cumbersome. Sometimes I think these rooms were built around it."

"Sounds like you miss your old sparsely furnished cottage in the woods."

"I surely miss the privacy of it. It gets exhausting living in a public place." Sarah sat up. "We better get going if you still want to go over to Carlisle today."

Forty–five minutes later Sarah's four–wheel-drive Subaru station wagon pulled up in front of the remains of the Centennial House. A once elegant red granite fountain stood empty by an old wooden signpost without a sign that now served as an anchor for the yellow police tape that cordoned off the sidewalk to the still smoking ruins of the hotel.

"Sometimes they smolder for days." Sarah spoke in a hushed tone that seemed appropriate for the death of such an awesome edifice. "Especially in the winter when the water freezes over parts of the building before the fire is completely out."

The fire in the Centennial had started on the third floor and worked its way up to the fourth before starting down. The efforts of the fire department had managed to save most of the first and second floor of the west wing, but the smoke damage was so intense that it seemed obvious that the rest of the building would end up being razed sometime in the future. The front porch roof, which had shaded relaxing vacationers in their rocking chairs for over a hundred years, had collapsed in one piece onto the front lawn, effectively blocking off the grand stone steps that led up to the front door. Ironically colorful, its turn–of–the–century pattern of red and blue shingles stood in contrast to the blackened clapboards and charred timbers of the rest of the hotel.

Tyler and Sarah walked around the edge of the property, surveying the damage in silence.

"And this is where the college used to be." Sarah indicated a grassy expanse through a border of trees off to their right. "But it's been cleaned up so nicely, you can barely tell where the building was."

Following a well–worn path that cut through the brush, they strolled out into the middle of the field. The early evening sunlight fell at a golden angle across the grass, giving the area the beauty and warmth missing from the dark shell of the Centennial next door.

"Is that a lake down the hill there?" Tyler shaded his eyes against the bright reflection of the light on the water.

"Yes, that was the main attraction of Carlisle as a resort town in the old days. That and the fresh mountain air." With the magnetism that all bodies of water seem to have, the lake beckoned them to come closer and enjoy its magic. But as they neared the wooden dock, which was badly in need of repair, Sarah grabbed Tyler's arm and made him stop.

"What's the matter?"

"Look. Someone is already there."

A slope–shouldered figure sat dejectedly on the edge of the dock, staring into the water, legs dangling. From the large mass of gray hair swept up on her head, it appeared to be an older woman. A few steps closer and they were able to see that she was wearing a brown tweed suit and nylons – her sensible high–heeled shoes were sitting on the dock next to her.˜

"Do you think she's okay?" Tyler whispered. "I mean, do you think she's contemplating suicide or something?"

Sarah snorted at Tyler's need to dramatize every situation. "I doubt it. I think she's just sad and wants to be alone."

"Well, she's not exactly dressed for a hike along the lake."

"Obviously she wasn't planning on feeling like this. Let's go." Sarah headed back up the hill at a fast clip, and reluctantly Tyler followed.

"Don't you think we should have tried to talk to her?" he asked, unable to let go of the intrigue he had created.

"No, I don't. She is clearly looking for privacy, something I have respect for, although I know you investigative types don't know the meaning of the word."

They walked the rest of the way to the car in silence, not wanting to argue and knowing that, if they spoke at all, they would disagree. "Let's see if we can find where the town library is," Tyler suggested. "I'd like to know when it's open — I'm sure they have a wad of information on the history of these old hotels."

They finally found the library around the corner from the main street. It was open from ten to one the next day and Tyler made plans to ride the mountain bike over first thing. They stopped to get some self–service gas at a small convenience store before driving home and Tyler could not resist making small talk about the fire/murder with the older woman behind the counter.

"Damn shame, isn't it? Nobody ever died in one a them fires before. Mother of the woman was just in here a little while ago. Had to come up and identify the body. What a sad thing to have to do." The woman's chubby cheeks and bright eyes made her appear ready to burst with the desire to divulge more of the succulent information she knew.

"Really. Where'd she come up from?"

"Well, the one what died was from Hawaii they say. Left a husband and a coupla kids there. Her mother lives in Connecticut so I guess the family figured it would be faster and easier if she just came up. Nice lady." She let out a deep breath, clearly relieved to be able to reveal more.

Tyler laid a bag of chips on the counter and pretended to search for something else in the racks. "She staying over?"

"Guess so. She's gotta claim her daughter's belongings that are still down at Brookside." The woman clucked her tongue and shook her head. "I hope I never live to see a day like that."

31

Tyler paid for the gas and the chips and hurried back out to the car where Sarah was waiting impatiently. "Sorry, but people who work in places like that always know what's going on. I had to pick her brain. Where is Brookside?"

"You mean those cottages on the edge of town? We passed them when we got off the highway. Just about the only place to stay around here now, I imagine. Why – you think we should rent one and have a romantic getaway?"

"No, but I think we should pretend we're interested." Tyler grinned at her puzzlement. "If my guess is correct, Mimi's mother should be spending the night there."

"Mimi's mother? You're not going to bother a grieving mother, are you?" Sarah's gray eyes widened with disgust and astonishment.

"No, I'm not going to `bother' her. I'm going to help her find out who murdered her daughter." He punctuated his dramatic announcement by popping open the bag of potato chips.

"And what makes you think she wants your help? She doesn't even know you. If she's smart, she's not talking to reporters. Even handsome, charming ones." Sarah's feelings about his idea were evident.

"I have a few good lines that have worked before. There it is, pull into the office. First we need to figure out if she's here."

"Well, did you find out where she's from, Sherlock?"

"Connecticut. And I also found out Mimi has a husband and kids in Hawaii. What are you doing?"

Instead of stopping, Sarah had driven in and was slowly cruising the gravel drive that ran along the semi–circle of tourist cabins. On a weekday in early May, only two cabins showed any signs of occupancy. In front of one was parked a sports car from Quebec; in front of the other was a sedan with Connecticut tags.

Tyler leaned over and gave Sarah a kiss. "Do you want me to come in or will I detract from your credibility?" she asked, her attitude softening up a bit under his touch.

"You ARE my credibility – but I think you better wait here. Most private investigators don't bring their girlfriends along." He gave her his most charming, conspiratorial grin but she didn't fall for it.

"Private investigators? Oh, come off it, Tyler, you don't have a license for that." She shook her head. With his sun-kissed curls and boyish good looks, Tyler could pull off just about anything, particularly when it came to women. And he was always willing to try something new.

"Well, how about private investigative journalist?" He said the last five syllables in a garbled whisper out of the corner of his mouth. "I love you; I won't be long."

As he knocked on the door, Tyler remembered the other reason he had wanted to stop at the front office. He didn't even know Mimi's mother's name.

"Yes?"

He was taken aback for a minute, not so much by the grief–stricken beauty of the aging woman, but by the fact that she was the same person who had been sitting alone by the lake a half hour before.

"I'm sorry to bother you at a time like this–" Damn, he wished he knew her last name – "but I heard in town you might be looking for someone to help you find out who–" He didn't want to say 'murdered' but then decided it might shock her into a decision – "who murdered your daughter."

She gasped a little before stuttering – "Well, yes, but I...who are you?"

"Tyler Mackenzie. I'd like to offer my investigative services to you if you're interested." His eyes were busy taking in all the details about her – the tortoiseshell combs holding up gray hair that still looked thick and luxurious, the patrician angles of her nose and cheekbones, her expensive cashmere sweater.

"How– how did you find me?" Her hand flew to her chest in a flustered gesture. He noticed the large diamond, her professionally manicured nails and the age spots below her knuckles.

33

"Oh, uh, the police, you know..." Tyler made an ambiguous gesture and then ran his fingers through his hair. "You must be very frustrated and angry at the injustice of it all. I am doing some work on the stories behind the various hotel fires in town here and thought I might be able to be of service to you as well. May I come in?"

She looked over her shoulder at the tiny room and bit her lip. "Actually, I'd rather talk to you somewhere else. I find this room overpoweringly depressing. Is there a restaurant where I can follow you for coffee?"

"Uh, sure." Tyler didn't have a clue where they could go. "My wife's in the car. Would you mind if she joined us?"

"Your wife?" Sarah snorted as she pulled into a parking space across the street from the Lakeview House. "You better keep your lifestyle out of the conversation or she'll never believe you."

"My lifestyle?" Tyler feigned surprise. "I live with you in West Jordan and my work takes me away a lot."

"Oh, please. Don't exaggerate."

Tyler could feel the tension between them mounting. "Don't blow this for me, Sarah."

"Oh, don't worry, dear." Sarah contorted her beautiful lips into a parody of a simpering grin. "I'm going to keep my mouth shut and just watch you work. Your kettle of hot water is only big enough for one to drown in."

Tyler did not reply. He knew from experience there was no point in retorting to Sarah's stinging sarcasm.

There was nothing particularly special about the Lakeview House except that it was the only place in town for supper and it did have a spectacular view of the lake. Looking for something more casual, they had stopped first at the Carlisle Cafe, but it was only open for breakfast and lunch. The Lakeview House was a typical family restaurant with wooden tables and paper placemats that featured scenic views of Vermont. It had a bland, American menu to match.

"Just coffee for me, please," Tyler told the waitress.

"Me, too," agreed Sarah.

"If you don't mind, I think I'll order something to eat. I'd rather not go out again after this." Mimi's mother ordered the Yankee pot roast. "You know, it seems almost too fortuitous that you came along when you did," she said after the waitress left them. "I've spent the entire afternoon wishing I could see justice done to whomever did this horrible thing to my daughter."

"Did you know she was coming to Carlisle for a visit?" Tyler asked.

"Well, yes, of course. She flew into New York and spent the weekend at my house in Connecticut before coming up here. But she was very mysterious about why." A frown wrinkled her high forehead. "She just said she had some old business to attend to. The police tell me their main suspect is some old friend of hers from college who was supposed to meet her here." Her expression grew troubled; her eyes were like blue skies suddenly darkened by gray clouds.

"She didn't mention any names of people she was coming to see?" Tyler drew a dark line down the side of the still empty page of his open notebook.

"Mr. Mackenzie, my daughter is a grown woman. What she does with her life is her affair. I don't pry." Uncontrollable tears filled her eyes. "Maybe if I had pried more, she would still be alive."

The waitress arrived with the coffee, giving Mimi's mother the momentary distraction she needed to regain her self–composure.

"Tell me about Mimi," Tyler said gently as he stirred his coffee. "What was she like?"

"She was beautiful, always so beautiful. She had beautiful long wavy black hair. She hadn't cut it in twenty–five years. She had two beautiful boys who looked just like her. They live on Maui. She was a real estate broker there. They have an incredibly exquisite house on the side of a mountain overlooking the ocean." She rambled on for

35

several minutes in disjointed recollections of her daughter's life, picking disinterestedly at the green salad the waitress had placed in front of her.

On an off–season, mid–week night, they were the only customers in the restaurant and the Yankee pot roast arrived quickly. Tyler realized that time was running out and he tried to steer the conversation back in a relevant direction.

"What about when she went to Carlisle College?"

Mimi's mother frowned again. "I never wanted her to go there. It was such a hotbed of counter culture. You know, drugs, sex, politics. But at that time she wanted to be a potter and Carlisle had a good pottery department. She dropped out after a couple of years, but she got a job and stayed here for another year anyway. I think she had some boyfriend whom she was living with that she didn't want to leave."

"Do you remember his name?" Tyler leaned forward eagerly.

She shook her head. "Nick...Neil...Nelson...Something that began with an N. I'm sorry, it was so long ago. I only met him once and I never liked him. He was dirty and sullen." She stared down at the pot roast with a look of revulsion clearly meant for the boyfriend whose name began with N.

"Can you remember any of her other friends from college?"

"There was a girl with blonde hair, very bubbly and sweet. They worked together at one of the old hotels that was still around at the time. She went out to dinner with us." The older woman's face flushed suddenly. "I don't know why I'm telling you this, but I remember she was wearing a white dress without any undergarments beneath it. When I realized that, I could barely finish my meal for wondering about whether my own daughter was wearing any. But that was how a lot of young women dressed back then. I was certainly glad when that era was over."

Tyler was beginning to feel frustrated. The things she was remembering were interesting but not particularly useful. "Any chance of talking to Mr. Farrell?"

"Steve? I'd rather you waited a bit, if you don't mind. He has his hands full coping with the two boys as well as funeral arrangements and what not. I'll be flying out to Hawaii day after tomorrow and I'll mention to him that you will probably be contacting him. What exactly are your fees, Mr. Mackenzie?"

Sarah gazed studiously at the last bit of daylight on the lake trying not to laugh as Tyler's face reddened. "Well, since I'm going to be researching the fires anyway, I'd rather wait and see what pans out as far as–"

"Mr. Mackenzie. I want to see my daughter's murderer brought to trial. I don't care how much I have to pay, but I have to know that you are willing to help me or I will find somebody else. Do I make myself clear?" Her perfect posture, distinct diction and imposing manner made Tyler believe she must have been a schoolteacher at some time in her life.

Tyler opened his notebook to a clean sheet of paper and pushed it across the table. "If you would write your name, address and telephone number in there, please, and the date that you can be reached at that number again after you return from Hawaii. I'll call you at that time and let you know what kind of progress I'm making and we can decide on a form of payment then."

She hesitated for a moment before writing. Tyler struggled to read her cursive script upside down so that he could call her by name. Diana Stellano from Westport, Connecticut.

"Mrs. Stellano, do you have any pictures of Mimi that you could send me? Maybe a current one and one from her college days? It would be extremely helpful." He could see Sarah shaking her head ever so slightly, just enough so that he knew she disapproved of the extent to which he was involving himself.

When they were finally alone in the car again, her temper exploded as he had expected it would after having kept her mouth shut for so long. "I asked you up here to help prove the innocence of the poor soul who is the popular choice for being guilty of this crime and within a few hours you've managed to get hired by someone else who would be happy to see you find enough evidence to put him in jail! What do you think you're doing?"

"I'm saving your friend a bunch of money," Tyler replied quietly. "Now he won't have to pay me. Look, Sarah, the truth is the truth. If he's innocent, whatever I find out is going to help both of them."

Sarah's silence acknowledged that she knew he was right. "Let's talk about something else," she said after a while. She didn't want to think about Reed and Mimi and Carlisle College anymore.

"How are things at the inn?"

"Actually, I'm a little worried. It's not making enough money and especially not at this time of year."

"But Woody always did okay, didn't he?"

"Yes, and that's because Woody did everything." Sarah felt a rush of relief at being able to air the troubled thoughts she'd been having. "He was the manager and the cook – all he had to pay was a bartender and occasionally a waitress. Now he has to pay me, a cook and a bartender. I've worked it out so that I tend bar on Peter's nights off and I do the cooking on Clive's nights off–"

"You?"

She grinned in the near darkness. "Yeah, scary thought, isn't it? He makes it pretty easy for me really. Anyway, these days, there's nothing left at the end of the week. A couple of weeks I've felt so bad I haven't paid myself. I'm thinking that I might have to let the bartender go and do that myself again. Then at least I could live off the tips."

"Have you talked to Woody?"

"I haven't wanted to spoil his good time, but I think I'm going to have to."

Tyler reached for her hand which was resting on her thigh. "Maybe I can help out some while I'm here." His offer had been genuinely innocent, but Sarah didn't want to take it that way.

Whenever they got together after several months apart, they couldn't keep their minds on anything for the first few days until they were sexually satisfied. After a couple of days of uninhibited lovemaking, they always felt closer and more in tune with each other. And sometimes during a serious disagreement, sex was the only activity they shared harmoniously, the only thing that could remind them of how strongly they really felt about each other.

Slipping her hand out from beneath his, Sarah moved his hand up into the warm recess of her crotch and grinned again as she spoke. "Well, you can at least help me enjoy life a little more."

CHAPTER THREE

Tyler felt a childlike rush of excitement as he took the mountain bike out on its first excursion. The heavy springtime dew sparkled in the strong May sunshine and the day held the promise of being much warmer by afternoon, maybe even hot.

"Don't forget that Reed is coming to have supper with us this evening. Try to be back by five." Sarah stood barefoot on the porch watching him get ready, wearing nothing but her silk robe. Her hair was pinned loosely up on her head with a large barrette and the several strands that had escaped accentuated the careless beauty that Tyler found so attractive.

"How could I forget? I have dozens of questions to ask him." He gave her a quick kiss on the lips before he hopped onto the seat of the bike and rode off down the street.

At the center of town he took a hard right onto the dirt road that led over the mountain to Carlisle. Almost immediately it became a sharp incline marked by sizable rocks and deep ruts formed by the recent run–off of melted spring snow.

Several times he had to get off and carry the bicycle over a fallen tree or around particularly soft mud. But once he made it over the mountain, the last few miles were a pleasant, easy ride through woods wearing the first fuzzy green haze of early leaves and smelling fresh and damp.

As he had expected, the library in Carlisle was deserted, abandoned on a gloriously warm spring morning for more seasonal pursuits. Mrs. Meade, the librarian, was more than happy to lead him to the shelf designated for town history. There were two scrapbooks of old newspaper clippings, a book of general town history which included a pictorial chapter on the era of the grand hotels, and a book entirely devoted to the lost hotels of Carlisle.

The history of Carlisle was more fascinating and unusual than Tyler would have expected. He was surprised to learn that at the turn of the century there had been over thirty hotels and boardinghouses in the tiny northern town, most of which were built between 1890 and 1900.

A hand–drawn map in one of the books showed a three–dimensional layout of the town in 1899 with each of the hotels neatly depicted as a white building with windows, their sizes and shapes drawn in careful scale. At the edge of town was a compound that looked like a castle with flags flying on four turrets. The map's key called it the Mountainside Hotel.

"Is this still around?" Tyler asked Mrs. Meade.

"The Mountainside? Oh, my, no. The big building burned nearly fifty years ago. I was a little girl and I remember the fire clearly. My father was a volunteer fireman then. The Mountainside was a small town in itself. It even had its own train station. A few of the annexes survived the big fire, but they were destroyed in another blaze back in 1977. The train station was the only thing that survived, although the train hasn't stopped there since before World War II. But Muriel told me that last time she was out walking that way she saw that the roof had finally caved in."

Tyler went back to his reading and tried to discover what had caused the demise of the once thriving summer tourist trade. Although his first rationale would have been the human fear of being caught in a burning wooden building, it turned out that the advent of the automobile was the real reason behind the short–lived era of Carlisle's grand hotels.

By the 1950s, many of the hotels had burned down and train service was discontinued. New uses were found for the few existing hotels. Camps and schools were obvious options, although most of the buildings were not winterized so their use was limited. A few establishments limped on halfheartedly for some years, converting their once elegant dining rooms and ballrooms into restaurants or summer nightclubs.

The books were really an overview. As Tyler pressed Mrs. Meade for more details, she quietly begged off. "I only know what I know because I grew up here. I'm not one of those people who really studied town history. Now if you want to talk to somebody who knows about the timeline of these hotels, you should talk to Wanda Kensington. She's had a lifelong interest in the history of Carlisle's tourist industry and seems to have a photographic memory for details, particularly about the fires themselves. Her husband's the town fire chief."

"Where can I find her?"

"She runs the Carlisle Cafe. I'm sure she'd be pleased as punch to talk to you. Seems she never gets tired of going over those old stories." She lowered her voice conspiratorially. "And most people around here are sick of listening to her."

Since it was nearly one o'clock and the library was about to close for the day, Tyler made some copies on an ancient and slow–moving copy machine and then rode his bike up the block to the Carlisle Cafe.

The sun was beaming down with a savage glare, and the mid–day heat that reflected up from the sidewalk was reminiscent of the hottest days of summer. The only twinge of coolness remaining in the air came with the occasional light breeze that rustled the newborn leaves on the trees.

The smell of cooked food coming through the open doors of the Carlisle Cafe made Tyler realize how ravenous his trek over the mountain had made him. Leaning his bicycle against the front of the building, he stepped into its dark, welcoming interior.

Apparently opened as a classic luncheonette some time back in the thirties or forties, the sturdy but outdated furnishings could have suited any place from tacky to sophisticated. As it was, the cafe made the most of the old–fashioned, polished wooden booths and lunch counter and the black and white linoleum floor. The mirror hanging behind the counter was etched around the edge with Art Deco designs. A couple of larger tables set against the back wall were covered with red and white checked tablecloths. Bushy hanging plants and tasteful prints added atmosphere and the young waitress wearing a batiked t–shirt, tight denim shorts, and white running shoes brought the whole package right into the 1990s.

Despite the rising heat, the place was nearly full. A group of women in business suits were eating taco salads at one of the large tables and most of the booths were occupied. They contained such a wide variety of people that Tyler could not easily pigeon–hole what kind of clientele the cafe catered to. "Small town" would probably cover it.

He slid into one of the few remaining booths and watched the waitress as she bounced swiftly from the tables to the kitchen to the cash register and back again. The lithe movements of her slim body and the corn silk color of her short springy curls spoke to her youth. When she suddenly appeared at his side with a menu, her sparkling blue eyes startled him with all the enthusiasm and enjoyment of life they seemed to hold.

"Nice day, isn't it? Would you like something to drink?"

She was a little breathless from her dance of the dining room, earrings still in motion, cheeks pink from the activity and heat. While she waited for his reply, her glance was darting from table to table, checking to see who was ready for more coffee or done eating. When her eyes finally focused on Tyler's face, she caught her breath and then dazzled him with a wide smile.

"You're not from around here, are you?"

He laughed. "How could you tell?"

She shrugged and laughed a merry sound that reminded Tyler of some wind chimes he had heard in Bali. "Because I know everybody who lives around here. Coke, Sprite, Diet Pepsi, coffee, iced tea?"

"How about iced coffee?" He noticed that she had two tiny earrings – a moon and a star – dangling from one ear; a large hoop hung from the other.

She made a face. "I suppose it's time we turned a pot into that. I'll be back in a few minutes for your order."

As he watched her waltz around the room, he realized he was already hopelessly captivated by her presence. A charming child, he told himself. Young enough to be his daughter. Nobody else in the room seemed to find her as enchanting as he did.

"Is Wanda Kensington here today?" he asked when she brought his iced coffee.

"In the kitchen as always." She tossed her head, indicating the door behind the counter.

"When would be a good time to talk to her?"

"Probably after two when we close up." She squinted her eyes at him suddenly. "Are you some kind of salesman?"

Tyler laughed. "Do I look like a salesman?"

She blushed ever so slightly. "No. You look like a male model for GQ."

It was his turn to blush. "Thanks a lot. My life's ambition."

"Does she know you?"

"Not yet. Does that matter?"

She straightened his place setting and the salt and pepper shakers. "No, I just wondered. She's my mother."

"Hey, Arden, can we get another basket of bread over here?" called a heavy man in construction overalls.

"Yeah, just a second, Buzz. Have you decided?"

"I'll have today's special." He pointed to the card that said "homemade beef stew and biscuits."

"Today's special. Yes, I think it is, isn't it?"

Her suddenly dreamy tone and play on his words made Tyler glance up quickly. Her sky blue eyes were assessing him provocatively. He'd seen more than his share of looks like that before. Usually it didn't matter, he could ignore a come–on as easily as a pesky fly. But he was strangely

44

attracted to this sprite. He suppressed an urge to leap on his bike and ride away as fast as possible.

A bell dinging insistently in the kitchen broke her reverie and she dashed off. Keeping his gaze focused on the kitchen door, he soon saw a woman poke her head out, give a hard look in his direction and then dash quickly back inside. Although she looked nothing like Arden, he assumed it must be her mother.

"She wants to know what you want to talk to her about," Arden announced as she placed his meal in front of him.

"I was told she was an authority on the old hotels in town. I'm working on an article about the life and death of the tourist business in Carlisle and I was hoping she could help me out."

Arden snorted. "Only her favorite topic. Damn, and I was hoping maybe you were the son of one of her long lost lovers and had come to town to tell her she'd been left a million dollars."

"Sorry." One of her long lost lovers? In the quick glance he'd had of Wanda, she hadn't impressed him as a one-time beauty. That didn't mean that a hard life couldn't have changed her looks drastically.

"So who's this article for?"

"A magazine I work for in New York, or anyone else I can sell it to."

"New York? You mean the news of that Hawaiian woman dying in that fire reached all the way down there?"

"You might say that. Do you think she'll talk to me?"

"How about do I think she'll ever stop?"

Hot beef stew turned out to be the wrong choice for such a warm day. Several times, he had to use a paper napkin to wipe the perspiration off his face.

"Looks like you're ready for a swim," Arden remarked as she cleared his dish away.

"The lake looks mighty inviting right now," Tyler admitted. "But I didn't bring a change of clothes and I don't relish riding home on a bicycle in wet pants."

45

"Is that your mountain bike out front? I've got one too. It's a gas this time of year. Listen, if you want to wait around half an hour, I know a great place to swim. And you don't need a bathing suit."

It was as blatant an invitation as he'd ever been given. An image of Arden kneeling naked by the edge of the water ran through his mind like a video on fast forward. He forced himself to shut it off. "Look, Arden—"

"What are you afraid of?" She had lowered her voice, but her eyes saw right through him.

"How old are you?"

She grinned. "Old enough to know enough. I'll be twenty next month."

"And how old do you think I am?"

"I don't know, twenty–six?"

He tried not to laugh at her youthful naiveté. Six years to her probably seemed as long as twenty to him. "Try thirty–nine. I'm going to be forty this year."

"Really?" She looked impressed. "You're in incredible shape for such an old geezer."

"So what would your boyfriend say to you taking an old geezer like me skinny–dipping?"

"Don't have a steady boyfriend. Listen, I'm not gonna jump your bones. I'm headed for a swim after work today anyway. If you want to come along, I'd like the company."

Turning on one heel and tossing the curls out of her eyes, she held the tray of dirty dishes up high over her shoulder and headed for the kitchen. Despite his resolve, Tyler still could not help admiring the tight curves of her buttocks beneath her shorts and her shapely, sturdy little legs. What could it hurt to have a quick swim with her? There was no way he was going to get involved with someone half his age, no matter how delicious she appeared.

He could not believe he was thinking about her like this. Resting his head in hands for a moment, he tried to concentrate on Sarah and the way she had made him feel only yesterday. But somehow right now Sarah seemed solemn and heavy compared with the lightness of Arden.

"Are you all right?"

Looking up he saw Wanda hovering over him with a frown on her face. Her short stiff hair was dyed an unnatural shade of black and teased up a little on top probably to hide a thin spot. The roundness of her face and the soft, slightly sagging skin of her cheeks were a sharp contrast to the thin lines of her lips and the hard darkness of her eyes.

"You don't feel sick, do you? I made that beef stew up fresh today, you know." The concern in her voice brought Tyler to attention. He stood up and extended a hand.

"Tyler Mackenzie. Thanks for coming out. And I'm fine. It's just the heat, that's all."

"If you think it's hot out here, you should check the thermometer in the kitchen." As she slid into the seat across from him, Tyler was able to note that, although narrow shouldered and small breasted, Wanda was more than just a little broad in the beam. It pained him to think that Arden might look like that in thirty years.

"Heartburn?" Wanda asked in response to the expression on his face.

"No, I'm fine." He had to snap out of this. He was beginning to feel oppressed by the sluggish afternoon warmth. Sipping some ice water, he said, "So I hear you are the last word on the old hotels around here."

"The last word?" She looked at him curiously and then laughed with a wheezing noise. "Yes, you might say that. Which hotels are you researching?"

"Oh, the Mountainside, the Centennial...Which do you think I should start with?"

"Well, those are good choices. You couldn't do a history of Carlisle's hotels without them. Both went down in spectacular fires..." Her eyes grew distant and reflective; he could almost see the specter of flames mirrored in them.

47

Tyler cleared his throat. "I hear your husband is the fire chief and that you know quite a bit about the various blazes the old buildings went down in."

"And my father was fire chief before him until he retired." Wanda's gaze came slowly back to earth. "My goodness, there is so much to tell. You'll have to be more specific, I guess."

"Well, let's start with the Mountainside since that was the biggest." He didn't want to just jump in with the Centennial even though that was his real reason for being here.

"Where to begin...it would take hours..." She suddenly flashed him a disarming smile and he was surprised to see a dimple appear in each of her soft cheeks. "Are you in town for a while, Tyler?"

"As long as I need to be. Why?"

"The best way to do this might be to take you on a little tour of the ruins and sites still around. That way I can make the history really come alive for you, the way it does for me."

"That sounds great!" Tyler was enchanted by the idea. He couldn't have asked for more. "What time is good for you?"

"Well, I can probably get someone in to cover lunch for me tomorrow...How about tomorrow morning at eleven?"

"I'll be here. Thanks so much, Wanda. This is more than I ever expected."

"It's my pleasure. What are you drinking, iced coffee? Arden, bring this man another iced coffee on the house, will you? Awfully hot for so early in the year, isn't it?" She stood up. "Gotta finish cleaning up the kitchen now. I'll see you tomorrow." Her impressive behind looked even larger as she retreated behind the counter.

"Sounds like she likes you," Arden remarked teasingly as she slid another glass of iced coffee in front of him. "She's not that friendly to most people."

"I guess we share a common interest." Every time she caught his attention, he seemed to lose his focus. His

48

purpose for coming to Carlisle today seemed to be slipping farther and farther away, a helium balloon that was floating out of his reach.

He had to put things into their proper perspective. Arden knew everyone in town. She could probably help him immensely. She could probably fill him in on invaluable information about who was in town the day of the Centennial fire. She could probably introduce him to others who could help. After all, if Wanda was her mother, then, for crying out loud, her father was the fucking fire chief.

But when he looked up from his drink, she had disappeared. Probably just as well, he thought with a certain amount of relief. He left his money on the table with a more than generous tip, and walked out of the now empty restaurant.

No cool breezes stirred the thick air in the center of Carlisle now. He hoped it would be cooler on the shady dirt road back to West Jordan. As he knelt down to tie a wayward shoelace before peddling home, something soft hit him in the back of the neck and skimmed across his shoulder.

He jumped back instinctively before he realized it was just a clean white bath towel. Glancing up, he saw Arden straddling her own mountain bike, a wide grin on her face. Another white towel hung loosely around her neck.

"You coming?"

How could he resist? Besides, he had made the rational decision that it would be useful to cultivate this young girl's friendship.

He smiled back at her and slung the towel around his own neck. It smelled faintly of perfumed laundry detergent. "I'll follow you."

Half a mile out of town, Arden took a right turn onto a narrow dirt path that quickly became a steep slide down what could only be termed as a ravine. Tyler slowed down to a snail's pace as he admired how easily Arden took the bumps and curves of the downward trail. She obviously knew the terrain well.

"Show off!" he called as he dismounted and walked his bike the rest of the way down. She was too far ahead to hear him. The sound of rushing water became louder and then the path ended abruptly by a pile of granite boulders at the edge of a wide stream.

"This is where you swim?" Tyler had to shout to be heard above the crashing of the fast moving water.

"A little ways down there's a natural dam and a deep pool. But we have to walk from here." She scrambled nimbly over the large uneven rocks, completely at ease and apparently very used to the beauty of her surroundings.

Tyler followed more slowly, becoming more uncertain of the wisdom of embarking on this adventure. The swollen stream was deep and fast and cold; it cooled the air surrounding it by several degrees. But as they rounded a bend, the water became suddenly quieter and gentler and much more inviting.

"Here we are," Arden announced dropping down on a large, flat, sunbaked boulder. "My private piece of heaven."

"Thanks for sharing it with me." Tyler flopped down next to her.

"Well, it's not really private. Lots of people swim here in the summer. But this time of the year, it's all mine."

"Arden, can I ask you a few questions about something I'm working on?" Tyler was surprised that he was actually able to focus on his long range goal right now.

"Sure. Like what?" She was kicking off her shoes and unbuckling her belt.

"Can you remember back to the day when the Centennial fire happened?"

"I should be able to — it was less than a week ago. My brain cells aren't that fried yet." She gave him a funny look.

"Did you work at the cafe that day?"

"Yeah, sure, why?" Her little shorts fell down around her ankles, revealing a pair of pale blue bikini underpants.

"Can you remember if there was anyone from out of town who came in for lunch that day?"

50

She turned to face him and frowned with one finger on her forehead. He could not tear his eyes away from a little tuft of blond pubic hair that had escaped from the narrow crotch of her underpants.

"I don't recall anybody. I mean, if there had been some real hunking dude or some super beautiful babe I'm sure I'd remember. But actually I don't think there was anyone I didn't know."

"Well how about if anybody acted unusual that day? Or if a couple of people had a fight or something?"

Her eyes narrowed suspiciously. "Are you some kind of cop or something?"

Tyler laughed at the look on her face. "I'm a journalist trying to write a good story, that's all. You know, human interest angle, whatever."

Arden slapped her cheek suddenly. "What am I thinking? SHE came in for lunch that day."

"Who?"

"The woman who died in the fire. The one from Hawaii. Only of course we didn't know who she was at the time. That she was going to die in the fire, I mean." Arden whipped her shirt off over her head and then stood looking down at him, her hands on her little hips, wearing only a stretchy peach–colored cotton bra and her underpants. The whiteness of her skin made her seem suddenly fragile. "Aren't you going in?"

"Oh, sure." Tyler quickly took his own T–shirt off and tossed it on the ground beside him. "So did you talk to her?"

"Well, nothing special. Just took her order, you know. Hey, where'd you get a tan like that already?"

"I just came back from Bali."

"Bali?" Her blank expression said it all as she kicked her batiked shirt aside.

"Indonesia. Like where your shirt is probably from. All right, so do you remember what she was wearing?"

"Red. A red dress with long sleeves. It looked fabulous on her because she had this really dark, frizzy hair."

"Was she fat, thin?"

"I don't know. She had really big tits, like out to here." Arden held her hand several inches away from her own small round breasts. "You know, I always notice when they're the kind that stick out over the table."

Tyler laughed at her description. Before he had a chance to ask her another question, she had unhooked her bra and slipped off her underpants. Glancing provocatively over her shoulder at him, she tilted her head meaningfully towards the stream, before executing a graceful swan dive off the rock and disappearing into the water. Seconds later she surfaced a few yards downstream with a breathless whoop.

"What are you waiting for?" she shouted, treading water. "Chicken!"

If he hesitated now, he knew he would never get in. Dropping his shorts and boxers, he leaped in after her.

The water was colder than anything he had ever experienced. As his head broke the surface, icy fingers seemed to be squeezing the warmth out of all his limbs and organs. His heartbeat seemed erratic and his lungs did not want to open up for air. Forcing his body towards shore, he dragged himself out onto the rocks. As he gasped for breath, he watched his skin turn red as though he was a lobster being pulled from the boiling pot. Arden materialized at his side.

"Why didn't you tell me we'd be swimming above the Arctic Circle today?" he gasped as she handed him his towel.

She shrugged and grinned. Her translucent skin was a bright pink as it fought to regain its warmth. Her tiny, pale pink nipples had hardened into rosebuds not much bigger than the goose bumps that covered the rest of her breasts. Oblivious to the cold and her nudity, she sat down cross–legged next to him.

"Refreshing, wasn't it?"

He laughed and shook his head in disbelief as he wrapped the towel around his waist. "I may not warm up again until fall."

"What you're supposed to do now is stretch out on that big sunny boulder over there. The sun will warm you right up, you'll see."

The warm granite did look very inviting and he wanted to put some space between himself and Arden's naked body. Spreading the towel, he stretched out on top of it, face down, not wanting her to be aware of the fact that he was more than a little aroused by her.

Amazingly enough, within a few minutes of baking in the sun he began to feel extremely relaxed and could even feel himself drifting towards sleep. He opened his eyes to see what Arden was up to. He did not even have to pick up his head to see her. She was sitting up on a rock, leaning back on her hands, eyes closed and face tilted up to the sky, her legs stretched out in a vee. Her uninhibited position was an open invitation to the sun. Or anyone else who was interested in looking or possibly doing more. She was a Maxfield Parrish print come to life.

Tyler filled his mind with the view of her perfect elfin body set against the glorious background of the mountain stream on a spring day. Then, as though drugged by the image, he closed his heavy eyelids and slipped helplessly into sleep.

Afterwards, he remembered that he had awoken at one point with an incredibly stiff neck and had rolled over onto his back to alleviate the pain. But by the time he was awakened from an exciting sexual dream by an even more erotic sensation, he had no recollection of changing his position and could not imagine how Arden had managed to roll him over without him being aware of it.

He opened his eyes just in time to see the top of Arden's white blonde curls lift up from his groin area as, in one agile motion, she swung her leg over him and slowly began settling herself down onto his very erect penis.

"Oh, my God, Arden!" He emitted a groan that was a cross between pleasure and horror as he tried to extract himself out from under her. "What do you think you're doing?"

"Don't tell me you don't want to do this," she said trying to push him back down again.

"Well, believe it or not–" Letting his physical strength overcome his mental weakness, he rolled the two of them over so that she was on the bottom and then quickly pulled himself out of her. "I don't." He looked around for his shorts but his clothes were on another rock several yards away.

"Look, I admit I may be a little bit physically attracted to you–" he called over his shoulder as he made his way towards his clothing.

"A little bit?" Arden snorted derisively, her ego obviously bruised. "That was one of the biggest attractions I've seen in a long time!"

He had to laugh in spite of the situation. "Okay, so maybe I'm a lot attracted to you. But that doesn't mean I have to have sex with you."

"But I know you want to."

"There's lots of things I want to do that I don't do! Besides, I already have a girlfriend. I've even had sex once already today!"

With his shorts in place, he turned to face her. Although she didn't say it, her body language clearly said, so what? Her hands were defiantly on her hips, her lips were pursed in frown and she was not going to be embarrassed into covering up her beautiful naked body.

Shit, he had to keep from blowing this connection. He would have to wait until later to deal with his own feelings about having actually been date–raped by someone half his age and half his size.

"Look, Arden." He moved close enough to touch her face. "I'm sorry if I hurt your feelings. I'd still like to be your friend and get to know you better."

He knew he was leading her on by the look of hope that lit up her eyes. "Okay. No hard feelings. Besides, I did break my promise not to jump your bones. I just thought ..." She shrugged and let the thought pass. "You leaving now?"

He looked at his watch. 4:30. Damn. He'd never get home by five – it would take at least two hours. "Yes, I'm already late for an important meeting. How about you?"

"No – I don't have to be anywhere until my aerobics class at seven. I think I'll stay here for a while. Probably won't be this nice tomorrow." She scratched her neck and looked up at the angle of the sun. "So – see you soon?"

"Definitely. I'm going to need more than just your mother's help with this story." That probably wasn't what she wanted to hear. "I'll call you in a couple of days. If anything comes up, I'm staying over at the West Jordan Inn." He hoped it wasn't a mistake to tell her that.

When Tyler left a few minutes later, she was still standing there on the same rock with her back to him, arms akimbo, stance defiant, watching the water rush by.

Pushing the bike back up the steep incline took several minutes longer than coming down. When he finally reached the road, his brow was damp with sweat again. He was really going to be late now. Sarah would be ripshit at him. She was never late when someone else's time was at stake.

Well, he certainly had never expected the day to turn out the way it had. How would he ever explain it to her and convince her of his innocence? And how innocent was he really? It made him think of all the stories he'd heard over the years of girls being reprimanded for getting themselves into compromising situations – "Well, it never would have happened if you hadn't invited him over when your parents weren't home," or "What did you expect would happen if you went to the drive–in with a fifth of Wild Turkey?" or "If you didn't want to have sex with him, why did you take off your clothes and fall asleep on a boulder stark naked?"

Surely Sarah had had a similar experience at some point in her life. And being a woman, she would be compassionate and understanding about what it felt like to be sexually victimized.

Yeah, right. Dream on. Tyler hoped the mud up to his axles would answer any questions about why he came home so late on a warm, sweet evening in early May.

55

CHAPTER FOUR

Sarah was trying desperately not to lose the sense of peaceful well–being she had been feeling all day. But as five o'clock became six o'clock and then six thirty and then nearly seven, she could not even remember the love and good will she had felt towards Tyler over coffee in bed that morning.

Reed had arrived promptly at five bearing a large bouquet of fringed red parrot tulips.

"These are exquisite!" she had exclaimed. "Where did you find flowers like this?"

"In my garden. I thought you'd like them. They remind me of you."

Sarah had blushed so deeply that she probably had actually resembled the tulips for a moment. "You do remember that I told you Tyler is more than just a friend, don't you?"

He had shrugged unconcernedly. "Story of my life. But doesn't stop me from expressing what I feel."

For the first hour they had chatted idly, sitting in wicker chairs on the porch, drinking margaritas, enjoying the unseasonably warm air. When Tyler didn't show up by six, Sarah's irritation began to show.

"You sure we shouldn't go look for him?"

"No, this is just like him. Gets so involved with what he's doing that he forgets what time it is. I'm glad this is a restaurant and we can eat whenever he gets here. If I had dinner on the table I'd really be pissed."

Reed raised an eyebrow. "I guess I'm glad I don't have to see that side of you."

Forty–five minutes and another margarita later, Sarah was becoming more worried than angry.

"What's the worst that could happen to him? That he'd have to abandon the bike in the woods and walk home? Lighten up. I'm prepared to spend the night and besides, this gives me more alone time with you."

Sarah frowned and did not reply for a moment. For a man accused of arson and murder and possibly facing a life sentence in prison, Reed seemed awfully relaxed. But maybe he was right. All she had was an incorrigible boyfriend.

"He just infuriates me some times. He gets so absorbed in what he's doing that the rest of the world disappears. It's like he has blinders on and can't see anything but the task at hand. Of course, I don't mind when that task is me..." She closed her eyes for a brief second as she remembered Tyler's face close to hers in bed, watching her intently as his fingers did magic tricks to her body that excited her to near explosion. "Would you like another margarita?" she asked, standing up abruptly and downing the rest of own drink.

Reed put his hand over his glass. "Not just yet, thanks."

By the time Sarah came back outside, Tyler had arrived and he and Reed had already shaken hands and started conversing. Tyler's bare legs were splattered with mud above equally encrusted sneakers and his khaki shorts were streaked with dirt from where he had wiped his hands on them. He was describing a portion of the road that seemed to have thawed beneath the surface between morning and evening where he'd sunk so deep he'd had to literally dig his bike out.

"Hello, dearest. Sorry I'm so late." He gave Sarah a peck on the cheek as though this was an everyday occurrence in their life, like he had merely been stuck in freeway traffic on the way home from the office.

"Where have you been–" she began to scold, but before she could put the question mark on the end of the sentence, he cut her off.

"I'm just going to run up and take a quick shower and wash this mud off. I'll be ten minutes max." He stepped inside the screen door and then, thinking twice, kicked off his muddy sneakers and left them outside on the porch before bounding up the stairs.

"Good thing the entrance to the bar and restaurant is around the side," Sarah remarked as she swept Tyler's tracks off the porch. "So – did your first impression of him inspire the confidence that he could help you?" She could not keep the cynicism out of her voice.

"Sarah."

"Well, Christ. You'd think a smart guy like him could figure out how much time it takes to get home fifteen minutes early so that he could shower before an appointment instead of after he's introduced himself."

Reed laughed and after a moment she had to join in. After all, it really was a small, humorous problem compared to the one they were about to tackle over dinner.

"I can't believe how ravenous all that exercise has made me. I bet I could eat two of every course." Tyler pushed his empty soup bowl away and leaned back in his chair. "So let's start with how you know Mimi."

"We went to Carlisle College together for a year back in the early 70s. Truthfully, I didn't know her all that well. She was the roommate of a girl I hung out with for a while. As I recall, she moved out of the dorm mid–year to live with her boyfriend."

"Did you ever sleep with her?"

"Tyler!"

"Now, Sarah, we're talking the early seventies here."

"He's right, Sarah. At a place like Carlisle, lots of us slept with people we barely knew." Reed shook his head slowly, staring off into the distant memories of his past. "No, to my knowledge, I didn't sleep with her. At least I don't remember it if I did." He grinned ruefully.

"Did you do a lot of drugs back then?"

"No, not me. Just the required amounts for socializing. Now Amber on the other hand–"

"Who's Amber?" asked Sarah.

58

"Amber was Mimi's roommate, the one who was my girlfriend for a while. Amber liked to live on the edge. Drugs, alcohol and especially sex. Since she and Mimi were so close, I assume Mimi probably had the same inclinations."

"So where's Amber these days?"

Reed laughed and shrugged. "I haven't seen Amber since the day I left Carlisle. We'd already ended our relationship by then. I walked in on her having this group sex thing one night. When I confronted her, she acted like it didn't matter that she and I were involved in a one–on–one way. She said it didn't change our relationship any. I decided I just wasn't interested in sharing diseases with everyone else at school. Or my girlfriend. And that was that."

Tyler was gorging on his salad, so Sarah took the opportunity to satisfy her own curiosity. "So, like how many were involved in this group sex thing?"

Tyler gave her a dirty look, but his mouth was too full to keep the conversation on track. Reed laughed again. Sarah was beginning to realize that his laughter was a nervous habit. "Oh, I don't know. Maybe seven or eight. More guys than women. But believe me, it turned a lot of people off when they heard about it. I mean, group sex as a fantasy is one thing, but as a reality..."

"Was Mimi part of it?" Tyler steered the topic back again.

"I don't think so. I can't really remember. I sort of doubt it, though, because she'd already moved off campus by then."

"Did you ever meet her boyfriend?"

Reed nodded emphatically as he popped a tomato into his mouth. "Mmmm. Real motherfucker, if you don't mind my language. Lived by himself in an old ramshackle house on the edge of town near the National Forest. Amber and I went out there a few times because she wanted to visit Mimi. The guy acted like he couldn't wait for us to leave. Real aloof, unfriendly type. Very possessive about Mimi. I could never see what she saw in him. Amber would laugh at me and tell me he was incredibly sexy. I thought he was a jerk."

"Do you remember his name?"

"Ned or Nick or something. I can't remember. I haven't thought about him in years."

"Was he a local or did he go to the college?"

Reed shook his head again. "Might've been local. Hell, if I can recall."

"Well, if he was local, he might still be around. And if he's still as possessive as you say, he might be our man." Tyler jotted a few things down in his notebook.

Both Reed and Sarah were duly impressed. "That's a great idea!" Sarah exclaimed. "Can you remember what he looked like, Reed?"

Reed shut his eyes for a moment and rested his chin in his hand. "Tall, maybe over six feet, dark hair, kind of shaggy, beginnings of a beer belly. One of those out of shape he—man types who could lift a car or knock you flat in a second. I still don't know where the sex appeal was."

"Do you think you could still find the house where he lived?" Tyler asked thoughtfully.

"Yeah, I think so."

They were all silent for a moment while the bartender cleared away their empty salad plates and served their dinners. It was almost dark outside now and Sarah lit the candle on their table as well as the candles on the other tables in the nearly dining room and then dimmed the overhead lights.

"What about Mimi? How did she look back then?" Tyler tested his Cajun catfish to see how spicy it was.

"Good. She looked good. Mmm, this chicken is excellent. She was kind of big – broad shoulders, big knockers, small waist but big hips. The kind of body that most men like to drool over. She had real thick curly black hair, pretty long, darkish skin, kind of a prominent nose. I think she was part Italian."

Tyler nodded. It matched Diana Stellano's description and what Arden had told him about the woman who had eaten lunch at the cafe.

"And now, the real question. Why do you think she asked you to meet her?"

"I don't have a clue. Maybe she just wanted to talk about old times. Maybe she thought I might know where Amber ended up."

"Do you?"

"Nope. I don't even know how Mimi got my address. Like I said, I never saw either of them again after I left Carlisle at the end of the semester in June." He held up a hand suddenly and swallowed a mouthful of food. "Wait a second, I did hear something about them maybe a year or so later. Doug Arbuckle spent a few days at my place on his way out West, he was a friend from school, and told me that Amber and Mimi were still hanging around Carlisle but had dropped out of the college. He'd seen them at the lake one afternoon, it must've been summer, but I can't remember what he said they were doing. I probably told him I didn't care, so he might not have told me at all."

"Where's Doug Arbuckle live?"

Reed shrugged again. "You got me. I think he grew up some place outside of Boston, maybe Wellesley or Weston, but when I saw him that last time he told me he was headed for Colorado. I have no idea where he ended up."

"How about Amber? Where'd she grow up?"

"Amber? I don't know if she ever grew up." His pale blue eyes grew distant again. "She always reminded me of Mary Martin in that Peter Pan TV special from the late fifties. But I think she spent her childhood in Manchester, New Hampshire. She didn't talk about it much, I was under the impression it wasn't particularly great as far as childhoods go."

"What was her last name?"

"Saint Pierre. Amber St. Pierre."

"Do you think her parents are still in Manchester?"

61

"Her father and stepmother, you mean? Her real mother was gone, I don't know if she was dead or divorced. I got the feeling there were a few types of abuse going on in Amber's home before she left for college. Only we didn't call it abuse back then. They weren't well–off, I know that, because Amber was on part scholarship, part financial aid and never had much money to blow. If I remember correctly she didn't even go home for Christmas that year. So, no, I don't know if her parents are still in Manchester. But if you're thinking of looking for her, I doubt that she would have settled close by them, if you know what I mean."

"Well, twenty years is a long time. She might have resolved her differences with them by now. They may know where she is."

"Twenty years?" Reed stared at the candle and drifted off again. "Sometimes twenty years ago seems like yesterday."

Over coffee and dessert, Sarah questioned Tyler about his day. Suppressing his feelings of guilt, he told them about what he'd learned at the library and Arden's description of Mimi coming in for lunch and about Wanda's offer of a tour the next day.

"Sounds really interesting," Reed remarked. "I never knew much about the history of those old places even though a lot more of them were still standing back when I was in Carlisle."

"I'd like to know more also," Sarah agreed. "Think she'd mind if you brought a few friends?"

Tyler was thoughtful for a moment. It could be helpful to have Reed along on a tour of Carlisle, possibly knock on a few of the closed doors in his memory. But he was not the most popular man in town right now. "You'd have to promise not to mention who you were," he answered finally. "I don't think the police in Carlisle would be too wild about the primary arson and murder suspect being given a tour of the grand hotels that burned down. But it might help jog your memory about a few things. I'd also like to go over in detail what you remember of the night you drove through Carlisle when Mimi was murdered. And afterwards we can see if you can still find your way to Mimi's boyfriend's house."

Later, as they got ready for bed, Tyler tried to find the courage to tell Sarah about his incident with Arden. But no matter how he worded it in his mind, it never sounded as innocent as he felt he was. And he knew what Sarah would think. Luckily she was too tired to sustain the anger she had felt towards his being late. But the air between them was still strained. Neither of them initiated any overtures of making love.

By morning the weather had turned overcast and the humid air promised rain. Donning foul weather gear, the three of them piled into Sarah's car and drove around the mountain to Carlisle. Reed wore Tyler's felt fedora which covered his hair and partially hid his face.

"Not that anybody but the town cops would recognize me. Of course in a small town like Carlisle, you never know where you might meet a town cop."

Sarah and Reed waited in the car while Tyler went inside the cafe to find Wanda. It was the lull between the breakfast and lunch crowds and the cafe was empty except for the savory smells coming from the kitchen. He poked his head through the swinging doors. "Anybody here?"

The only person he saw was Arden, who was filling salt and pepper shakers on a counter in the middle of the room. She was wearing a long white apron that hung below the hem of her shorts and made her look even more childlike. Her face lit up like a sunrise when she saw Tyler.

"My mom just ran home to change her clothes and to pick up Mary McGillicuddy to fill in for the lunch shift." Arden wiped her hands on the apron and came around the counter to stand unreasonably close to him. "You want a soda or something?"

63

"Uh, no thanks. I've got some friends waiting in the car. I'll just stay outside until Wanda shows up."

Arden shrugged and pouted a little. "Suit yourself. I'll see you later then. My mother thought she'd bring you back here for a late lunch after the cafe closed."

As he hurried back through the dining room, Tyler wondered nervously if the mother had the same designs on him that the daughter did. Wanda was coming up the sidewalk just as he stepped out the door. She was accompanied by a white haired woman with a body like a flour sack. "I'll be with you in a second," she called as she hurried by him. His brief glance of her indicated that, although she was wearing tight Levis and sturdy shoes, Wanda was also wearing excessive eye shadow and lipstick, and something with a red silky bow beneath her jacket.

He glanced back at the car. Reed and Sarah seemed to be laughing conspiratorially about something. He was beginning to think it had been a mistake to bring them along. Everything was starting to feel like a mistake. He opened the driver's side door.

"Sarah, why don't you sit in the back with Reed and I'll drive?" he suggested. "Let's try not to mention Reed's first name – just say he's your cousin from..."

"Minnesota," Reed volunteered. "Well, that's where I am from, where I grew up."

As Tyler was pondering how they had overlooked that piece of information the night before, Wanda approached him, slightly out of breath.

"Do you mind if a couple of friends tag along with us?" he asked her immediately. "They were really excited when they heard I was going to get the history of Carlisle's hotels from a true expert." He flashed her his widest smile, the one he knew caused Grand Canyon dimples to appear in his cheeks. "I thought it would be easier than trying to repeat everything for them later."

Overwhelmed by his attention, Wanda giggled like a teenager. "Why not? The more the merrier," she replied, trying to slide her oversized behind gracefully into the

64

passenger seat. "Now, Tyler," she went on when she was finally settled, "Where would you like to start?" She did not even turn to acknowledge the presence of Sarah and Reed.

"Well, with the Mountainside, if you don't mind. That was the grandest hotel of all, wasn't it?"

"Yes, it certainly was. Why don't you make a U–turn after this red car passes by and we'll head over to that part of town." Wanda slid into command quite naturally and was soon effortlessly directing the event.

They toured the ruins of the Mountainside's personal train station, the carriage barn that amazingly enough still housed an old stage coach and a 1932 limousine, the foundations of the stables, the overgrown tennis courts and the remains of the formal gardens. They finished with the grand stone staircase that stood at the edge of a grassy field as a memorial to the once spectacular hotel building.

"Do you remember the fire?" Tyler asked.

"How could I ever forget? It was probably one of the most impressive events of my childhood. My father was the fire chief, don't forget, so my family was quite involved. He didn't come home for three days and nights; my mother would make big pots of soup for all the fire fighters and we'd bring it over to them. Let me tell you, they had a terrible time with that fire. It was windy and below zero and the water hoses kept freezing up. At times they could barely contain the blaze. We heard they could see the glow at night all the way over to Jordan Center. Yes sir, if you ask me, nothing that exciting ever happened in this town again."

"Anybody die in that fire?"

"Susie Jenkins' dad. He got hit with a falling beam when the west wing collapsed. Thank god, it was winter or that place might have been full of guests."

"How did the fire start?" asked Sarah.

Wanda shrugged. "No one ever really knows how these fires get started. Arson most likely."

65

Reed shook his head. "Why would someone want to burn down the classic works of intricate architecture that these old places were? It hurts my heart to think of it."

"The carpenter's lament." Sarah gave Reed a tiny grin.

"So aside from Susie Jenkins' dad, has anyone else died in any of the other hotel fires around here?"

"Nope. Well, not counting this last tragedy at the Centennial House." Wanda began walking back to the car and Tyler quickly fell into step with her.

"Did you know the woman who died in that fire?"

Wanda shook her head. "Apparently she was from out of town."

"I thought I heard somewhere she'd gone to Carlisle College back when."

Wanda's derisive snort expressed her opinion more eloquently than her words. "Us town folks didn't have much truck with those college kids. They were a bunch of hippy weirdoes who brought all kinds of bad influences to the village. Most of us heaved a big sigh of relief when that place closed down. Except for the fact that a lot of local people lost their jobs."

Behind her back Tyler gave Reed a look that meant *don't say a word.* "Any of the college kids stick around town after the school closed?"

"A few. I think Ernie Bascom went to the college if I'm not mistaken. He's our plumber – lives over to Jordan Center."

Tyler could see Reed's jaw drop and then he silently mouthed the words, "I knew him."

"So where to next?" he quickly asked Wanda.

"Well, why don't we go by some place that's still standing? The Barrister, round the other side of the lake, is a wonderful example of a typical resort hotel."

As they all got back into the car, Tyler realized that in order to win Wanda's confidence, he was going to have to come back alone. He had a feeling that, if he tapped the tree just right, she would be a sap bucket overflowing with all kinds of information that could help him.

An hour later, when a light drizzle finally became driving rain, they decided to call it a day and return to the cafe for lunch. They hung their wet coats and hats on the old-fashioned coat rack by the door. A couple of solitary diners sat at the counter and there were still a few tables of customers, but it was obvious where they were supposed to sit. They all crowded in to the booth on the end which had been set with a white tablecloth and a centerpiece of early lilacs.

"My goodness, Wanda, you really shouldn't have gone to all this trouble. I'm the one who should be taking you out to lunch," Tyler commented. He and Wanda were squeezed in together on one side, Sarah and Reed on the other.

"I didn't go to any trouble," Wanda laughed. "I had Arden do it all." She squinted suddenly at Reed who was sitting across from her. Tyler realized too late that the seating arrangement was a mistake. Wanda had lots of time to study Reed whose face and hair were now totally exposed without his hat. "You remind me of someone, Andy," she remarked thoughtfully. They had told her Reed's name was Andy.

"Well, maybe you've seen me before. I had a cousin who went to Carlisle College and I used to visit her here. Maybe you just saw me around."

Sarah's and Tyler's eyes met as they both held their breath waiting for Wanda's response.

Wanda shrugged. "Maybe that's it." It was obvious she wasn't convinced.

Across the room, Tyler saw a man and woman suddenly put their heads together as they whispered and stared pointedly at Reed. He swallowed the lump in his throat. Hopefully they would be too polite to say anything.

"You know we don't really have a whole lot of time," he announced in a worried voice. "I hope you haven't planned a three course meal here, Wanda. We have to get Sarah back to West Jordan for an important appointment at the inn."

67

"That's right. The, uh, my accountant is coming by to go over my taxes. I'm, uh, a little late in filing this year." Sarah grimaced, but not because of the taxes. She did not lie with the easy grace that Tyler did.

"I guess I didn't catch what exactly it is you do in West Jordan, Sarah." Although Wanda was speaking to Sarah, she was still scrutinizing Reed's face.

"I manage the West Jordan Inn. You know it, of course, it's very well known in these parts. You'll have to come by for dinner some night, on the house, of course," Sarah was rattling on, a little nervously, trying to redirect Wanda's attention.

"Have you even been over there, Wanda?"

"Oh, sure. Not for a good many years, I don't get out much at night anymore because of this place, but I had my share of drinks there in my younger days."

"Did you know Sarah's mother is the one who did that big stained glass window there behind the bar?"

"Your mom was Winnie Scupper? She did the window in our church when I was a little girl." Safely distracted at last by a topic of greater interest to her, Wanda finally let her gaze stray from Reed and began a lengthy discussion with Sarah about the famous glass work her mother did before she died in her early thirties from a mysterious and accidental fall off a bridge.

The rest of the meal seemed to proceed without a hitch, but an underlying tension lay close beneath the surface. One of the men sitting at the counter spun around and did a double take at Reed. As Arden passed by, he pulled her aside and whispered something in her ear. Her musical laughter filled the room as she pulled her arm away and went on with her work. "You're crazy," she called over her shoulder.

"We really have to go." Tyler stood up, but he was trapped in the booth by Wanda's bulky frame. He put his hand on her shoulder. "I'd like to set up another time to get together, if you don't mind. There are still a number of places I'd like to see."

68

"And next time we won't slow you down with our presence." Sarah took hold of Reed's arm and they both stood up as well. She maneuvered Reed out of the restaurant as quickly as she could, leaving Tyler to make his further arrangements with Wanda.

As they reached the car, Sarah heard the cafe door slam and saw that Tyler was right behind them. She also saw Arden come racing out after him and grab him around the waist in a very familiar way. She could not hear what Arden said but saw Tyler shook his head firmly saying no. Then, flashing her his most promising grin, he pulled away and came towards the car.

"What was that about?" Sarah's tone was full of meaning.

"Tell you later." He climbed into the driver seat. "Now, Reed, let's see how good your memory is. Which way do we go to Mimi's old boyfriend's house?"

Fifteen minutes later Tyler slowly drove the car into the last yard on a dead end road, having passed the nearest neighbor at least half a mile before. Outside a rundown farmhouse that was badly in need of a paint job, three fierce–looking pit bulls barked and strained at their chains. It was an easy assumption that whoever lived there was probably not home since there were no vehicles in the yard that appeared to work, not counting several rusting hulks that were parked permanently in the woods at the edge of the property.

"Yeah, this is the place all right. Barely looks any different than it did twenty years ago, except there are more junk cars."

"Should we knock on the door?" Sarah asked. "He might have a wife who stays home without a car all day."

"Barefoot and pregnant? That would be his style. Damn, I wish I could remember his name."

To answer that question, Tyler backed up to the battered metal rural delivery mailbox perched precariously on a rotten two–by–four at the end of the driveway.

Flipping it open he pulled out a stack of mail. "Mr. Neil Richelieu."

"Neil! Damn, that's right." Reed smacked himself on the side of his head. "I can't believe he still lives here.

"Nothing for Mrs., or Mr. and Mrs., Richelieu." Tyler stuffed the mail back into the box. "Well, I guess we'll come back another time. Maybe we ought stop at that last house and see what the neighbors have to say about him."

The "last house" turned out to be a modern log cabin that did not look like it had been around at the time that Mimi had lived with Neil. A short bald man and his white-haired wife came to open the sliding glass door together.

"Neil? You're looking for Neil?" The man seemed stupefied by the idea. "Never seen the man have any daytime visitors since we retired here eight years ago. Keeps to himself, people say he's more than a little crazy."

"Bob, shhh! They might be family or something."

"Well, if they're family they know he's a little crazy. But if they're family, how come we've never seen their car before?"

"We're not family," Tyler assured them quickly. "Reed here used to know Neil back when the college was around, just thought he'd look him up."

"Oh, you knew him back then? They say he used to be quite the womanizer when he was younger. Now he don't seem to care about nothin' but those damn dogs. Wish he'd get rid of them. Martha and I are afraid of taking a walk in that direction for fear them dogs might get loose."

"Does he work somewhere?"

"Oh, yeah. I believe he's a welder out to that body shop on the highway. Set of biceps on the fellow like I've never seen except in the movies. Not someone to mess with."

They thanked Bob and Martha and got back in the car. "Well, that's one small success for the day, anyway," commented Tyler as they headed back along the dirt road into town. "We'll have to figure out what our approach will be to this guy and which one of us should do it." He felt

70

relieved that now he at least had something to report back to Mrs. Stellano.

"Do you have to head back home tonight or can you stay over again?" Sarah asked Reed. "I think it's useful to have him on hand, don't you, Tyler?" Her voice had an oddly casual tone to it that Tyler could not fathom.

"Definitely. I'd like to try to contact a few of those other old college people you mentioned. They may remember things that might help us."

"Well, I can't think of anything more important on my agenda right now that trying to save my own life." This time there was no question about the underlying feelings when Reed laughed loudly at his own remark.

Someone was pounding on the bar with a beer mug and yelling her name. "Sarah! Sarah! Wake up!"

Was she so tired that she had fallen asleep on her feet? As she struggled slowly towards the end of the bar the pounding began again. Then suddenly someone was shaking her by the shoulders and forcing her to sit up in bed.

She opened her eyes to see the bedroom lit by an eerie orange glow. "Tyler, what the –"

The wail of a siren pulling into the parking lot brought her to her feet. A quick glance out the window told her everything. The old barn across the yard was a tower of flames.

Sarah grabbed the first clothes she came into contact with, an old sweatshirt and pair of Tyler's pants, and dressed as she ran down the stairs. Tyler was close behind her. She unlocked the outside door and flung it open, much to the relief of Brian Evans, the local policeman who had been pounding on it.

"We need you to move your cars out onto the street so that the fire engines can get in," he explained rapidly.

"I've got the keys to the Subaru. Sarah, you better wake Reed up so he can move his truck." Tyler raced out into the yard and Sarah ran back inside.

71

"Sarah, make sure your windows are shut tight!" Brian called after her. "They're gonna hose down this side of the building so that it doesn't go up."

A dozen thoughts ran through her mind as she hurried up the front stairs. She prayed that Reed was still in bed and sound asleep. Without stopping to knock, she tried the door handle to his room. It was not locked and she quickly threw the door open.

Reed was curled up in a ball under the quilt, snoring loudly. She was sure there was no way a person could fake a snore like that.

"Reed, Reed, wake up!" She had no time for gentleness in waking him.

He sat up abruptly and looked around at his surroundings blankly. Then, seeing the flashing lights and the color of the sky outside, he leaped out of bed and ran to the window completely unconcerned for his own nakedness. Even in the midst of a crisis, Sarah could not help but take a second to admire his sturdy muscular physique before she scooped his pants off the floor and threw them at him.

"Hurry! You've got to move your truck!"

"My God, Sarah, what happened? Who did this?" He followed her, barefoot and shirtless, down the stairs.

"I have no idea. We just woke up and the barn was already on fire. Damn, I wish I had an inventory of what was in there. We just used it as a storage shed. I hope nothing valuable of Woody's was there."

When they reached the door, Reed faltered at the sight of the police cars and the growing crowd. He grabbed Sarah's hand and pressed the keys to his truck into it. "You do it, Sarah. I can't go out there."

"Reed!"

"They'll think I did it, I know they will. Somebody did this on purpose to set me up, I'm sure of it."

Sarah's jaw dropped and then closed again with firm resignation. "If you hide out in here, you will only seem more guilty. Come on, I'll go with you." Hooking her arm firmly through his, she led him across the parking lot to his truck.

To her relief, nobody paid the slightest attention to who Reed was. They were too intent on controlling the growing blaze. But she knew there would be questions to answer later and that Reed was right. He would be first on the suspect list.

The three of them stood on the side porch for the next two hours, watching the volunteer firemen of West Jordan squelch the raging flames. The ancient, dried timbers of the barn burned neatly and rapidly, but the occasional explosions from cans of gasoline or paint or other unidentifiable substances made the situation unpredictable and dangerous. Dawn was breaking by the time the building had been reduced to a smoldering, charred heap of rubble.

"I feel responsible for this, Sarah," Reed repeated for the third time. "Even if it wasn't done to set me up, somebody may have been trying to let you know what they think of you helping me out."

Or maybe it has to do with nosy journalists poking into business they shouldn't, she thought, but could not bring herself to say.

"Look, I'll build you a new barn, how's that sound?"

"Don't be silly. Insurance will cover it." Sarah sat down on the edge of the porch and sipped a cup of coffee.

"No, I mean it. It's the least I can do to help you out. Go ahead and claim the labor and even bill me, but I'll turn the money back over to you. It'll help you out here a little."

"Okay, we'll talk about it later. But I think your time has come now." A couple of men with clipboards were headed towards them accompanied by Brian Evans.

"Mr. Anderson, we'd like to speak to you alone inside if we may. Sarah and Tyler, Mr. Johnson will take your statements out here."

Sarah squeezed Reed's hand before they led him away and then rested her forehead on her knees for a moment.

She felt Tyler's arm creep around her back. The weight of it was reassuring. She lifted her head and straightened up.

"Ms. Scupper, can you give me the names of anybody you can remember who visited this establishment last night..."

CHAPTER FIVE

"Tyler! Phone call!"

Tyler looked up from the game of chess he was playing with Reed to see Sarah holding out the cordless phone to him from behind the bar.

"Who is it?" he mouthed.

She put her hand across the receiver. "Arden?" She shrugged.

"Thanks. I'll be back in a second, Reed." Tyler carried the phone out into the front lobby. "Hi, Arden. What's up?"

"I was wondering if we could get together this evening."

"Get together?"

"And talk. There's some stuff I think I ought to tell you about."

"Uh, sure. The only problem is I'm expecting a few really important calls tonight. How about during the day tomorrow?" It had to be safer to see Arden in the daytime; he still didn't trust her motives. "Your mom's supposed to give me a tour of Maple Hill and the old college site. How about after that?"

Tyler couldn't tell if she was sighing or just taking deep breaths on the other end of the line. "No, I'd rather meet tomorrow night. I'll meet you at nine at the Springhouse."

"The Springhouse?"

"It's the bar in the old annex of the Barrister Inn. We can go somewhere else and talk."

"Okay. See you then." Tyler shut the phone off and sat on the edge of the front desk for a moment, intrigued by what she might want to tell him. He'd been hitting nothing but dead ends in the last few days. Doug Arbuckle could not be tracked down. None of the St. Pierres in the Manchester area had ever heard of anyone named Amber. His hotel tours around Carlisle with Wanda were a gold

75

mine of historic information, but had brought him no closer to the answer of who might have murdered Mimi. He'd left a message on Neil Richelieu's answering machine the night of the fire and again today, but had no response. He hoped Arden really had something to tell him and it was not just another sexual trap.

He still hadn't gotten around to telling Sarah about the afternoon at the river. In the last few days since the barn had burned down, she'd been fairly stressed out. It had taken a lot of talk and trust to convince the cops that Reed had not set the fire. Arson specialists had determined that it had probably been a misplaced cigarette butt tossed in the wrong direction by an exiting patron of the bar, but no one could be certain. Sarah had been really nervous about calling Woody in Florida to tell him about the fire, but once he found out that nobody had been hurt, Woody had been very relaxed about it.

"None of that stuff I had stored in the barn is doing me any good down here," he said. "So I guess I'm not going to miss it." He had been extremely pleased that Reed was going to clean up the site and rebuild the barn in a more useful, modern design.

Tyler jumped as the phone in his hand rang into his thoughts. "West Jordan Inn."

"Yeah, is there a Tiner Mackenzie stayin' there?" a voice growled in his ear.

"Tyler. Yes, that's me. Who's calling?"

"This is Neil Richelieu. You been leavin' me these messages on my machine about me callin' you. What's so important?"

Tyler sat at the desk and searched the drawers for a pen and some paper. "Thanks for calling back, Neil. I heard that you were an old friend of Mimi Farrell."

"Who?"

"Oh, I'm sorry. You probably knew her as Mimi Stellano."

There was a short silence at the other end of the line.

"Yeah, I knew a Mimi Stellano once. What about her?"

"When was the last time you saw her?"

There was an ugly snarl of laughter. "I ain't seen her in close to twenty years. Damn good thing too. She ruined my fucking life."

"Really? How'd she do that?"

"Fuckin' walkin' out on me the way she did. Made me look like a piece of no–good shit couldn't control his own woman." The man had clearly worked up a good beer buzz before he called. "Workin' as a cocktail waitress at that place, PRETENDING to work as a cocktail waitress, I should say. She was really a cock–FUCKING waitress, screwing guys for money so she could split for Hawaii. Like screwing me wasn't good enough–"

"Neil, you know about the Centennial fire, don't you?"

"What about it?"

"You heard there was a woman who died in that fire, didn't you? A woman named Mimi Farrell?"

"You mean – my Mimi?"

"Look, Neil, I'm sorry to be the one to break it to you–"

"You're not breakin' nothin' to me. The fuckin' bitch deserved to die." There was pause while he swilled something and then belched. "Shit, you tellin' me she was up here and didn't even come to see me? After I was the one made her into a real woman, she should come crawling on her knees, beggin' for forgiveness." His words were more slurred now and Tyler realized there was a strong possibility that Neil was not telling the whole truth.

"Look, Neil, maybe we can get together tomorrow night and you can tell me more about Mimi–"

"Tell you nothin'! Who the hell are you, anyway? And why're you calling me to tell me my Mimi's dead?" Tyler could hear suspicion fall over Neil like an executioner's hood. "Bet you're some cop trying to get me to admit that I did it. Just cause I got outa hand with Millie McPherson that time, they're always tryin' to pin stuff on me. But Millie deserved it too. Flauntin' her butt in front of them guys at the races –well, fuck you too, buddy!"

At the sound of the dial tone, Tyler shook his head and shut the phone off again. If there ever was a man with motive, Neil was it. Finding out anything more about him would be the hard part.

Walking back into the bar, he saw that Reed had abandoned their chess game and was sitting at the end of the bar, laughing about something with Sarah. Sarah had gone ahead with her money–saving plan and let the weekday bartender go, and was covering those shifts herself for now. But business seemed to have dropped off a bit once word got around that Sarah was sheltering and siding with a suspected murderer who might have burned the inn's barn down. Some folks came by once or twice out of curiosity, but mostly it was just the old regulars now, the ones who trusted Sarah's judgment as much as they had trusted Woody's before her.

But watching Sarah's eyes sparkle as she talked with Reed, Tyler found himself wondering, with a surprising twinge of jealousy, about Sarah's judgment.

"That was Neil Richelieu," he announced. "A man with a motive if there ever was one. But gaining his confidence is going to be a trick for Houdini."

"Maybe he'd talk to me," Reed suggested. "You know, an old acquaintance who happened to be in town and stopped by for a chat."

Tyler shook his head. "If he knows you're the prime suspect in the murder of `his Mimi', he'll eat you alive. No, I'm going to have to work on some other angle to get close to him."

The next morning he arrived at the Carlisle Cafe on his bike promptly at 10:30 as planned. The weather had become more typically seasonal, cloudy and cooler, with the sun showing a flash of itself now and then. Wanda had gotten permission to take him on a tour of the Charlemain Hotel, one of the few original structures still standing in this town of hidden history. He was starting to get sick of seeing empty fields where some incredible edifice or other had once stood. Despite his detailed questioning of how each particular building had burned, Wanda always seemed rather vague when it came to specifics. He was going to have to pay a visit to the newspaper archives soon to fill in his story.

The restaurant was empty except for Arden who was sitting on one of the counter stools, reading a magazine. Her bare legs dangled, not quite long enough to reach the footrest. Tyler had noticed that no matter what the weather, Arden always wore shorts that displayed as much of her shapely little legs as possible.

"My mom went home sick." Instead of saying hello, Arden patted the stool next to hers and dazzled him with a smile.

"Well, that's too bad." Tyler remained standing. "Anything serious?"

"No, just one of her migraines. She gets them from time to time."

Tyler frowned, wondering what he could do now to make this visit to Carlisle worth his while.

"But, you know, there is something going on in town that you might find interesting." Seeing that Tyler wasn't going to sit next to her, she put her feet up on the stool beside her and spun it back and forth a little, a teasing gleam in her eye.

"What's that?"

"They're starting the excavation of the old Cherry Lodge site today. Some investor bought it and wants to put a condo village there. They're down there now bulldozing what's left of the old cellar hole and the barn and outbuildings. Wanda didn't think you'd be interested, but I thought you might be able to use it for your story. It's sort of an end and a beginning, you know what I mean?"

"Yes, I do." Tyler was touched by her fresh perception of what he was doing. He could see why Wanda, with her obsession for history, wouldn't want anything to do with the excavation of Cherry Lodge. "How do I get there?"

"Take the road around the lake. It's about half a mile on the left hand side. You can't miss it – it's the place where the backhoe is digging and the dump truck is filling up." As he turned to go, she added," We're still on for tonight, right?"

The excavation site was impossible to miss because of the number of cars, including some police cars, that were pulled haphazardly off the road onto a shoulder that was nothing more than grass and a ditch. As he inched his bike slowly by, he could see a small crowd gathering near an enormous fresh pile of dirt and debris that had obviously been moved just that morning. He parked his bike at the edge of the driveway and walked back to join the oddly silent group.

They were nearly all men in a variety of work clothes, many of whom wore beepers on their belts. The expressions on their faces were not exactly welcoming when they saw Tyler approaching, so he walked as nonchalantly as he could toward a large older woman standing on the edge of the group.

"What's going on?" he asked quietly, at the same time straining to peer down into the freshly dug hole that everyone else was staring into. All he could see were the backs of three large cops and another, even larger man, with a shovel, who seemed to be delicately poking in the dirt.

"They found a body."

Her curt reply was all Tyler needed to hear. He tried to get a better view by sidling his way up the side of the rock pile but he was quickly waved back, with a threat to the crowd in general to stay clear of the hole.

One of the cops turned and shouted a question at a broad–shouldered, gray–haired man who stood slightly apart from everyone else. "Lou, what year was it this place burned down?"

"Seventy–four, I think it was."

"It was Halloween, remember?" another older man volunteered. "We had all the fire engines down t'th'other side of town for the bonfire at the school."

Tyler realized with a start that the man named Lou was Wanda's husband, the fire chief.

"That's right. The place was already a goner by the time we got here. There was no way we could've saved it."

"By God, it's a woman," the man with the shovel exclaimed loud enough for everyone to hear. "Look at her jewelry."

"Don't touch anything," one of the cops warned. "Go gently now, Bud. We want to keep everything as intact as possible."

"Definitely a fire victim," the first cop shouted back up at Lou. "Why don't you come on down here?"

Lou was frowning as he half climbed/half slid down into what Tyler now saw was the old cellar hole of the original hotel. "But we went through the rubble with a fine tooth comb afterwards," he said as he came towards them. "You know, looking for probable cause – oh, sweet Jesus!"

Tyler could see the color draining from Lou's face as viewed the remains of the corpse. The crowd edged closer, trying to get a better look at what Lou was seeing.

"Yeah, Happy Halloween, huh?" The cop turned around to face the others. "There's nothing to see folks, nothing left but a skeleton. You might as well all go about your business. You can read about it in the paper next week."

Nobody moved.

"Wonder who she was?" mused the same older fireman who had fought the Cherry Lodge fire all those years ago. "Wasn't nobody reported missing around that time, I know we checked into that."

"Maybe someone would recognize her jewelry if they'd just let us get close enough to look," muttered the woman next to Tyler.

Tyler had been thinking the same thing, trying to figure what excuse he could use for getting down into the hole. Lou was backing away now, up the steep slope

81

towards Tyler, giving him a slightly better window on what was going on. Now he could see the excavator still carefully clearing around what must be the skull. As he tossed a small shovelful of dirt onto the hillside just below Tyler, there was a glimmer of something shiny flying through the air with it.

Whatever it was had landed just to the left of Lou who was still struggling up the hill with his eyes glued to the macabre scene. A quick glance around told Tyler nobody else had seen the object fall. With what appeared to be an impulsive gesture, Tyler took a few bold steps down the slope and grabbed Lou's arm.

"Here, let me help you," he offered, at the same time letting his camera case fall to the ground. "Oh, just a second." As he bent down to pick it up, his fingers dragged across the dirt until they came in contact with a small sharp object. Keeping it between his hand and the camera, he assisted Lou back up to the edge of the site.

No one questioned his motive. The older man was still as white as a sheet. Tyler was somewhat surprised by his reaction; as fire chief surely he had encountered death before. Although Wanda had mentioned that no one had ever died in a hotel fire before Mimi. And a skeleton was a different matter altogether.

"Are you okay, Lou?" the big woman asked him.

Lou took a deep breath. "Fine, fine." He took a handkerchief out of his pocket and wiped his face. "It's just a little upsetting that we might've let this happen, no matter how long ago it was."

While the focus was on Lou, Tyler slipped his hand into his pocket and let the object go. The sharp point on it had left a dark impression on his palm. "You're Wanda's husband, aren't you?" he said, turning to Lou. "I'm Tyler Mackenzie," he went on in response to Lou's blank look. "I'm doing an article on the old hotels in Carlisle and Wanda's been giving me history tours. She knows a lot about these old places and when they burned down."

82

Lou looked at him oddly as though his thoughts were very far away. "Nice to meet you," he said distantly. "I have to get back now." As he turned abruptly and walked down the driveway, most of the eyes in the crowd followed him.

"Pretty shook up, wasn't he?" commented somebody.

"Yeah, I think he's mad he was never able to nail Richelieu for any of the fires, and now especially this one."

"Was Neil Richelieu a suspect in this fire?" Tyler asked the man who had just spoken.

The man laughed bitterly. "Richelieu's always a suspect. But don't print that in your damn article. There ain't never been any proof."

"All right, everybody out of here now. We're going to set up a barrier while we wait for the forensics experts to get here. Come on, everybody, move it out."

Grumbling, the crowd began to disperse. Tyler walked back to his bicycle, wondering what to do next. There were suddenly so many new, unanswered questions. It was probably time for a visit to the archives room at the Jordan Weekly Record. If he took the main roads home instead of the trail over the mountain, he would have to go right through Jordan Center. It was a route he would normally avoid because of the traffic, but there were some things he wanted to know.

About a mile down the road something sharp stabbed his upper thigh and he pulled off onto the shoulder. He shoved his hand into his pocket and pulled out the mysterious object.

It was an earring. Blackened and dull and dirt encrusted, it began to come to life as he rubbed it clean on his khaki shorts. There was a yellowish stone in a circle of silver with two curved points on the top, like horns. It dangled from a silver post that had once hung in the dead woman's ear. The back of his neck prickled as he looked at it. He knew he should probably give it back to the police. Instead he pocketed it and rode on.

By the time Tyler pulled into the parking lot of the inn it was early evening and he was beat. The ride home on main roads through Jordan Center was much longer, with just enough traffic to be unpleasant for a bicyclist. Reading the microfiche in the archives of the local newspaper had been tedious as well. Luckily, because of his tours with Wanda, he had specific names and dates to look up that helped him zero in on the right weekly issues.

Neil Richelieu was indeed mentioned as a possible suspect in the Cherry Lodge fire but no one had been able to pin any evidence on him so the case had been dropped. But a history of suspicion brought his name up more than once in the ensuing fires following Cherry Lodge. Each time he was dismissed for lack of evidence. It certainly made Neil look like the next best person for Tyler to investigate.

All he wanted now was a beer and a bath. He wished he hadn't committed himself to meeting Arden later on. He wanted to concentrate on Neil. In the morning he would go out to the welding shop on the highway where Neil worked and feel him out. But then again, maybe Arden could be helpful in that aspect too. After all, she did know everyone in Carlisle.

As he locked his bike to one of the back porch posts, he realized with a start that the charred remains of the old barn were gone. Reed had hired a backhoe to come in for the day. The debris was cleared out and the old dirt foundation was smoothed over. When he stepped inside the lounge, he found Reed was busily working on his blueprints for the new building at a table by an open window. Sarah was conversing with a couple of local forest rangers at the bar. When Tyler didn't approach her, she excused herself and came over to where he waited by the door to the upstairs.

She was wearing a short black knit dress. It had a low scooped back with buttons reaching from the back waistband to the hem. It emphasized the lean angles and long curves of her body. Her dark hair was loose instead of braided tonight and her flushed cheeks added to her ripe, healthy beauty. Tyler wished he was staying home tonight instead of meeting Arden.

"What's up, Tiger?" she greeted him amiably with an old nickname. "How was your day?"

"Productive enough. Did you hear anything about the body they found at Cherry Lodge?"

"Body? No! You're kidding? What's Cherry Lodge, anyway?"

Tyler quickly explained what had happened that morning. Sarah was invaluable when it came to picking up local gossip at the bar. "So talk it up tonight. See if you can find out if anyone knew who it was. I've got to clean up and run out again. Mind if I use your car?"

"I'm not going anywhere. That gives me the creeps, Tyler. Someone dead there all these years and no even missed her."

"Oh, somebody somewhere probably missed her. Just no one from around here. She had a lot of jewelry on; it might help identify her." Tyler remembered the earring in his pocket but he did not show it to her. He knew Sarah would give him hell for taking it and he didn't have time for that now.

Giving her a quick kiss on the lips, he said, "Wait up for me. I won't be back late."

The Springhouse Bar in the Barrister's Annex was not hard to find but Tyler was surprised by how many cars were parked outside this small building in the middle of nowhere. The bar was actually downstairs in what had once been the springhouse for the old Barrister hotel. It was smoky and filled with people and Arden had to shout to make herself heard.

"Tyler! Over here!" She waved to him from a seat at the end of the bar. She looked young and pretty in a blouse of loosely crocheted lace over a camisole and a diaphanous skirt made from yards of some crinkly material. He realized with a guilty sense of responsibility that she was probably too young to drink in a public place.

"Hi!" Her conspiratorial smile flashed like a movie marquee to let everyone around her know that something special was going on between her and Tyler. She slipped her arm through his and pulled him towards her. He could feel her brightness and energy already beginning to melt his determined stoicism. The touch of her little hand gave him an uncertain feeling in his stomach. Her spell was beginning to work on him again.

"What are you drinking? I'll buy you one."

"Oh, just a beer. I have to drive later."

"Oh, you're not BWI tonight?"

"BWI?"

"Biking while intoxicated. They can't bust you for that you know." Her Tinkerbell laugh carried above the noise.

"What are you drinking?" he asked, wondering if it was just plain cola in the tall glass in front of her.

"Dark rum and coke. My favorite." Her moon and star earrings danced on her little ears as she tossed her head towards the bartender.

As soon as he managed a few swigs of beer, Tyler decided to get right to the point. "So tell me, sweetheart. Why'd you bring me out to this dive on a dark and windy night?"

She giggled. "This isn't a dive. The Springhouse is the coolest place for miles around. Ooops! No pun intended." Tyler was beginning to realize that Arden was not drinking her first rum and coke of the evening. He watched her down the glass in front of her as though she were drinking water through the straw. Before she could order another for herself, he made a hasty decision.

"Why don't we go outside and sit by the lake and talk?" he suggested. "I noticed a dock next to the parking lot."

He had known the romance of the suggestion would appeal to her even more than the being seen with him in her popular hometown hangout. She made a big show of saying goodbye as he helped her on with her cardigan and led her to the door. She was just a little unsteady on her feet.

"Whoops, I forgot my backpack. It's on the floor where I was sitting." She waited just inside the doorway while Tyler retrieved it for her. He was surprised by the weight of it.

"What have you got in here?" he asked, slinging it over his shoulder as they went out.

"Oh, just a few things I thought might come in handy." She led the way through the parking lot towards the dock. The night air was cool enough to seem very refreshing after the smoky bar.

They sat down at the end of the dock and let their feet dangle above the softly lapping water. Almost immediately they were awash in a flood of headlights as a car pulled into the parking lot. A door slammed and loud music blasted through an open window.

Tyler and Arden both laughed. "Not particularly serene, is it?" Tyler remarked.

Arden leaped to her feet suddenly and walked to the other side of the dock. "Come on, I have a better idea."

"What's that?" Tyler asked, but she had already turned around and lowered herself off the edge. "What are you doing?" In two seconds he had crossed to where she had stood.

"We'll take this dingy out onto the lake. Nobody'll bother us out there. Toss me the backpack."

Tyler looked at the sky. It was a clear night lit by a half moon. "You sure about this? Have you done this before?"

"All the time. One of those quaint local pastimes. Undo the rope before you get in."

"Whose boat is this anyway?"

"Ralph, the owner of the Springhouse. He won't mind, I've borrowed it before."

Tyler threw her the rope and the backpack and then slid off the dock into the boat himself. It was a little metal three-seater, about six feet long, and dry in the bottom, which he took as a good sign. As he settled himself into the middle seat, Arden reached over and pushed the boat clear of the pilings. It began to drift slowly away from shore towards the open expanse of the water. The lake was small enough that Tyler could see the twinkling of lights on the far shore.

"Where are the oars?" he asked, feeling beneath the seat for them.

"Oars?" Arden's tone was so odd that Tyler look up at her sharply. Her face was only partially visible in the moonlight, but because he knew what he was looking for, the mischief dancing in her eyes was as bright as day. "What oars?"

"Arden!"

For a moment he considered jumping ship and swimming ashore. It would serve her right for playing a trick like this on him.

"Tyler, we do this all the time. That's half the fun of it. The boat almost always ends up in the same place. The current always brings you down to the east end of the lake by the Mountainside."

"And then what do we do? Walk back at two in the morning with the boat on our backs?"

Oh, Tyler, lighten up. It's an adventure. We'll be fine. I've got a blanket and a bottle of wine and a flashlight in here." She reached for her backpack and began pulling things out. "I even remembered to bring a corkscrew."

"Good Christ! Were you planning this?"

She giggled. "In a way. But I didn't expect it work out quite so perfectly."

Tyler closed his eyes and put his head in his hands. He could not believe he had let her trap him this way again. He wondered if she really had anything to tell him or if that was all just "part of the plan" too.

At the sound of the cork popping out of the wine bottle, he sat up. In a less than polite manner, he reached over and helped himself to the bottle, upending it into his mouth. Cheap California burgundy. "All right, Arden," he

said finally. "Now we're really all alone. So what is it you need to tell me about?"

CHAPTER SIX

Sarah poured herself another margarita. She carefully washed the shaker and strainer and set them in the rack to dry before letting the final dish water out of the bar sink. Switching off the last of the lights, she picked up her drink and made her way through the semi–darkness towards the front sitting room of the inn. It was not a room that was used very often but it had a cheerful atmosphere, as well as a comfortable couch and armchairs. And Sarah thought she could control her moody feelings about Tyler a little better if she didn't wait for him upstairs in the apartment.

He seemed to be worse than ever about keeping to a promised time frame. As much as she envied and admired how impulsive and spontaneous he was, she could not ignore her innate sense of trust and responsibility. Consequently he still drove her crazy. Woody said their personalities complemented each other, that Sarah was earth and Tyler was water, and together they could grow anything. But these days it seemed more like Sarah was fire and Tyler was the air that fanned the flames between them.

Sitting down on the couch, she made a conscious effort to stay calm and relax. Tyler would have a perfectly valid explanation as to why he wasn't back before midnight when he said he'd be back early. He always had a good excuse.

"Hello? Oh, it's just you, Sarah." Reed peered around the corner of the doorway. "My room is just above here and I thought perhaps someone was breaking in. I didn't expect to see you."

"Well, Tyler's not back yet and I thought I would just hang out in here for a bit. I won't make any noise."

But instead of going back upstairs, Reed sat down at the opposite end of the couch and turned to face her. "Everything okay? You look a little gloomy."

"I'm fine." She gave him a small smile to prove it. "You know, I always worry when Tyler doesn't show up when he says he going to, even though I should know by now that I shouldn't. It just makes me a little tense, that's all."

"Well, turn around and sit here." Reed patted the middle cushion of the sofa. "I'll give you a back rub to relax you."

Sarah tilted her head quizzically and raised her eyebrows.

"A back rub, Sarah. I actually took a few massage courses at Carlisle College – I think you'll find I'm quite good at it."

Sarah put her drink on the floor and moved into the position he indicated. She didn't say that it wasn't Reed whom she couldn't trust, it was herself.

"Oooh, good dress for a back rub." Reed admired the low cut of her black jersey dress. "I'm just going to slip it a little lower off your shoulders so I can get a better grip. There. Now just let your head fall down on your chest. That's it. Just relax."

His fingers were so strong and self–assured that she could do nothing but give herself up to his touch. "Massage classes in college?" she murmured.

"It was Carlisle College, don't forget. There were plenty of other less orthodox classes than that. Visual Relaxation, Midwifery, Stone Wall Building. I wish I could think of some of the others. I remember Amber had some wild dance class. It was called something like Snow Dancing. I mean can you imagine a whole semester devoted to something like that?" He laughed.

Sarah was beginning to feel like jello under his masterful hands. She could feel her body sinking lower into itself.

"This posture isn't good for you." He stood up. "Why don't you just stretch out on the couch? I can kneel on the floor." Gently he guided her head down onto a pillow as she lifted her legs up behind her.

"You're going to make me fall asleep," she mumbled, grinning into the pillow. "I won't be able to hear Tyler when he comes home."

Reed moved her hair away from her neck and smoothed it back from her temples. "Well, that wouldn't be the end of the world, now would it?"

"Wanda and Lou aren't my real parents."

"Really?" Was that all she had wanted to tell him? Tyler hoped that he didn't sound disappointed as he waited for Arden to go on.

"I always thought they were when I was little. My last name was Kensington like theirs and they told me I was their child. I called them Mom and Dad. I still do. They're the only ones I know." Arden reached out in the darkness for the wine bottle, her fingers closing over Tyler's for a brief second. After a few swallows of wine, she went on.

"Anyway, the summer I was twelve there was this kid, Kevin Bascomb, who kept making fun of me, saying I was the abandoned bastard child of some hippie chick from the college. He said he knew it was true because his father had told him and his father had gone to the college so he knew.

"When I asked my parents about it, Wanda denied it immediately. But after I went to bed I heard my parents having a really big fight and the next day my dad told me that it was true that I was adopted. He gave me all this crap about how they loved me like their own – I shouldn't call it crap because I'm sure it's true – and that Wanda was really sensitive about it because she could never have kids. He went on and on about how I was the best thing that had ever happened to her and finally I asked him if he knew who my real mother was."

Slightly out of breath, Arden paused with her intuitive instinct for the dramatic.

"Did he?" Tyler asked obligingly.

"Yes, he knew her quite well, he said. She was a college student who rented a room from them when I was an infant and who wasn't quite mature enough to take care of me. He said Wanda did most of the mothering when I was a baby and that one day my mother just took off and never came back. I was about eighteen months old at the time and he says I never missed her, I was so used to him and Wanda taking care of me.

"Well, I was pretty moody about it after that. I got kind of obsessed with wanting to find my real mother and all. Wanda couldn't stand it, it made her really mad. Finally to make me quit asking her all the time, my dad gave me a name and an address of someone who had been a friend of my real mother's. So I sent this letter off and waited and waited but there was never an answer. I was heartbroken, of course. I started hasseling my mother again, asking her if she still had any of my mother's belongings around. Finally to get me off her back she gave me the only thing she had kept."

Arden flicked on her flashlight at this point and shone it at her ear where the tiny crescent moon hung. It was made of silver and inlaid with a smaller moon made of turquoise. It looked like typical trendy jewelry from the early seventies.

It was an interesting story but Tyler still could not grasp why she thought he would be interested. "So who was the person you wrote to and where did he or she live?"

"Well, all I had was the name M. Stellano and a post office box in Lahaina, Hawaii."

Having been lulled into a state of complacency by the water, the wine and her voice, Tyler was suddenly wide awake. "Stellano? In Hawaii?"

"That's right. When I heard that a lady named Mimi Farrell from Hawaii had died in the Centennial fire I didn't make the connection at all. It had been years since I thought about that unanswered letter. But then yesterday I was looking at a copy of last week's Jordan Record that a customer had left in the restaurant. And when I read the article about the fire I discovered that her maiden name had been Stellano."

Tyler's mind could barely work fast enough to keep up with the new possibilities this opened up. "So you think that Mimi was a friend of your real mother's from the college?"

"Yes. And I have this terribly guilty feeling that maybe she was coming to find me after all these years and tell me where I could find my mother. What if it's my fault she came here? If she hadn't come here, she wouldn't have died!" Arden was definitely working herself into a state of hysteria. Tyler reached over and grabbed her hands between his.

"Arden, I know for a fact that she was planning to meet someone else that she knew from Carlisle College the night she died. She wrote him a letter and told him she was coming. You can't blame this on yourself. It's possible she never even got your letter. Maybe she'd already moved from Captain Cook by the time it arrived. Twelve years is a long time, you know."

"Yes, I know, but still..." She was trying not to cry now and he could feel her body trembling with the effort. "I guess it's really myself I feel sorry for. She was the only chance I ever had of finding my real mother. Now I'll just never know."

With a quick movement that rocked the boat dangerously, Tyler moved to share her seat and she moved aside to accommodate him. He slipped a comforting arm around her shoulder.

"Arden, I might be able to help you find your mother. You probably aren't aware of this, but finding missing people is actually something I'm rather skilled at."

"Really? You would help me?"

"I'll do my best. But you're going to have to tell me everything you can think of about your mother. Like for starters, what was her name?"

Arden giggled a little. "Well, that's one thing I can tell you but it may be the only thing. My mother's name was Amber St. Pierre."

Sarah was falling asleep under Reed's expert massage. "I don't want to fall asleep," she murmured. "Talk to me, Reed. Keep me awake."

His touch changed instantly to a light, feathery stimulating sensation. As he ran his fingers up and down the inside of Sarah's thighs, she began to think that maybe things were going too far. Rolling over on her back, she propped her head up against the arm of the couch and looked at him through heavy–lidded eyes. He took her feet into his lap and began to rub them while he looked at her.

"I can't begin to tell you how erotic you look to me right now with that sexy dress falling off your shoulders and your hair all long and messy."

"Reed." Sarah pulled her feet away from him and in closer to her own body. "That's not the kind of talk I meant."

"I don't believe you for a minute but if that's what you want to pretend..." he shrugged and reached for her feet again. "I can behave. We don't have to make babies."

"Make babies?" Sarah choked on her laughter.

"Well, I think about that at my age, you know. Here I am in my mid–forties, no steady relationship and no future generations. I used to say I wanted to have kids, but not until later, when I was ready to settle down and be responsible. And here I am responsible and ready and no one to have babies with."

"Actually I know what you mean. I'm getting to that now or never age, at least you don't have to worry about that, and I'm in a relationship with a guy who comes and goes like he's never going to settle down. How could I have kids with someone like that?"

They were silent for a minute, each feeling their own personal pain on the subject. Finally Reed spoke as he stroked one of Sarah's feet. "That was one of the reasons I responded to Mimi's letter. All those years ago when Doug Arbuckle visited me, he told me that Amber had a baby she claimed was mine. I was bitter – I told him that there was no way Amber could possibly know if it was me or ten other guys. She just figured I was probably the easiest sucker of the bunch and that she could stick me with child support. Years later, when I never had any other kids, it began to haunt me. What if it had been mine? How would I ever know? So when Mimi wrote and said she needed to meet me with about something, my mind immediately ran in that direction. But I guess I was never meant to know the answer to that particular question."

"Reed, why have you never mentioned this before?"

"I don't know. It's not really relevant. It's just kind of a fantasy I've built up in my head over the years. And besides," he lowered his voice and looked down, "it seemed like it might give me more of a motive for murdering her."

"How do you mean?"

"Like maybe she told me something I didn't like hearing about the subject of my possibly fathering a child. Besides, it's all just conjecture. Like I said, I'm sure Amber sent Doug Arbuckle with that message just to con me into getting back together with her again. I'm sure real life with a squawking infant was not the piece of pie she was used to. Men were probably running the other direction when they saw her coming."

"I think it's time we called Mimi's husband and see if he knows what her reason for coming to Carlisle was. Oh, but probably we ought to let Tyler do that. This is really his baby. Sorry, wrong choice of words."

They laughed together and Reed reached over to grasp both her hands in his. "Jeezum crow, Sarah. Why don't you give up on him and come to bed with me?"

"I met your father today, did he tell you?" Tyler pulled his feet onto the seat, doubling up his long legs, as Arden spread the blanket out on the bottom of the boat, smoothing it as she pushed it beneath the seats.

"No, actually we didn't talk much tonight. He was in an odd mood and Wanda was still in bed with her headache. There – now if we put our heads up there, this seat will be just over our middles and your feet will have to go under the next seat as well. But it can be done."

"You've done this before, you mean."

"Of course." Arden wriggled into position beneath his seat and then stretched out comfortably. "See. And we get a great view of the stars."

"Did your father mention the body they found at the Cherry Lodge excavation?" He looked down at her face, just barely lit in the pale light of the half moon.

"No, he didn't have to. It was all anyone talked about at lunch today. Apparently they think some woman must have died in the fire. Nobody had any idea of who she was." Arden giggled a little. "I know I shouldn't laugh, it's so gruesome, but like it was almost a direct rerun of the conversation a few weeks ago after the Centennial fire. It was too weird."

"It is a morbid coincidence, isn't it?" Tyler shook his head. "But it's highly unlikely that there's any connection between a woman who died in a fire eighteen years ago and a woman who was murdered in one this month."

"I know. But still. It was weird. Aren't you going to lay down here?"

"In a minute." They had finished the bottle of wine and Tyler was beginning to feel very drowsy. He wanted to talk to Arden a little longer before he crawled under the seats onto the blanket. His long day was catching up with him and the soft motion of the boat was sure to put him to sleep as soon as he was in a prone position.

"So do you know this guy Neil Richelieu who lives in Carlisle?"

Arden gave a derisive snort. "The old lecher. Of course I know him. He's a gross pig – I wouldn't have anything to do with him."

"You sound like you speak from personal experience."

"Yeah, he's come on to me more than a few times. Thinks he's God's gift to women, but really he's just a disgusting old drunk. His muscles don't turn me on. Why do you want to know about him anyway?"

Tyler wondered how much he should tell Arden about what he was doing. "Well, his name has come up because he's been a suspect more than once in these hotel fires."

"Yeah, but they say he always has an iron–clad alibi."

"Did you know that Mimi Stellano lived with him when she was in college?"

Arden sat up and peered intently at him in the darkness. "You're kidding me, right? You mean he was her boyfriend? My God, she looked so together."

"Well, he might have been different back then. It could be that when she left him, he never got over it. Been mad ever since. But think this through with me for a minute. If Mimi lived with Neil, then Neil must've known some of her friends."

"Like my mother!" The excitement disappeared from her voice as quickly as it had come into it. "But I'll be damned if I'll go groveling to him asking about her. Besides, he's nutso."

"I've got to get over there to talk him anyway. I'll ask him for you."

"Well, don't mention my name. I don't want him to have any good reason for coming after me. Besides, he talks when he's drunk and if it got back to Wanda that I was still trying to find my real mother, it would break her heart. I don't want her to know unless I really find out something. It just wouldn't be worth it."

Tyler couldn't seem to stay upright any longer. He slid down onto the blanket and maneuvered his long body into position next to Arden. "I'm exhausted," he mumbled, resting his head on his arm and closing his eyes. "Are your parents going to worry when you don't come home?"

"Are you kidding? They won't know the difference. My room is in the basement and it has its own outside door." She flung her arm over him and snuggled closely.

"Basement. Sounds kind of damp." He wasn't sure if he'd even spoken the words or if he'd just dreamed that he said them.

"No, it's got windows all along one side and it's full of plants. It's warm and cozy like a greenhouse."

Tyler was asleep before she had finished speaking.

When Reed leaned over and kissed her, Sarah found that she could not keep herself from responding. She knew that, if things had gone differently from the start, she would probably be enjoying an intimate relationship with him by now. But the way the situation was at this point, it was totally inappropriate. Even if she was steaming with anger at Tyler and this man was melting her heart.

"Do you want to go up to my room?" Reed asked presently. Her face was buried in his shoulder as he gently stroked her hair.

She shook her head. "I can't do it and feel good about it, so what's the point? Another time, another place, another lifetime. If or when Tyler and I call it quits, you'll be the first person I look up." She glanced at her watch. "And at this rate, I may be calling on you in the morning."

"Damn, I wish we weren't such rational adults! I'd like to throw you down on that rag rug right now and make wild, passionate love to you until you had to beg for mercy. Or more."

Sarah put a finger to his lips. "Stop. Don't talk about it. Don't make us both crazy." Detaching herself from his embrace, she stood up. "I'm going to bed now. Let's not forget to ask Tyler to call Mimi's husband tomorrow."

"Yeah, I've got to be up early anyway. The lumber I ordered for the barn is coming. Then I think I'm going to go back over to my place for a few days. Got to try to keep my regular life from losing its shape. See if I can get a couple of the guys I usually work with to come over and help me get the frame up."

But Sarah knew that his real reason was to put a little space between them to cool things down. She felt bad for him but what could she do? Awkwardly they said good night and then went their respective ways to bed.

When Tyler woke up a few hours later, he was chilled through and in desperate need of relieving his bladder. He managed to disengage himself from Arden, who was wound around him like an ivy vine, and then lurched toward the side of the rowboat on his knees. There was no option but to pee into the pristine waters of the lake.

The moon had set, making visibility even more minimal than before. He pressed the button on his watch to light up the digital readout – it was nearly 3:00 AM. At this latitude and at this time of year it would start to get light in less than hour. Looking up at the shadows of the treetops against the sky, he could see they had drifted into a narrower part of the lake than where they had started. Hopefully they would run aground soon.

Shivering, he crawled back down beside Arden, lying as close to her body as he could so that he could wrap the edges of the blanket around them like a cocoon. Arden stirred and rolled over so that their bodies fit together like spoons in a drawer. She helped him adjust the blanket over them and then pulled his arms around her, slipping one of his hands under her shirt and placing it over one of her perfect, small round breasts.

Tyler lay motionless and wide awake, trying not to disturb the envelope of warmth they had created around themselves. He tried not to think about the nipple growing hard beneath his palm or about the swelling in his groin area. He thought about Amber St. Pierre and Mimi Stellano Farrell. He tried to work out a timeline of what little he knew about them and where they had lived and who had known them. But he could not transcend what was happening between the two earthly bodies pressed against each other for warmth in the bottom of a rowboat adrift on a lake.

With just the slightest amount of movement, Amber slid her long skirt up so that her smooth bare buttocks were right up against the bulge in his crotch. He was not surprised that she wore no underpants, or perhaps she had slipped them off some time earlier. Nor was he surprised that he could not keep his free hand from exploring the warm curved surfaces she had made accessible to him. It was something he had wanted to do since he first laid eyes on her.

His nose was buried in the nape of her neck. He was overwhelmed by the fresh smell of her skin and the shampoo scent that lingered in her hair. He tried to think about Sarah and the inn and his editor in New York. He reminded himself that he had a deadline on his story about Burma, which he'd barely even started. But no matter how far away he sent his mind, he could not get away from what was happening right now. His fingers could not stop exploring, could not stop turning his secret fantasies about Arden into a reality that moaned with pleasurable sensation.

"No intercourse," he whispered into the ear inches from his mouth before he began probing its depths with his tongue.

Arden's only response was a sigh of pleasure.

For the next hour he stroked and caressed her body to orgasmic plateaus that echoed across the surface of the lake for any living creature to hear and wonder about. Twice she begged him desperately to come inside her. Although he continued to refuse, he did not stop her when she finally undid his pants and gave him his own opportunity to fill the dawn with the uncontrollable sounds of sexual gratification.

A jarring thud on the outside of the boat brought him smartly back to reality. His head was swimming as he raised himself on his elbows and looked around.

"My God, we've come to shore," he announced, feeling a mixture of relief and sadness. The guilt would come later. His interlude with Arden was over and he knew it was a fantasy he would never indulge again.

The boat had hit a broken branch of a tree that protruded out into the water. They were floating by a very dense stretch of woods but just across the narrow inlet was a row of summer cabins, mostly uninhabited. He realized that the sky had been light for some time now and he wondered if their activity would have been visible to the few year–round inhabitants of the lakeside cottages had they been awake.

Arden sat up. She had managed to shed most of her clothing and was wearing only her cardigan; her body was still a moist and open invitation to Tyler. Her curls were tangled and her cheeks unnaturally rosy. In the pale light of dawn, with a light mist rising off the lake, she could have been a dryad or a druid or whatever those ethereal English tree spirits were called.

Tyler pushed the boat free of the sodden branch and it moved slowly on with the current. He could see their journey's end not five hundred feet away where the lake emptied into a narrow stream next to a manmade sandy beach. He turned to Arden and took her hand.

"Just so that things are perfectly clear between us," he said. "This was a once–in–a–lifetime event. There will never be anything resembling a repeat of this. When we get out of this boat, what happened between us is in our past, our very private past."

"Well, I wish we could stay here forever then." She pouted like a petulant ten year old, and Tyler shivered a little, wondering where his sanity had disappeared to for the last hour.

"Look, I want to help you find your mother, but I can't do it unless we can relate to each other as just friends. I wish I could have controlled myself and kept my hands off of you, but I just couldn't. I'm sorry."

"No, you're not."

His eyes met hers. She was right. He wasn't sorry. But it was out of his system now. His burning desire was gone and in a way he felt cleansed.

Something scraped across the bottom of the boat and he looked over the side. The water was shallow now, shallow enough for him to leap out and haul them in to shore. There was no modesty left between them. He dropped his pants and climbed out of the boat.

"So how do we get back to the Springhouse from here?" he called over his shoulder to Arden.

"We walk or hitchhike. It's only about four miles. Other times we've hung out on the lake until it's really morning so that there's some traffic and it's easy to get a ride."

Other times. He shook his head. Exhausted as he was, he wanted to get back home as soon as possible. To put this bizarre incident behind him. To sneak into bed beside Sarah. And to wake up with the energy to continue putting together the new pieces of the ever–increasing puzzle surrounding Mimi's death.

CHAPTER SEVEN

It was after six A.M. when Tyler lifted the sheet and crept quietly into bed next to Sarah's sleeping body. He lay perfectly motionless for a few minutes, listening to the even rhythm of her breathing. Suddenly unable to stand himself, he slipped out of bed and headed for the bathroom, shutting the door silently behind him. The old, claw foot tub beckoned invitingly – a hot bath was exactly what he felt like right now.

Ten minutes later he had finished scrubbing the guilt off his skin and closed his eyes to enjoy the relaxing warmth of the steamy water. He began to make plans for the day – a few hours of sleep, then he would call Wanda and ask her some questions about Amber St. Pierre. Chances are Wanda hadn't made the connection of Mimi Farrell with her old tenant. He would not mention Arden's revelation. But finding Amber might mean solving both mysteries with one blow. He would also make a trip over to the body shop where Neil was a welder, get a look at him anyway, maybe get a chance to set up a meeting under some other auspices.

The slamming of the toilet seat lid made him open his eyes. Sarah sat down hugging one knee to her naked chest, and regarded him with pursed lips and a sour expression in her sleepy eyes.

"Hi," he ventured quietly.

"Hi." There was not a shred of warmth in her greeting. "Are you just getting in now?"

"Well, a little while ago. I'm sorry if you were worried. You won't believe what happened." He watched for any change of emotion but her face was a steel mask of controlled feelings.

"I'd believe just about anything could happen to you. Except why you couldn't find a damn telephone and give me a call."

"What if I told you I couldn't call because I was stuck out in the middle of a lake in a rowboat with no oars?"

Sarah snorted in disbelief. "So I guess the truth must really be a lame excuse this time if you expect me to swallow that one." She stood up abruptly and walked out of the bathroom.

"Sarah—" Tyler got to his feet and grabbed a towel. The water running off his body created a river on the floor as his followed her into the bedroom. She was sitting in bed, with the covers pulled up under her arms.

"Goddam it, Tyler, it's six fucking thirty in the morning. What kind of relationship do you think this is? After all these years, I feel a great sense of responsibility for you and your crazy life and of course I'm going to worry when you don't come home until eight hours later than expected. Tell me you don't feel that sense of responsibility towards me. Go ahead and tell me. Then I can throw you out once and for all and find myself a grown—up man instead of an aging boy."

"Oh, come on, Sarah. I'm sorry, I really am. But I really was stranded out on that lake last night. There was nothing I could do."

"Alone?"

"No, I was with Arden. She actually told me some very—"

"You're telling me you spent the night in a rowboat with Wanda's daughter? That sexy little number who wears her shorts too short?"

"Sarah. She tricked me into it. She—"

"So did you sleep with her, Tyler? Did she trick you into that too?"

"Sarah! Why are you so mad at me this time? I'm not on some kind of 9 to 5 office schedule. I have to go with what's happening, follow my leads when they show up—"

"You did sleep with her, didn't you?"

Tyler did not answer her, he just met her icy gaze with his own smoldering look. Something else was going on here, Sarah had never showed any signs of sexual insecurity in their relationship before. Over the years they had both admitted to trying out other lovers during off times and had also both admitted that nothing ran even a distant second place to what they shared. In fact, Sarah rarely got mad with him, sad and frustrated sometimes, but almost never angry.

He could see now that she had dark circles under her eyes as though she had not slept much. Maybe her short fuse could be attributed to lack of sleep.

"Look, I'm sorry if I kept you up last night—"

"Oh, don't worry your self–centered head about it. I was in good company."

"Damn you, Sarah, what the hell do you think I'd be doing in West Bumfuck, Vermont, if it wasn't because you called me to help a distressed 'friend' of yours? I've gotten so wrapped up in this problem YOU laid on me that I can't even remember when the deadline for my Burma Road story is. Now if you'll excuse me," he grabbed a pillow off the bed, "I've had an exhausting night. I believe I'll go sleep on the couch downstairs."

"Well, at least you've got that part right, buddy!" she shouted after him.

He was halfway down the stairs before he realized that all he was wearing was a towel wrapped around his waist. Too proud and too weary to go back into the bedroom, he continued on his way to the front sitting room. Wrapping himself up in an old crocheted, multi–colored afghan, he dropped his body onto the couch and pretended that he would be able to sleep now.

He knew he must have finally fallen asleep when the sound of voices in the front hall woke him up.

"You know, I'd like you to come over and see my place some time." Reed's voice. "I don't suppose I could talk you into coming with me today."

106

"It's tempting." Sarah's voice. "But I don't have anyone to cover for me tonight."

"It's kind of like having a baby."

"Yeah."

Tyler heard the screen door slam as they moved out onto the porch. He stayed motionless, intent on catching their conversation.

"Everything okay between you and Tyler?"

"No." A sullen pause. "Did we wake you this morning?"

"Not really."

"Not really?"

"I was already up." Reed laughed a little.

"I'm sorry we were so loud. So you're off?"

"Yeah, I'll be back in a few days. After last night I need to put some space between myself and this scene for a little while."

After last night? Tyler could not keep himself from sitting up now and trying to see through the lace curtains covering the windows to the porch. Reed and Sarah were just out of his view and the sudden silence between them was unnerving.

"You have my number, right?" Footsteps sounded on the steps and then crunched down the path towards the parking lot. Their voices faded away.

"Shit." He could not believe how angry he felt. Angry at himself, at Sarah and Reed, and especially at Arden. Why did it suddenly seem as though he couldn't trust anyone anymore?

He rose quickly and headed upstairs to dress before Sarah came back inside. From the upstairs bedroom window he had a clear view of Reed and Sarah leaning against the side of Reed's truck. Reed's arm was around Sarah's shoulders and they were both looking at their feet and talking.

"Damn." Talk about putting some space between himself and his situation. He didn't think he could get out of the building fast enough this morning. But he needed to

107

make a couple of phone calls first. He looked at the clock —
it was already after ten.

"Wanda? It's Tyler. How are you feeling?"

Better, thanks. Just a migraine. I get them now and
then."

He had to get right to the point. "Look, I came across
something interesting yesterday that I wanted to talk to
you about. In connection with Mimi Farrell's murder."

"Really? What's that?"

"Well, it's seems Mimi's best friend was a girl named
Amber St. Pierre who rented a room from you for a while."

There was a very long silence on the other end of the
phone. "Is that right?" Wanda replied finally. "I don't recall
anybody named Mimi Farrell."

"But you do remember Amber, don't you?"

"Well, yes. It was a long time ago, about twenty years,
I'd say. It didn't really work out and we never rented any
more rooms to college kids after that." Wanda turned away
from the phone and yelled across the restaurant kitchen to
somebody.

"Mimi's last name used to be Stellano. Does that ring
any bells?"

"Look, Tyler, this isn't a good time to talk. I'm behind
after being out yesterday.

"Can I come by later this afternoon then?" He would
have to bicycle to Carlisle anyway, there was no way he'd
be borrowing Sarah's car today.

"Okay. Why don't you meet me over at my house
around four?"

Tyler hung up and looked out the window. Reed was in
the cab of the truck now but he and Sarah were still
talking through the window.

He quickly leafed through the yellow pages of the phone
book. There was nothing in Carlisle under "Welding" but
there was a "Highway 29 Body Shop" listed under "Auto
Body Repair."

"Is Neil Richelieu working today?"

"Who wants to know?"

"His uncle."

"I don't have no fucking uncle." The phone was slammed down.

Well, he knew where to find Neil.

The sound of an engine starting made him look out the window again. Sarah was giving Reed a goodbye kiss through the window of the truck. Feeling sick to his stomach, Tyler grabbed his daypack and his shoes. He'd get his morning coffee from the West Jordan Village Store. As he headed down the back stairs, he heard the front screen door slam. He would be on his mountain bike and headed into town before Sarah discovered he was gone.

Not that she would care.

That bitter thought accompanied him most of the way over the mountain to Carlisle.

The Highway 29 Body Shop stood on an open stretch of newly paved road just past the cottages where Mrs. Stellano had been staying, which reminded Tyler that a call to her was long overdue. The body shop was an ugly, prefab building of pale green corrugated metal. Its substantial size was dwarfed by the size of the junkyard beside it.

There was no mistaking which of the two men eating lunch in the office was Neil Richelieu. His Arnold Schwarzenegger muscles gave him away as much as his surly greeting.

"Yeah?"

At close range, Tyler saw that the only his upper body was truly muscular. Beneath his pecs rode a beer belly the size of a small keg. His head had that sort of square shape to it that Tyler had associated since high school as belonging to dumb jocks; his closely shaved crew cut had a subtle salt and pepper effect. His features might have been good—looking if years of scowling hadn't frozen them into a permanent squint and frown.

"Neil Richelieu? I'm Tyler Mackenzie. We spoke on the phone a few nights ago. You called me over at the West Jordan Inn." Tyler extended his hand.

Neil started to use the side of his jeans to wipe the mustard off his own hand but stopped himself midway. "You're the fuck who called me about Mimi, right? Hell if I've got anything to say to you. I ain't talking about Mimi anymore, you got that?"

Tyler wondered what Mimi could possibly have seen in such an unsavory character. Perhaps he had been different twenty years before.

"Fine," he said as pleasantly as possible. "But how about Amber St. Pierre? You must have known her too."

"In the biblical sense you mean?" Neil guffawed a few times, trying to catch the eye of the weasel–faced fellow eating a baloney sandwich next to him. "Yeah, I knew her and both ways too."

"You mean intimately?" Tyler felt foolish being so formal, but he couldn't bring himself down to Neil's level.

"Yeah, intimately." Neil mimicked Tyler's tone in an embarrassingly accurate way. "She was one of the hottest chicks I ever knew. Loved to fuck, didn't care who or what. Or who was watching."

Weasel–face wheezed with delighted laughter. "I don't remember that one."

"Hell, she was long before you came to town. That was back when those college hippies over–ran everything." Neil's face darkened suddenly with the memory.

"She as good as that Melissa you talk about?"

Neil snorted. "No comparison. I mean, I've laid dozens of women, I love women, but Amber was in a class by herself."

"So she was your girlfriend for a while back then?"

"Hell, no. I just fucked her now and then. When the situation called for it." The sandwich in Neil's hand rested uneaten on his knee now as he began to disappear into what seemed be unsettling thoughts.

"When the situation called for it?" It seemed like an odd way to put it.

"Yeah, you know, she was my Mimi's best friend. Sometimes we had a what do you call it, menage a trois, sometimes I fucked her to teach Mimi a lesson. Shit, I said I wasn't talking about Mimi!"

But Tyler knew he couldn't keep himself from bragging about his sexual conquests. It was a useful thing to know. "So what ever happened to Amber?"

Neil shrugged. "Hell if I know. She lived down to Lou Kensington's. They probably got some kind of address for her. Why do you want to know, anyway?"

"I work with an insurance company in the southern part of the state. She's got a good size life insurance policy coming to her if we can find her."

"Lucky her." Neil resumed eating his abandoned sandwich, apparently back to present times.

"Somebody told me she had a baby back then. Do you remember that?"

"A baby?" He shook his head. "Never saw any baby. She didn't look like nobody who'd ever had a baby. Didn't act like anybody's mother either." He nudged his companion. "Hard to picture somebody's mother giving head, ain't it?"

They laughed loudly together. "Nah, she had a tight little ass and these nice hard tits. She and my Mimi were like night and day." The darkness crossed his face again.

"Do you remember if she had a boyfriend?"

Neil shook his head. "Didn't seem to care if she did. Too bad you weren't around back then to get a piece of the action," he said to Weasel–face. "Lots of those college girls liked to give it away for free, didn't have to pay them nothing, didn't even have to buy them drinks. You don't see too many chicks acting like that anymore."

"So what about this Mimi chick?" Weasel–face asked, eager for more sex stories. "Was she a good fuck too?"

Tyler ducked instinctively as Neil's fist shot out and hit the other man in the face at the same time his baloney sandwich smashed into the wall behind him. Neil definitely

111

had a sore spot in his shriveled psyche when it came to Mimi.

A half–filled soda can flew by Tyler's shoulder, narrowly missing his head. "You get the hell outa here, insurance man! You're ruining my fucking day, you hear?"

Tyler didn't say goodbye.

He still had a few hours to kill before Wanda would be home so he rode down to the Carlisle library to see if they might have anything useful to him in their archives. He told Mrs. Meade, the librarian, that he wasn't exactly sure what he was looking for, maybe some old catalogs from the college that might have names of people who would remember Mimi or Amber.

"Carlisle College? You know who could help you out on that one? Irma Blumchek. She worked in the registrar's office at the college and when it closed, she took all the old records home for safekeeping. Grade transcripts, of course, are available from the State Department of Education in Montpelier. But she managed to get everything else out before the contents of the building were auctioned off. I mean, there was a whole file of final theses that were going to be dumped, projects that students worked hours on that she felt someday one of them might want. She has the enrollment records and yearbooks and things like that."

"Does she live nearby?" Tyler could not conceal his excitement.

"Just up on Maple Avenue. Third house on the right. It's yellow with green shutters. Lots of irises growing along the porch."

He stood outside the Carlisle convenience store, rapidly consuming a turkey sandwich and a soda, before following Mrs. Meade's directions to Maple Avenue, less than a quarter mile away.

Irma Blumchek was a plump, white–haired elderly lady, a Norman Rockwell image of the perfect, small town grandmother. She wore a faded yellow apron over a nondescript gray print dress and orthopedic black shoes with square solid heels. Her soft voice held just the trace of an unidentifiable Eastern European accent. And she was delighted to help Tyler.

"Oh, please come in. I like to think I rescued all these papers from destruction for some greater purpose than filling up my back bedroom. I'm sure we can find something to help you. I have the files on all the registered students."

He followed her up a polished wooden staircase with a neat Oriental runner tacked to the middle of the steps. He got a fleeting glimpse of fringed lamps, doilies and bureau scarves as they moved through the house, exactly as he might have expected.

In the back bedroom there were three walls piled high with dated cardboard boxes. They surrounded a high double bed covered with a tufted chenille bedspread. "I couldn't bring the file cabinets," Mrs. Blumchek said mournfully. "They were being auctioned off with everything else to help pay the college's bankruptcy debt. But if you tell me what years you are looking for..." Behind thick glasses, her dark eyes sparkled with excitement.

Tyler told her approximately what years he thought he needed. To his surprise, Mrs. Blumchek's face lit up with a smile when he mentioned Mimi and Amber's names. "Oh, of course, I remember them! They were both such sweethearts..."

He frowned a little as he watched her searching the boxes. So far nobody else had referred to them so nicely. But it seemed quite possible that Mrs. Blumchek brought out the good side of people. And she probably had no idea of Amber's unorthodox sexual activity.

"Oh, and also Reed Anderson. We might as well look at his file also."

"Do you mind my asking why you want this information, Mr. Mackenzie?" She did not look up from her search as she spoke and it occurred to Tyler that she would probably treat a possible ax murderer out for revenge as sweetly as she was treating him. It was not a pleasant thought.

When he told her that Mimi Stellano was the same woman who had been murdered in the Centennial fire, she sat up on her knees and stared at him. After a moment, she took a deep breath and remarked, "Oh, dear. How very sad. I never even think of them as aging, let alone dying. Oh, here you go. Frederick Reed Anderson, would that be who we're talking about?"

She passed him Reed's student file to look at while she continued her search. As Tyler began his perusal of it, he realized the gold mine of important personal information that Irma Blumchek was sitting on. Here was a copy of Reed's student identity card with a picture of a young Reed with an enormous head full of curly reddish–blond hair and a handlebar mustache. He received a perverse pleasure in seeing that the beard Reed wore these days hid a weak chin. His file was full of glowing reports on his achievements in his two years at Carlisle. He had apparently helped design the conversion of an old barn building at the college into an outdoor theater. His application and emergency information confirmed his story of growing up in Minnesota. The only smudge on his golden record was an arrest for drug possession which was later dismissed as a misdemeanor due to "extenuating circumstances." Whatever that meant.

By the time he was done, Mimi and Amber's files waited for him as well. Mimi's file followed a stormy couple of years, with notes from her advisor about meetings he had with her after she moved off campus mid–year and in with a local man of questionable reputation. There was an angry letter from Diane Stellano castigating the school for letting her daughter do such a thing. The last item in the file was a letter from Mimi herself requesting an extended leave of absence from the school until she could "get her personal life together."

Amber's file was the most disjointed of the three, but Tyler was able to find answers he thought he might never see. Her mother's name was Rochelle St. Pierre Parker. Her father was Cyrus Parker, remarried to a stepmother,

Marie. Tyler quickly scribbled down their address, now twenty years old, in Manchester, New Hampshire. A lengthy letter from Amber's high school guidance counselor explained that Amber came from an abusive home situation, had run away on numerous occasions (skipping school as well), and that they had reason to suspect she had experimented with illegal drugs. Next was a statement from the college admissions office saying they thought Amber would benefit greatly from admission to Carlisle and they recommended a full scholarship, which apparently had been granted.

He was struck by the similarity to Arden in the mischievous expression Amber wore on her college ID picture. Her hair seemed to be blonde, but it was longer than Arden's and not as curly. Suspended from a chain around Amber's neck was the little silver moon inlaid with blue that Arden now wore as an earring. He decided that, although they had similar delicate bone structure, they did not really look that much alike.

Unlike the previous two, there were a few failing notices on classes in this folder. There was also a mention from Amber's advisor that, at the school physician's recommendation, she had been spoken to about her promiscuous sexual activity. The next item of interest was a letter from Amber herself stating that she planned to continue with her schooling up until the time she gave birth and requesting that the school allow her to keep the baby in her dorm room with her. It was duly noted on the bottom of the letter, that this request was declined and that Amber had been informed that she would have to move off campus following the child's birth. Wanda and Lou Kensington's had been offered as a suggested place to rent.

The last document in Amber's file was an application for the continuation of financial aid. It stated the Kensington residence as her address and her place of employment as the Darby Mountain House. Occupation: cocktail waitress.

The rattling of delicate china brought him back to the present. Mrs. Blumchek had just placed a tray of homemade chocolate chip cookies and lemonade on top of one of the cartons. Tyler sat up quickly from where he had been comfortably sprawling across the double bed as he read.

"I didn't mean to disturb you. I thought you might be hungry."

Oh, you didn't have to do this. You've done me a great favor already. Besides, I'm just about finished." Biting into one of the cookies, the thought fleeted across his mind that maybe Mrs. Blumchek would rent him a room in her house and take care of him. Banishing the fantasy, he asked, "Do you remember the Darby Mountain House?"

To his surprise, the rosy color of her cheeks seemed to deepen ever so slightly. "Who could ever forget it? A house of very ill repute. Why do you ask?"

"Because Amber listed it as her place of employment. I wondered if it was still around."

"Amber worked there?" Mrs. Blumchek sounded shocked and he pointed it out to her on the application he had just read. "Oh, as a cocktail waitress. But still. I can't imagine how the poor child could stand being associated with place. I mean, nobody talked about it, but everybody in town knew what went on there."

"What went on there?"

"Well, nobody could ever prove it, but people say it was a, you know, a whorehouse. Edwin Keeler took it over when it failed as a hotel back in the fifties. He turned the dining room and ballroom into a nightclub and supposedly closed off the top three floors of bedrooms. But after the place burned down in the seventies and nobody could prosecute him, old Ed confirmed all the stories people had been telling about the place. Of course, lots of people say he burned the place down himself for the insurance."

"Can you think of anybody else who might have worked there at the same time as Amber?"

"I certainly wouldn't have a clue, I never set foot in the place in my life, but I'm sure old Ed could tell you."

"He's still alive?"

Despite her outraged demeanor, Mrs. Blumchek chuckled. "It's only been about fifteen years since he lost the place. When you get to be my age, that's not a very long time. Last I heard he lived in the subsidized housing project for the elderly over in Jordan Center."

Somewhere in the house a grandfather clock softly chimed four, reminding Tyler of his meeting with Wanda. "I'm sorry, I have to run. I'm supposed to meet Wanda Kensington at four."

He gathered up Amber's file and neatly placed it back inside the folder.

"Oh, I'm sure Wanda must have some stories to tell. And I'm sure she knows more about the Darby Mountain House than I do. But please feel free to come back any time if there's anything else I can help you with..."

On the short ride over to Wanda's house, Tyler found himself wondering why she hadn't mentioned the Darby Mountain House to him. It certainly sounded like some of Carlisle's most colorful history. But obviously she didn't like to talk about much of anything that had to do with Amber. He wondered what kind of success he would have this afternoon.

Wanda was waiting for him at her kitchen table and her reception was less than warm. Her defenses were up and he knew that the chances of getting the information he wanted were slim unless he found a new angle to approach her with.

"Look, my editor isn't too excited about this hotel history story and he wants me to work in the murder angle of this ex–Carlisle college student who comes back to town and ends up dead within hours of her arrival. I found out from people who knew Mimi that Amber St. Pierre was her best friend in college and that Amber lived with you for a

117

while before she left town. It's just an off chance, but I thought you might still have a forwarding address for her."

Wanda looked at him intently for a moment, apparently trying to size up just how much he was going for. Then she shook her head, her dark hair moving from side to side across her face. "Nope. No address. Only know she was going to Hawaii to visit that friend of hers, this Mimi that was killed."

So she was lying to him now, probably for the same reason she had lied to other people about it before; to keep Arden from finding her true mother and abandoning the woman that had raised and loved her for twenty years.

"I hear she worked at the Darby Mountain House while she lived with you. Maybe they had a forwarding address where they sent her last paycheck."

Wanda shook her head. "Would have burnt up with the place if they did. No, when Amber left she disappeared from the face of the earth for us. She always talked about leaving her past behind and starting over and it must be what she did. She never contacted us even once after she left."

Tyler took a deep breath before the next question. "And what about the baby? Did she take her with her?"

Wanda's face turned pale and her eyes narrowed. "What does her baby have to do with any of this? Who told you about her baby?" Her voice had a high–pitched nervousness and a reckless quality to it now.

"There was a note in her college file about it—"

"Her college file? How did you get a hold of that? I'm beginning to think you're just a common snoop, Tyler Mackenzie."

Tyler smiled his most disarming smile. "That's not the first time I've been called that. Now tell me why this makes you so upset. Was there something wrong with her child? Did it have a congenital birth disease or something like that?"

But Wanda was on her feet now, one hand on her hip, the other clearly pointing the way to the door. "I don't have to talk to you about any of this. You have no right to come here prying into the past. Now get out of my house! And don't expect me to help you with your so–called story anymore!"

Well, this was obviously a sore spot with Wanda, just as Arden had promised it would be. As he went out the door, he could hear her inside, still yelling obscene threats after him.

Lou Kensington was just coming up the walkway from the driveway as Tyler came down the porch steps. "What's my wife throwing a fit about now?" he asked pleasantly. "You trying to sell her some encyclopedias or a vacuum cleaner? I'm sure she told you we already have both."

Tyler found it curious how calmly Lou reacted to a stranger walking out of his house with his wife screaming obscenities after him. Obviously it wasn't the first time this had happened. "Mr. Kensington?" He offered his hand. "I'm Tyler Mackenzie, we met briefly the other day at the Cherry Lodge excavation."

"Oh, yes, that journalist that Wanda's been giving history lessons to. The one my daughter is deeply infatuated with."

Tyler could feel the color coming to his face. "She's not really, is she?"

"Oh, I wouldn't worry about it. She falls madly in love with someone new every few months. She's a flighty little thing, not quite ready to settle down yet. So what's Wanda all worked up about? Do I dare to go inside?"

Lou stood there in front of him, his hands in the pockets of his khaki work pants, his plaid flannel shirt still tucked in neatly at the end of a day's work. He looked solid and dependable, square jawed and clear–eyed, his silver gray hair catching a few glimmers of the afternoon sun. Tyler suddenly had an inkling of what a good father he had probably been to Arden. He decided to take his chances.

"My editor wants me to explore the murder angle of the most recent hotel fire here so I've been trying to locate a woman named Amber St. Pierre who was apparently the close friend of Mimi Farrell, the woman who was killed." Lou's smile became slightly strained–looking at the mention of Amber's name. "I've heard that Amber lived with you at one time and I wondered if either you or your wife had any forwarding address for her."

Lou shook his head and turned away. "No, I'm sorry to say we never heard from Amber after she left us."

"She never intended to come back for Arden?"

Lou turned sharply. "How do you know about that?"

"Her college records," Tyler lied. "I looked through them today at Irma Blumchek's. On an application she mentions next of kin as a daughter named Arden. It was just pretty obvious."

Lou took several strides down the path back towards the driveway and Tyler quickly followed him. "Now I understand why my wife blew up at you," he muttered in a low voice. "She's very touchy about the whole thing. She doesn't like people to talk about the fact that Arden isn't our natural born child and most folks in town don't even know.

"You see, it turned out Wanda couldn't have children and she was still adjusting to the idea when Amber moved in with us when she was about to give birth. Wanda just doted on that baby from the moment it was born. Instead of being jealous, Amber was glad to have Wanda take over. She didn't want to be tied down to the responsibility of a baby. The only thing she did for that infant was, uh, you know, breastfeed it. Wanda did everything else, even made the baby a nursery upstairs next to our bedroom because Amber worked late nights."

"Over at the Darby Mountain House."

"That's right." They were standing in the back yard now, under a cluster of apple trees. Looking back at the house, Tyler could see the basement apartment with its wall of large sunny windows and its private entrance that Amber had once occupied and that her daughter lived in now. "There were some serious discussions about leaving Arden with us for the winter while she went to Hawaii. She had this fantasy about living on the beach in a grass shack with the baby and eating coconuts and pineapples. Used to make us shudder."

"But when she did finally leave for Hawaii she never came back."

"That's it in a nutshell. Never saw her or heard from her again. When Arden got older she wanted to try and contact her natural mother and I've never seen Wanda so crushed in her life. By then she thought of Arden as our own. And by all rights she is. We've raised her since the night she was born. But you can understand it, a child's curiosity and all that. I gave her the address of the friend Amber had gone to visit in Hawaii but there was never any response and Arden had to give up on the matter. So if we don't bring the subject up, we have a calm and peaceful household. I'm sorry you had to stumble in on our family's secret."

There was a finality to the way Lou spoke, as though enough had been said. But it was not enough for Tyler. "Where'd you find Mimi's address in Hawaii?"

"Mimi's address?" He looked confused. "Oh, a letter came for Amber a few days after she left, from an M. Stellano. I, uh, had tucked it away in case Amber ever came back." He had an odd expression on his face. "Despite the hatred my wife has cultivated for Amber over the years, I was always very fond of Amber. Wanda had no sympathy for a woman who turns her back on her beautiful baby. Granted, she wasn't a good mother. But I think she just wasn't ready, she was still a girl, she was too unsettled. She was a good person and she had a big heart. At times Arden reminds me a lot of her."

"Did you ever open that letter?"

"The letter? No, when there was no response, I threw it on the fire. I was afraid Wanda might come across it and at the time I didn't need anything to fan her anger."

Tyler had a gut feeling that Lou was lying, that he still had that letter, and that maybe his feelings for Amber had been more than just landlord and lessee. He was certainly protective of his wife's position, but he did not seem as defensive of it as might have been expected.

"Well, thank you for explaining all that to me, Lou. I know now how I overstepped my boundaries here today. I'm sorry if I alienated Wanda, please tell her I didn't mean to." Tyler swung one leg over his bicycle in preparation for departure. "Hey, do they have any leads yet on who that skeleton was they found yesterday?"

Just like the day before, he watched the color drain from Lou's florid face. He shook his head. "Nope. Nothing."

"It bothers you, doesn't it? Losing a life to a fire, even though it was so many years ago and you probably couldn't have saved her."

Lou nodded sadly. "It really does."

Tyler rode off thinking how lucky Arden was to have such a sensitive man for a father. He thought briefly about riding over to Jordan Center and talking to Edwin Keeler. But it would be late by the time he got there and even later by the time he got home. Lack of sleep and too much exercise was catching up with him – he was no longer able to go for days on nervous energy the way he had in his mid–twenties and early thirties.

Well, Sarah would already be working by this time and he ought to be able to crash upstairs without running into her. A few solid hours of sleep and he might be able to deal with their relationship better.

He headed east on the main road out of Carlisle towards the Darby Mountain pass. The sun was low enough now to shine directly in the eyes of the oncoming drivers, making it increasingly difficult for them to see Tyler riding on the edge of their lane. After a few near misses, he crossed the road, feeling safer riding with the cars headed in his own direction.

A few minutes later he heard a car come up right behind him and continue to tail him even though there was plenty of room to pass by. He glanced over his shoulder but was instantly blinded by the setting sun. Unable to see the car or driver, he motioned for them to pass him.

122

A moment later there was a sickening jolt. As his bicycle was rammed from the back, he held tightly to the handlebars but it was no use. The car bumped him again and the bike veered out of control. The last thing he remembered was flying head first through the air, over the shoulder of the road and into an embankment of raspberry bushes, as the car gunned its engine and whizzed by.

CHAPTER EIGHT

Both the bar and the dining room were exceptionally busy, even for a Friday night. Sarah was thankful that she could keep her mind occupied. She didn't have much time to wonder where Tyler was and or to be angry at his continuing irresponsible behavior towards her.

Around half past nine a large, burly stranger came through the door and sat himself down at the bar. He ordered a Bud draft. "I'm looking for that insurance investigator who's staying here," he announced to Sarah without any other introduction.

"Insurance investigator?"

"Said his name was Mackenzie."

A few seats down, a couple of regular customers burst out laughing. Sarah glared at them warningly. "Tyler Mackenzie? Yes, he does stay here, but as far as I know he hasn't come in yet in tonight."

"Well, guess I'll have to have a few beers and wait for him then. Got a piece of information might be worth something to him."

Sarah watched him out of the corner of her eye as she worked and wondered who he could be. When he removed his greasy denim jacket, his t–shirt could not disguise an overwhelming set of upper body muscles. He finished his first beer in the time it took her to ring up a dining room check for a party of four.

"Refill?"

He gave a surly nod. When she turned around with another brimming mug, she could tell his eyes were boldly appraising her body as though she were no more alive than a Penthouse centerfold. Working behind the bar she was used to that kind of attention, and usually it was easy to ignore. But there was something unnerving about his attention, something almost psychopathic in his gaze.

"You know, Tyler may not come back tonight. Just in case he doesn't, let me get your name and number." She flipped over an ordering pad and picked up a pen.

"Neil Richelieu. He knows my number."

Sarah forced herself to finish writing his name before looking back up at him. This was the guy who was their prime suspect in the murder case, the guy who could keep Reed from taking the rap for something he didn't do. She hadn't known Tyler had finally made contact with him.

Suddenly it seemed important to her to keep him there until Tyler showed up. She continued refilling his mug as first the dining room and then the bar emptied. She tried to make small talk with him but he didn't seem much interested in anything except staring at her breasts under her sleeveless sweater. She was usually quite adept at slinging some caustic sarcasm at men who blatantly undressed her with their eyes but she kept her remarks to herself this time. Her stinging barbs probably wouldn't have penetrated his scaly hide anyway.

"Well, looks like he may not show tonight." She wondered what she was going to do if she had to throw this guy out. "What kind of case is it you're helping Tyler with?" she asked casually as she began to break down the bar for the night.

"He's trying to locate some chick I used to know, a friend of my ex–old lady's. Says she stands to collect a bundle of insurance money. I thought maybe some of it might fall my way if I helped him out."

"Oh, right." Sarah nodded like she knew what he was talking about. "And what's this chick's– this woman's name again?"

"Amber. Amber St. Pierre. You ever know her?"

Sarah sucked in her breath. Reed's college girlfriend. The one he'd been telling her about just last night. "No," she exhaled. "Why? What was she like?"

Neil laughed for the first time, showing a mouthful of surprisingly white teeth. "She's not the kind of chick you talk to women about."

"Oh." Sarah dumped out a bucket of ice to fill the uncomfortable silence. "So were you able to help him out? Do you know where she is?"

"No, but I remembered something after he left."

"And what was that?"

"There are a bunch of boxes of her stuff in my barn. I don't know how they got there, my old girlfriend must have let her store it there or something, all I know is one day, I don't know how many years ago even, I was poking around up there looking for something and came across this stack of boxes."

"How'd you know they were hers?"

"Because "Amber's Stuff" or something like that was written on the outside of them all. I thought Mackenzie might want to give me some money to look through them. Might find something that tells him where she went."

Sarah was not sure why Tyler needed to find Mimi's old best friend so badly but she knew Neil was right. This was an opportunity Tyler would not want to miss. He'd be sorry he hadn't come home earlier tonight. Trying to ignore her own vindictive thoughts, she felt she had some questions of her own to ask. For Reed's sake.

"So what was your old girlfriend's name? The one who let Amber leave her boxes there?"

"What difference does that make?" Neil asked suspiciously.

Sarah shrugged. "I thought maybe if they were such good friends, she might know where Amber is now."

"Not a snowball's chance in hell. She's dead."

"Oh. I'm sorry to hear that."

"Yeah, I was sorry to hear it too. She was the one that died in the Centennial fire a few weeks back." Neil stared morosely into his beer.

"Really? Had she come to visit you?" Sarah hoped he wouldn't realize how much she was assuming.

"Hell if I know. I'll never know now. Just as well I didn't see her or they might've tried to pin that fire on me too."

"What do you mean? Have you been wrongly accused of setting something on fire before?" Sarah continued to scrub down the bar sink the same way she had been for the last ten minutes, afraid to change position in case he changed his talkative mood.

Neil snarled a jeering chuckle. "Guess you weren't around when Cherry Lodge got torched?"

Sarah shook her head. "Before my time."

"Yeah, well, somebody took it into their lame–brained head to point the finger at me, I never did find out who exactly. But in the end they couldn't find any loopholes in my foolproof alibi and they didn't want to drag my star witness into court so their precious theory that I was their arsonist got tossed on the dump."

"Really? So what were you doing at the time the fire started?"

"I was in bed with the wife of a prominent community figure. She saved my ass bigtime."

"But I thought you said you didn't do it."

"I didn't. But I still could've ended up in jail for a crime I didn't commit. Happens all the time. Hey, you wanna go get a drink with me somewhere else when you're finished your shift here?"

Sarah was taken aback by the sudden change of subject. "Uh, not tonight, thanks. Maybe another time." She tried not to let her utter revulsion at the idea be too obvious. If only there was only some way to ingratiate herself with Neil without leading him on sexually. She had a feeling that he might just spill lots of old secrets if he thought it would get him into her pants.

"Well, I gotta tell you, you're one hot–looking mama. I'd be happy to show you a good time anytime you're ready. What's your name?" He stood up and began to put on his jacket.

127

"Sarah." She felt weak with relief that he wasn't going to push the issue.

"Well, maybe another time then, Sarah. At least the night wasn't a total waste. Give ol' Mackenzie the message for me, will ya?"

"Sure." She didn't move until he was out the door, at which point she ran quickly to lock it behind him. Her heart was pounding furiously and she wished she could calm down and think straight.

She heard the grandfather clock in the front hall begin to strike midnight. Another midnight and Tyler wasn't home yet. As she focused once again on her ongoing irritation with him, she could actually feel herself calming down a little.

Maybe this time it really was over between them. Maybe when Reed came back she would be ready to say yes.

The telephone woke her from the heavy depths of the first hour of sleep. "What is it?" she mumbled almost incoherently into the receiver.

"Is this Sarah Scupper?" It was a woman's voice, very professional and very awake.

"Yes. Who's this?"

"Jane Reese, I'm the supervising nurse at the emergency room of the Regional Hospital in Jordan Center. Tyler Mackenzie asked me to call you to let you know he's been admitted here."

"What? What for?"

"He's been in an accident. Nothing too serious but we're keeping him until morning for observation. You can call in the morning and find out if he's ready to be discharged."

"An accident? What kind of accident? Can I talk to him?"

"He's resting now. We'll see you in the morning." She hung up, her chipper voice still ringing in Sarah's ear.

Sarah turned on the light and sat up, wide awake now. Tyler in the hospital? A perverse thought crossed her mind almost immediately. What if it was some nasty trick he had cooked up, having a woman call and pretend she was a nurse in the emergency room, saying he was under observation when the only thing he was really under was her?

She was disgusted with herself for not trusting him anymore. But then an even more disturbing thought occurred to her. What if someone had him hostage somewhere and had called her with this bizarre hospital story just to keep her from calling the police when he never came home?

Crazed by her own imagination, Sarah opened the yellow pages of the phone book and dialed the number of the hospital. "Can you put me through to Tyler Mackenzie's room please?

"One moment. I'm sorry, no calls are permitted to Mr. Mackenzie's room until tomorrow morning at which time you can ring him direct in room 204. And for your further information, most of our patients are not allowed to accept calls after 10 PM."

"Of course. Sorry."

Sarah paced up and down the length of the bedroom a few times before she realized there was really nothing further she could do at two in the morning. Sleep would have to suffice.

She did not bother to call the hospital in the morning because she was heading there whether Tyler would be discharged or not. Tossing and turning until dawn, she had been forced to admit to herself that, beneath those deceptive surface emotions, her attachment to Tyler was still very deep.

She did not bother to check in with the admissions desk, but headed directly for the elevator and room 204. Unfortunately it was a small hospital and a new healthy face was easily recognizable. The nurses at the floor station waved her towards them.

"Who're you looking for?"

"Tyler Mackenzie."

"Came in late last night," the other nurse informed the first one. "Cute guy in 204. You can go on down, honey. He's eating breakfast."

As she walked away, Sarah heard the nurse continue to describe Tyler's "tight little buns" that she "wouldn't mind having a piece of." She shook her head. Tyler had the same effect on women of all ages. Even if he was partially unconscious from a concussion.

She gasped as she turned into the doorway of his room. Even from twenty feet away she could see the deep scratches running across his face and down his arms. He grinned at her expression and flipped the sheet off his legs. Beneath the hospital gown, they too were crisscrossed with scratches of various widths and lengths. One of his ankles was wrapped in an ace bandage.

"You should have seen me last night before they washed off the dried blood. I looked like I'd survived an atomic bomb blast."

His flippancy brought Sarah back from her astonishment at his appearance. Underneath it all, he was obviously fine. He extended one hand to her across the breakfast tray.

"Thanks for coming." The hand that squeezed her own was missing the skin from most of its knuckles. "I was afraid you were still mad at me."

"Well, I am, but never mind. What happened to you? Why did they keep you here anyway?" She sat next to him on the edge of the bed and helped herself to a piece of toast and some of his coffee.

"Because I was unconscious for a few hours. They wanted to check me for concussion, etc. I wouldn't look so bad if it weren't for those raspberry bushes. Of course if they hadn't broken my fall, I might be a lot worse off."

"So tell me the details. I'm imagining the worst."

"Someone in a car deliberately ran me off the road. They did!" he insisted in response to Sarah's dubious look.

"You sure you didn't just fall asleep at the wheel? Or should I say wheels?"

He described how the car had slowed down, bumped into him and then purposefully bumped into him again. He told her about flying through the air, rolling through a thicket of raspberry bushes and bumping his head on a rock. The next thing he knew it was pitch black around him and he had no idea where he was until he tried to move and the raspberry thorns ripped some new scratches in his arms. Then he saw the stars through the leaves and heard the sound of a car on a highway and remembered what had happened. When he attempted to disentangle himself again, he discovered his left ankle would not hold him up without intense pain.

An hour later, gritting his teeth he had managed to crawl out of the raspberry thicket and back up to the highway on his shredded and bleeding hands and knees. The first car that passed him had stopped and here he was.

"So it sounds like the bottom line is that somebody is trying to warn you off or get you out of the picture," Sarah remarked when he was finished. "What exactly have you been on to in the last couple of days?"

She moved over to the Naugahyde guest chair and propped her feet up on the bed. Tyler settled back against the pillows, wincing a little, and then told her about Arden's quest to find her real mother who, it turned out, was Amber St. Pierre, old girlfriend of Reed and best friend of the recently departed Mimi Farrell.

The details about Arden's letter to Mimi, Wanda's reaction, and Lou's explanation left Sarah's head spinning. "And when, in all this, did you see Neil Richelieu?" she asked.

"Before I visited Irma Blumchek who used to be the secretary in the college admissions office. Why – do you suspect him of this prank as much as I do?"

"No, I mean, yes, I mean, I hadn't really thought about it yet. He showed up last night at the inn looking for you."

"Yeah, probably wanted to see if I made it home after he ran me off the road. Did he leave looking smug and satisfied?"

"Lewd and lascivious is more like it. He said he'd remembered some boxes of Amber's stuff that were in his barn. He thinks Mimi must have let her store them there. He thinks you'll pay him to look through them."

"He told you all that? The man has never spoken a civil sentence to me yet."

"Well, I don't think he has the hots for you."

Tyler laughed. "No, I don't think so. What else did he tell you?"

"What's it worth to you to know?"

Tyler laughed again to cover the relief he was feeling. Sarah was actually being playful and flirting with him.

"Dinner for two in Key West?"

"All expenses paid?"

"But of course."

"On New Year's Eve."

"Whenever you say."

"Okay. Deal. He told me that he'd been the prime suspect in the Cherry Lodge fire –"

"Well, we already knew that. But it's still amazing that he confided that much to you," he added hastily.

"Don't cut me off. And he said that the reason he never went to trial was that his alibi was that he'd been in bed with wife of some Carlisle bigwig that night and apparently somebody didn't want that fact dragged out in court."

Tyler whistled. "Incredible. He's eating out of the palm of your hand. You can't stop now. You've got to do this part of the job for me, Sarah."

"Oh, no, I don't. You're not feeding me to that beast. Not even for dinner for two in Tahiti."

"Oh, come on–"

"Give it up, Tyler! You can't con ME with your charm and dimples and tight buns. I know you too well for that."

He sighed. "Okay, then don't do it for me. Do it for your friend Reed. If you can get the beast to confide in you, maybe you can help pin Mimi's murder on him and save Reed's hide."

Sarah frowned and looked out the window at two doves pecking at the gravel on the hospital roof.

"Or maybe you'll fall in love with the beast and when you kiss him, he'll turn out to be a handsome prince and you'll live happily ever after in his palace with his singing servants who have resumed their true shapes after years of being cruelly transformed into barking pit bulls."

She tried not to smile. "So what happens when he gets me alone and tries to put the moves on me? He's not exactly harmless."

"We'll get you some mace. But I think you can handle it. I've seen you handle much bigger assholes than him in the bar. Besides, I've got this damn sprained ankle. I can't do anything for the next few days. You can go over there today and tell him I sent you to look through the boxes because I'm laid up. Try and keep it purely professional."

"What exactly would I be looking for?"

"An address book, old letters, bills, I don't know what. You'll know what's important when you see it. And you know what else? While we're in town, I need you to drop me off at an old age home where a guy named Edwin Keeler lives. I wonder if we can find some crutches around here..." Impatiently, he pushed a buzzer on his nightstand.

Sarah stood up and looked down at him seriously. "So what about you and Arden?"

"What do you mean?"

"Are you having a meaningful sexual relationship? Or is this just one of those lustful midlife crises where you need to prove to yourself that even though you're about to turn 40, younger woman are still attracted to you?"

Her spiteful words stung him in places he hadn't known he was hurting. The tears in her eyes told him more than her words. Once again he took her hands in his own battered ones.

"Look, our love means more to me than anything, even if I'm not very good at showing it. Even if I don't act very mature for my age. No, don't say anything, I'm not done yet." He handed her a tissue to wipe away her tears and shot a warning look at the nurse who was entering the room. "You're not completely innocent here either. I know how attracted you are to Reed's rock–steady earthiness. But you and I complement each other, you know, black and white, the sun and the moon, fire and water–"

He didn't understand why she suddenly stared at him so oddly.

"Together we make a complete circle. A perfect universe."

When the nurse returned a few moments later she had to clear her throat sharply to let them know they were not alone.

Sarah managed to convince Tyler that he was not in any condition to interview a fragile old man in a nursing home. His appearance alone was enough to distract anyone from confiding in him. She suggested that perhaps instead he ought to settle himself comfortably onto the couch at home and make a few phone calls. One in particular, the call to Mimi's husband in Hawaii, seemed to be long overdue.

"He might be able to tell you right off the bat where Amber is. And he certainly must have a better grasp than anybody else does on why Mimi was coming here to meet Reed."

Tyler counted the days and decided that Diane Stellano would agree that a decent enough interval had passed since the funeral. When Sarah left him an hour later, he had his foot elevated on a stack of pillows, his notes were spread out around him on the couch. and a pot of coffee and various snacks were within easy reach on the end table. He was cursing the fact that it was only 5 AM in Hawaii and that he would have to wait several hours to make his most important call.

He had watched Sarah get ready to leave with a bit of apprehension at his own idea. She was wearing black jeans and a black t–shirt; at his suggestion she added a short jacket with deep pockets that she could easily stash things in. He also suggested that she replace her leather boots with running shoes; she didn't have to ask why. She also plaited her hair into a tight braid which she then wound up and pinned into a low bun at the back of her neck. He had never seen her do her hair like that before. The severe style made her look like a librarian, but she seemed to think it was appropriate.

"I don't want it in the way," she explained. "And I may be crawling in some filthy places, you never know."

"Be brave," had been his parting comment to her.

As she drove to Carlisle, she ran through all the possible scenarios she could think of and how she would handle them. She hoped Neil would at least be home so she could get the ordeal over with. It was Saturday – he could be anywhere.

When she pulled into his yard, she knew immediately that he wasn't there. The dogs strained on their chains, barking hostilely at her. The dirt–covered parking place next to the back door was bare except for the black spots from leaking oil that had accumulated in one area.

Damn, she didn't want to have to hang around and she sure as hell didn't want to go home and come back. She looked around. The house was constructed in traditional, centuries–old, Vermont style with the barn connected to the back of the house and usually accessible through a breezeway to the kitchen. Houses had been designed that way to make it easier to care for the animals in the dead of a snowbound winter. Well, there was only one barn; if the boxes were stored there, she should be able to find them whether he was home or not.

Spurred on by the idea that she could accomplish her task without having to see Neil at all, she boldly slammed the door of her car. Ignoring the frenzied yelps of the pit bulls, she marched into the open door of the barn. Just in case the wild, growling dogs managed to pull free of their chains, she slid the wooden door shut behind her.

It took her eyes a minute to adjust to the dim quality of light filtering through the dingy, dirt–encrusted windows. The downstairs of the barn had obviously been in use for a number of years as a garage/repair station. There were work benches littered with tools and a few engine blocks in various states of disassembly. A narrow set of wooden stairs against the back wall led up to the next floor. If anything was stored in the barn, it was probably up there.

Gingerly she put her foot on the first well–worn step, but it seemed quite sturdy. Climbing quickly to the top, her heart sank a little at the sight of the second floor. What had once been an enormous hayloft was now an attic storage area for a man who had never thrown anything away. She picked her way through broken appliances, rusted tools, split lawn hoses and boxes of old magazines. She was about to give up and come back later when she found what she was looking for.

Three cardboard boxes and a couple of garbage bags, each labeled with red magic marker in the same way that Neil had spoken of them. "Amber's Stuff." The handwriting was cute and girlish.

Without a second thought, she dragged the first box out onto the floor and opened it up. Books. College textbooks and worn–out paperbacks. She scanned the titles quickly; Stranger in a Strange Land, On the Road, Electric Koolaid Acid Test, a couple of Carlos Castaneda books, a dog–eared volume on astrology. No surprises here.

She untied one of the garbage bags and peeked inside. Clothes. She dumped them unceremoniously onto the floor. A musty winter coat and a pair of Sorrells topped the pile. A floppy felt hat and matching mittens. She was starting to feel a little creepy about poking through somebody else's belongings. But it was for a good cause, she reminded herself, as she began stuffing the clothes back into the bag. Three pairs of worn–in, size six blue jeans, a couple of wool ski sweaters, another clean pile of folded turtleneck shirts in a variety of colors, several pairs of neatly rolled up socks.

It looked like Amber's entire winter wardrobe, left behind when she took off for Hawaii.

She picked up the last few items; a couple of tiny pairs of bikini underpants, some black tights and a short nylon slip. Retying the bag, she hauled out the next one and dumped it on the floor. The contents of this bag were more haphazard than the first. There were several dresses that spoke more to the style of the early 70s than the rest of the clothes did. There were two very short denim skirts and a pair of platform shoes. A couple pairs of cut–off shorts, some halter tops and T–shirts, a pair of sandals and a short white bathrobe of some sleazy synthetic material. Two T–shirts that sported a large blue crescent moon beneath the words "Blue Moon Lounge."

Obviously the summer clothes that Amber could not fit into the backpack required for all world travelers of those days. As she piled the clothes back into the garbage bag, one item made her pause and frown. A purple and black bikini bathing suit that still had a price tag on it.

Sarah shook her head and put it back in the bag with the rest of the clothes. Maybe Amber had changed her mind about it or it hadn't fit.

Two more boxes to go. The next one looked as though someone had swept off the top of a dresser right into the box. Hairbrush, mirror, lipstick, safety pins, barrettes sat in a jumble on top of the rest of the contents. A double picture frame held two photos; one of a round smiling baby, a solitary tooth showing proudly in its bare gums, the other of two smiling young women with their arms around each other that had to be Mimi and Amber. Sarah put it aside and went on.

There were half–burned candles, a macrame wall hanging, some rolled up posters, and a shoe box. Gingerly prying the shoe box out, she carefully took off the lid, now soft and soggy after years in an unheated barn. Inside were letters, bank statements and bills. Putting the shoe box off to one side, she attacked the final box of the three.

An old patchwork quilt was folded on top of everything else. Spots of mold now marred its colorful geometric pattern. Sarah lifted it carefully out of the box to see what was beneath. There was a straw hat and an empty woven straw bag. There was an alarm clock, an embroidered pillow and something lacy. But what caught her eye was a well–worn, brown leather shoulder bag. It took all her to strength to pull open the rusty zipper that held it closed.

Her brow wrinkled in puzzled distress as she viewed the contents inside the old purse. A checkbook for an account at the Jordan National Bank. A comb, a mailbox key, a handful of loose papers with notes on them. Half a month's worth of unused birth control pills, moldy and disintegrating in their package. And a Moroccan leather wallet that held thirty dollars in small bills and change, as well as a driver's license, a student ID, a library card, and a social security card.

The sound of truck tires on gravel brought her situation sharply into focus. Quickly repacking the box, she stuffed the contents of the shoe box into the pockets of her jacket and then took it off and folded it inside out so that nothing showed. Throwing the strap of the gaping leather bag over her own shoulder, she hung the jacket across it; there was no time to wrestle with the zipper now.

Backing away, she gave a quick final look at how she had left "Amber's Stuff." That's when she saw the item she hadn't connected with the pile of possessions before.

A dusty red frame–pack was propped up against a wooden support beam behind the stack of boxes. A crescent moon was embroidered on the front pocket in a neon shade of blue.

The sound of Neil's voice cursing and shouting at his unseen intruder sent her quickly down the stairs and across the dirt floor of the barn. She heard the back door of the house slam open and Neil's muffled threats as he searched his home for his unfortunate visitor. She took the opportunity to slip out the barn door and run around back to where the junk yard began.

"Hello!" she called, but her throat was so tight that nothing came out, but a high pitched whisper. She cleared her throat and tried again. "Hello! Neil! Hello!"

She made her away through the overgrown brush along the back side of the property and came out on the front porch. At the sound of her voice, the dogs went wild again and she knocked nervously on a front door that looked like it hadn't been opened in years.

"Who the hell are you?" Neil appeared at the end of the porch, carrying a double–barrel shotgun.

"It's me, Sarah, from the bar last night. I was just walking around the yard looking for you. Don't shoot!" She gave a half–hearted laugh and held her hands up in front of her.

Neil lowered the shotgun and an odd leer lit up his unshaven face. "Didn't expect to see you so soon, lady. How'd you find me?"

Sarah shrugged. "I just asked around town." She looked down at her feet, pretending to be shy, and noticed the patches of dusty dirt on her knees from kneeling in the attic of the barn. "I came by with a message from Tyler Mackenzie for you."

"Oh, really? And what's that?"

Still grinning, Neil leaned against the wall of the house waiting for her reply. Either he didn't believe this was her reason for visiting him or he couldn't wait to hear the results of his own handiwork on the highway.

"He got run off the road last night and is laid up for a few days with a badly sprained ankle. He said he'll be by as soon as he can, to see what you've got for him." She took a deep breath and inhaled the unpleasant smell of his beer–saturated body. She began to walk back towards her car. "Your dogs make me a little nervous. Would you mind calling them off?"

"Fudge! Fungus! Quit yer bitchin'!" He threw a rock in their direction and the pit bulls instantly quieted down. Neil fell into step with Sarah.

"So what do you say? You want to go out for a drink with me some night?" Neil obviously took her personal visit to him as a sign of interest.

She swallowed hard. "Sure." Her reply did not sound very convincing, but Neil didn't seem to care. "I'm off tomorrow night. Where should we meet?" She was not going to get into a car and go some place with him, that was for sure.

"How about over at the Springhouse? Do you know it?"

"Of course. How about for cocktails around five?" The earlier the better, and there would still be lots of daylight left.

"Sounds great. Sure you don't want to stay for a beer now? I've got some cold Bud in the fridge."

"No thanks. I've got work to do. Gotta go. See you tomorrow." Still clutching the old purse with its precious hanging cargo, she slid into the seat of her car. Before she could grab the handle, Neil wedged his body between the door and the car.

"Okay, baby. I'm looking forward to it." His eyes were shining in that frightening, psychotic way and for a moment he rested his thick fingers on her forearm. Trying not to shudder, Sarah started the engine and revved it a little.

"Gotta go," she said again with forced brightness. He took the hint and moved aside so she could shut the car door. With a perky little wave, she sped out of the yard.

At the end of the road, she pulled off onto the shoulder and allowed herself to collapse over the steering wheel for a few minutes. She took several deep breaths and then at last she allowed herself to think about the events of the last hour. Suddenly she was trembling uncontrollably and her shirt was damp with sweat. But it was not because of her planned encounter with Neil. It was because of the undeniable implications of what she had found in the barn.

CHAPTER NINE

"And this," Sarah said, taking a pair of sunglasses out of a red leather case, "is my final piece of evidence. Nobody, I mean nobody, goes to Hawaii without their sunglasses."

"Or their driver's license. Or a brand new bikini. So if she didn't go to Hawaii, where did she go?"

"I can't believe she'd go anywhere without her wallet. Or her hairbrush."

"Well, I've gotten the impression that she was fairly irresponsible and spaced out. Maybe she packed up her purse by mistake and left without it."

Sarah shook her head. "The more I think about, the more I'm sure I was looking at the entire inventory of Amber's personal possessions. And to my mind that can only mean two things – she was either kidnapped or she was killed."

"My God, Sarah, you're starting to sound like me." Tyler shifted the position of his leg and winced; his body was beginning to feel extremely battered in places. "But you have to remember we're talking about Vermont's golden era of communes, gurus and anti–materialism. Maybe she just decided owning things was not where it was at for her."

"Lame. You know you agree with me." Sarah sat down at the table and peeled a banana. "The question is why would anybody want to kill or kidnap her?"

"And who?"

"Well, unfortunately the who seems pretty obvious to me."

"Then why would he tell you that her possessions were in his barn? Why wouldn't he just get rid of them years ago?"

Sarah stuffed the banana into her mouth; she had no answer to that question. "Let's look at all this stuff," she said, pulling the stacks of old envelopes out of the jacket pockets she had shoved them into. "Maybe there are some answers here."

They quickly sorted them into three piles; bank statements, personal letters, and miscellaneous documents. The last group included pay stubs from the Darby Mountain House – the final one, dated October 28th, 1974, they had discovered in Amber's purse. Amber's birth certificate was there; Arden's was not. An envelope from Kingdom Travel included an itinerary for a one way ticket to Hawaii with a stop in San Francisco, departing November 4th. There was a postscript at the bottom reminding Amber to pick up her ticket by Friday because the office would be closed over the weekend.

"I wonder if the ticket is here someplace," Sarah murmured half to herself.

"Well, when you have an airline ticket where do you keep it?" Tyler countered.

"Usually tacked to the bulletin board by the telephone. Or in my purse, I suppose. It definitely wasn't in her purse."

"It seems to me that this ticket to Hawaii was the most important thing in Amber's life. So maybe she kept it some place very secret and safe."

"Speaking of Hawaii," Sarah reached for another banana. She felt ravenous now that the danger of her escapade was over. "Did you get a hold of Mimi's husband yet?"

Tyler shook his head. "I left a message on his answering machine. It could be that he's screening all his calls right now and may not call back. I'll try again later. Hey, speaking of Hawaii, look at this. These letters are from Mimi herself." He unfolded the musty old notebook paper and began to read aloud.

"Dear Amber, Life is great on Maui, hurry up and get here before you're snowbound in Vermont! I am working in

142

a health food store now and living upstairs with the owner. Don't laugh, but I think I'm in love again. This time for real! He's the opposite of Neil, sweet, gentle, doesn't need to prove his manhood all the time, he's kind to animals and I bet he's never raised his hand to a woman in his life."

Tyler raised his eyebrows and looked at Sarah. "Wouldn't surprise me a bit about Neil," she responded. "Go on."

"Unfortunately we don't really have any room for you to stay, but you're welcome to crash on the living room floor until you find a place. (Jason isn't the type to invite you to sleep with us, so don't come here expecting that.)"

"Hmmm, what does that tell us?"

"There are lots of people who camp on the beach too. You might enjoy that. But I have to tell you, I think it would be very difficult if you bring the baby. I don't think you'd ever find a set–up like the one you've got now..."

As Tyler read on to the end of the letter, Sarah picked up another one and began to quickly scan it. "Wait a second, Tyler, listen to this! *I think your idea about trying to contact Reed is a good one. Maybe he'll believe it if he hears it from you. He at least ought to know. You know, just in case something ever happens.* What do you think that's all about?"

"I don't know. Let me see that one." She handed him the letter and looked through the others. "This is odd, this one is addressed to Mimi with a stamp on it and Amber's return address. But it was never mailed and damn, it's sealed shut."

"Jesus, you're so moral. Hand it over here."

But Sarah held the letter just out of Tyler's reach. "Don't you think you should at least let Arden be the one to open it? Don't you think it might bother her that we're going through her mother's private things? I mean, in the end, it will all rightfully be hers. Shit. I just realized I left that picture frame sitting on the floor of the barn. I put it aside because I thought she might want to have it. Damn."

"What picture frame?"

"Oh, it was one of those old double frames, the hinged kind, and one side was a picture of Arden as a baby, and the other side looked like Amber and Mimi. I hope Neil doesn't notice it. I'll have to go back over there and get it somehow."

"Wait till he's at work on Monday. Now give me that letter. I'll take full responsibility for opening it. I'm sure wherever Amber is, she's forgotten about it by now."

Sarah slowly placed it in his hand and then watched him rip the end open. "It's dated October 29th. *Dear Mimi, It's all set! I'm picking up my ticket tomorrow. I decided to stop in San Francisco on the way. I've always wanted to go there and one of the women I work with at the Blue Moon has a brother there I can stay with and it won't cost me any extra. I should be in Hawaii by mid November at the latest.*

"It'll be good to get away from here. This thing with Mr. K. is starting to get a little too heavy for me. It's turned into something that happens every night after work. I'll be glad to leave it behind."

"Who do you think Mr. K. is?" Sarah interrupted.

"Probably Edwin Keeler, her boss at the Darby Mountain House. I'm seeing him tomorrow; maybe I can find out more. Anyway, where was I? *I ended up not calling Reed or writing to him or anything. I mean what's the point? Arden is perfectly happy here and Wanda assures me they will always think of her as their own. She pushes me to consider letting them adopt her. I know I'm not ready to be a mother but still. Some day I may be ready and then I will probably want her back."*

"That's a hell of an attitude!"

"Shhh, wait till you hear what she writes next. *Besides, Reed didn't believe me when I was pregnant, why should he believe me now? Although if he saw Arden, he would probably know—"*

"Oh, my god. He's her father, isn't he?" Sarah felt a chill run from the top of her head to the tips of her fingers and toes.

"*—immediately that she's his child*," Tyler finished in a reverent tone. "*She looks just like him.*"

They sat there in silence for a few minutes, awed by the truth. Finally Sarah spoke. "Do you think they look that much alike?"

"It's hard to know with his beard and all. And he told us he stopped seeing Amber because she was sleeping with so many other guys."

"But that was after they'd had a monogamous relationship for a few months. If you count back nine months from Arden's birthday, it might become pretty obvious."

"IF he can remember the actual dates when they hung out together."

"Oh, hell, I'm sure he can. In college everything goes by season and event. I'm sure he can remember what time of year it was and an accurate time frame."

Tyler nodded thoughtfully. "When is he due back here?"

Sarah gave a small sigh. She was not really ready to deal with Reed's return. "Probably tomorrow night. My guess is he'll want to start working on the barn on Monday."

"I'm thinking we ought to get the two of them together and see what happens."

"It would probably make Reed very happy. He told me he wished he had kids." Sarah stood up abruptly. "Do you need me to get you anything? I've got to get to work downstairs."

After bringing him a fresh cup of coffee, she headed off to work, obviously absorbed in some deep thoughts of her own. Tyler knew it had something to do with Reed and once again he felt those painful pangs of jealousy. But as he reached for the coffee, his foot slipped off its pile of pillows hitting the table and the pain in his bandaged ankle superseded all else.

By morning the swelling had gone down considerably and he could even put a little pressure on his foot. The rest of his body, however, felt as though it had been used as a demonstration model on how not to be a chiropractor. His neck was only slightly stiffer than his hip, which felt only slightly more twisted than his right shoulder. A hot bath and some limbering stretches took care of the majority of stiffness and he was hobbling around the apartment without his crutches by the time Sarah came up to help him to the car.

"I thought you weren't supposed to put any weight on that." She blocked the doorway holding out his crutches.

"Let's just get down the stairs first and then I'll use them." He shouldered his day pack and limped towards her.

Shaking her head, she helped him down to the first floor and out to the back seat of the car.

"All right, so where are we going now?"

"To the Stately Oaks Retirement Center. It's a subsidized housing complex for the elderly. It's on Barre Avenue in Jordan Center."

"I know where it is." Sarah seemed rather moody this morning and Tyler did not force any conversation with her. They rode the entire distance in silence, pulling into a horseshoe cluster of one–story apartments. A middle–aged woman wearing a volunteer's badge was on her knees planting petunias and marigolds along the sidewalks. She directed them to Ed Keeler's door.

The doorbell was answered by a short, slope–shouldered octogenarian stooped over a cane. Tyler found himself eye to eye with the top of a bald head, its few wisps of white hair accented by a generous sprinkling of age spots.

"Come in, come in! Nice to meet you!" His warm welcome of strangers was surprising; perhaps he did not get many visitors. He extended a gnarled hand first to Sarah and then Tyler. "Always nice to meet a couple of new young faces," he explained as he led them into a combination kitchen/living room. "That's what I miss most about losing the old hotel. All those nice young people. And especially all the pretty girls."

There was no missing the lascivious wink he gave Sarah as he motioned them to sit on his brown velvet couch. Edwin himself sat in a padded rocker by a large picture window that looked out into the courtyard. Sarah noted that the place was surprisingly clean and then realized that cleaning was probably part of the package that came with living in the retirement center.

"I'm not staying," she said hastily. Tyler had insisted that Ed Keeler would definitely not talk about the seedier details of his operation if a woman was around. "I'm just making sure Tyler's all set here and then I've got some shopping to do at the Grand Union."

Tyler was settling himself into a corner of the soft couch, trying to unzip his backpack and turn on his tape recorder without seeming too obvious. Sarah waved him a silent goodbye and slipped out the door.

But Edwin was already oblivious to what was happening in the room around him as he prepared himself for a dissertation on his favorite topic. "So you want to hear about the old days of the Darby Mountain House."

For the next twenty minutes or so Edwin recited a well–memorized history that dated back to the late 1800s. Tyler did not want the old man to wear himself out talking about the grand hotel era so he cut to the chase.

"Well, actually I'm not that interested in the really old days. I'd like to hear about the nightclub you had there in the early seventies."

"The Blue Moon? Well, you know, when I bought the hotel in the late fifties it was nearly condemned. There was no way I could bring all the plumbing and electric fixtures up to modern code. I thought I might as well have thrown my money down one those old rusted toilets until I came up with the idea of turning the ballroom into a lounge. It took a while for the place to catch on until I started hiring decent bands and dressing the waitresses in sexy uniforms.

147

By the early seventies it was pretty popular with a certain kind of crowd."

"So you never put the upstairs room to use again?"

Ed laughed merrily. "Now who said that? I guess you've come here with some knowledge of the former goings–on of my hotel. Aren't too many young men your age didn't get their first taste of you–know–what any place besides the Darby Mountain House."

"Is that right?"

"Damn tootin'. Only in the summertime, mind you. Couldn't keep those drafty upper floors heated in the winter. Of course, it was what you might call an 'open secret' in those days. As long as no trouble came out of it, the cops looked the other way. It was a discreet little operation that kept everybody happy. After the place burned down, it became sort of a legend and now everybody likes to be nostalgic about it." He snorted. "As though any of those town gossips ever set foot in the place."

"Did you have any trouble finding girls to work for you?"

He shook his head. "It was optional for them. Just because they worked in the club, didn't mean they had to work upstairs. There were a few real dumb bunnies working for me who never even caught on!" He laughed again. "No, usually it was just one or two girls a season, college girls most of the time who wanted to pick up a good handful of extra cash during the summer. I'd always watch them for a month or so before I'd even suggest it to them. See how they worked the floor, see how they related to the customers. Some of them would be shocked and just flat out say no; or they'd try it a few times and find it wasn't for them. I never forced anybody to do anything they didn't want to. It wasn't like I was a pimp or something. Jesus Christ!" The idea made him laugh some more.

"Do you remember a girl named Amber that waitressed for you?"

"Amber, sweet Amber, how could I ever forget Amber? She was such a hard worker, but she always had such a good time. Customers loved her, she was what they used to call a 'liberated woman.' No inhibitions with that one. Now see, there was a perfect example of the kind of girl who was right for our 'alternative service.' Found out after she'd been there for a week that she'd gone to bed with the band. Not just the lead singer, mind you, but the whole goddamn band! I pulled her aside and said 'Listen, honey, you could be getting paid good money to have this same good time.' Well, and now this is the part I can never quite understand about some girls–"

Edwin leaned forward to make sure he still had Tyler's attention. "She didn't like the idea of getting PAID to screw these guys! But when I told her how much money she could make if she would screw the next band coming in for me, her eyes got all shiny and she told me how she was trying to save up money to go to Hawaii with that dark–haired girlfriend of hers. Jeez, what was her name, she worked for me too..."

"Mimi? Mimi worked for you?"

"That's right. Mimi. Yeah, they were quite a pair, night and day, those two. Mimi with all that long dark hair and those big suck–me jugs and little blonde Amber with her tiny mouthful of a figure. Mimi was the one that men lusted after – on really hot summer nights I used to let them wear just their little mini–skirts and bikini tops with a short open vest on top. Guys would just follow Mimi around panting, not realizing that Amber was the one who would take it off for anybody."

"So did, uh, Mimi earn any extra cash while she worked for you?"

"Now see, she was one of that kind I was telling you about. She tried it a coupla times but she couldn't relax enough, she didn't enjoy it. I don't think she really knew how to have fun with the place like Amber did, she was too serious. I almost thought the two of them had something kinky going, they were such close friends."

Tyler was nearly speechless by now. He could not believe that Edwin Keeler would tell all these personal stories to any interested person off the street. But he was just a lonely old man who loved to talk and who, at one time, had led an interesting life that he knew people liked to hear about. Tyler cleared his throat.

"So what about you? Did you ever get in on the action?"

He shrugged and laughed a merry, wheezing laugh. It made Tyler think of dust balls scattering in the breeze from a window. "Now and then. But that wouldn't have been very professional, now would it? Speaking of professions, what did you say yours was?"

"I didn't. I'm a private, uh, insurance investigator. I've been trying to locate Amber St. Pierre because she stands to inherit some life insurance but I keep running into dead ends. You ever hear from her after she left here for Hawaii?"

"Nah, not a word. Fact of the matter is, she never showed up for her own going away party. Turned out she left on her trip a few days early without even saying goodbye. But I'll never forget how we all sat around in our costumes waiting for her to show up–"

"In your costumes? You were having a costume going–away party?"

"Well, it happened to coincide with Halloween and the full moon. And a blue moon at that. So it was an auspicious occasion all around."

"A blue moon? I'm sorry–"

"Well, our lounge was named the Blue Moon, I have mentioned that, haven't I? And Amber had this thing about blue moons, she was into all that astrology shit, and so we thought we'd have this great surprise party for her. Only she never showed."

"Oh. But I'm still not sure what you mean by a blue moon."

"When there are two full moons in a month, the second one is called a blue moon. You know the expression, once in a blue moon? Of course you do. Everybody does. Well, you only get two full moons in a month maybe once every three or four years. So it's kind of a special occasion. We used to

150

always have some kind of wild party at the club on those nights."

Tyler suddenly remembered the little moon earring that Arden wore with the turquoise blue inlay. She said it had been her mother's.

"She ever talk to you about her baby?"

Edwin shook his head. "Hell, no. I don't think she wanted people to know she came with any kind of baggage like a kid. I didn't know when I hired her and the way I found out was pretty bizarre." He shook his head again at the memory.

"How was that?"

"One night a few weeks after she'd been working I saw her walking around with these two big wet spots over her tits. I asked what she'd spilled on herself and she looked down and said something about leaking milk again. Only time I can remember her being kind of embarrassed. I asked around town and people told me she had a baby that Wanda Kensington took care of most of the time. The Kensingtons are the ones who might know where she is. Have you asked them?"

Tyler nodded. "They don't have a clue. Or they're not saying. Is there anybody else still around who worked with Amber back then? Somebody who might have heard from her?"

Old Ed thought for a moment. "Ricky Sims was the bartender in those days. He has the real estate office in Carlisle now. And there was a girl we called Willow. I thought I saw her at the post office a few years back with a flock of kids. Bigger than a house, lost her shape entirely, barely recognized her. Lost all the records when the place burned down and it's hard to remember who was there exactly when."

"When exactly did it burn down?"

"Last day of March, 1980. Off season, all closed up, of course. I was down in Tampa, playing golf when I got the news. Don't know why I didn't stay down there. Thought maybe I could make a go of it in some other place up here back then. But the insurance money wasn't even enough for a down payment on something else. And old Chief Bilodeau was retiring that year and that young upstart they hired in his place made it clear to me he wasn't going to look the other way. The old chief was always happy to overlook any laws I might be breaking as long as he got his monthly freebie. So I retired." Edwin sighed and rocked his chair a little. "Led a quiet life ever since."

Tyler thought about Amber's letter again, the one about "Mr. K." "You know, for some reason I was under the impression that you and Amber had some kind of thing going after hours, that you two were more than just friends."

"Don't know where you got that idea. I loved Amber almost like a daughter, but physically–" he shrugged. "She wasn't the type that made my dick hard. I'm an old–fashioned tits and ass man from the fifties. I like them better when they look like a Penthouse centerfold. Old what's her name, Amber's friend there, Mimi, now she made my mouth water. But she lived with that lunatic biker. I remember he came into the Moon a couple times and caused a scene when somebody just made a comment about Mimi. He was too violent. I had to have the bouncer keep him out after that."

Through the window, Tyler could see Sarah coming up the path to the front door. "Ed, did you hear about the woman who died in the Centennial fire last month?"

"Of course I did. I watched the six o'clock news. I keep up with the world."

"Did you know that it was Mimi, the same girl you've been telling me about?"

Sarah was quietly letting herself into the apartment.

"No! Really? You're sure? Oh, that's a shame. A damn shame. I'm sorry to hear that." Sinking back into his memories, Edwin Keeler seemed to shrink into himself, shutting out the ugly news of the present.

Tyler gestured with his head that Sarah should announce her presence.

"I'm back!" she called brightly. "How was your talk?"

"Just great," he replied loudly, stumbling to a standing position on his good ankle. "Look, Ed, if you remember anything else about Amber that might help me find her, will you promise to call me? Here's my number." He pressed a business card from the West Jordan Inn into the old man's hand.

As quickly as he had slipped into the past, Ed was back to the present. "Sure, sure," he said, getting slowly to his feet to see them to the door. "I still can't believe she didn't stay in touch with the Kensingtons. I mean, they kept her baby, didn't they? Most of the old timers in town knew about that. People used to talk about her living with them, saying she ruined things between them for a while."

Tyler stopped his slow march to the door and looked at him. "In what way?"

"Oh, it was just crude gossip. Things like," he lowered his voice in an attempt to keep Sarah from hearing, "She gave Wanda the baby and she gave Lou the blow jobs. And knowing Amber," he shrugged, "well, who knows?"

"Mr. K! I can't believe we didn't make that connection!" Tyler smacked the side of his head. "It makes perfect sense now."

"It's sad. It's just plain sad. Doesn't it get you down finding out all these dysfunctional things about people's pasts?" Although Sarah didn't bring it up, Tyler knew she was referring to the things she and he had found out about her own mother and father.

"Do you know what a blue moon is?" Tyler asked abruptly changing the subject.

"You mean like 'once in a blue moon'? Sure, it's when there are two full moons in a month. I went to a blue harvest moon party last year."

"Well, maybe I'm the only person in the world who didn't know what it meant."

"Oh, maybe it's just something us country folks know about," she replied with an exaggerated Vermont accent. "What brought that up?"

He told her about the Blue Moon Lounge and Amber's obsession with blue moons and Arden's blue moon earring and the blue moon goin– away party that Amber never made it to. "That one was on Halloween, no less."

"So that only strengthens the idea that something suspicious happened in those last few days."

"That's right, and somehow you're going to worm the truth out of that scumbag, Neil. Now, let's talk about what you're going to do when you meet him tonight. Damn, I wish I could be there to back you up."

Sarah blinked a couple of times as her eyes adjusted from brilliant daylight to the darkness of the underground bar. The handful of cars in the Springhouse parking lot assured her that at least she and Neil wouldn't be the only patrons of the place at this time of day.

Tyler had reminded her that she needed to drink something that she could nurse slowly and not get too drunk on. She ordered a dark imported beer and sat down at a table in the back, away from the bar but with a good view of the door. The bartender eyed her with curiosity and undisguised interest. She smiled to herself, thinking how surprised he was going to be when he saw who she was meeting.

She and Tyler had argued about how she should dress; she had wanted to wear a shapeless black linen dress that she felt sexually safe in. Tyler had told her she ought to give it to Goodwill, he didn't care if it was fashionable and comfortable, it made her look like shit. In the end they had settled on a pair of loose–fitting cotton pants knit like a fine soft sweater and a matching tunic, both in a light ivory color. Sarah had rarely worn the outfit; she was afraid of staining it when she worked and it was too fancy for just hanging around in.

"Wear your hair down, it makes you look younger and more vulnerable. And wear some funky jewelry."

"I don't own any funky jewelry. I hate to think what I'd look like if I let you tell me what to wear every day."

It had turned out okay, the outfit made her feel comfortable, elegant and even a little bit confident. It also helped her keep her distance from Neil when he strode in a few minutes later. He was wearing a clean white T–shirt with his jeans and his freshly–washed hair was still wet and shiny. The hair on his chest was so dark that Sarah could see the outlines of it through his T–shirt along with the intimidating structure of his upper pectoral muscles.

She swallowed hard as he approached the table, swaggering a little, knowing that every man in the room was watching him. "Hey, baby. You're lookin' good. Real good."

Two hours later, he was effusively pouring out the injustices of his life between shots of whiskey and bottles of beer.

"Nothing ever seems fair," he said banging his elbows down on the table and staring mournfully at her. "That insurance investigator comes to see me, not about a big settlement for me, but about some old chick I used to know who's about to inherit millions."

"How well did you know her? Maybe she'll give you something for it if you help him find her."

"How well did I know her? I ain't seen her in twenty years, that's how well I knew her."

"Did you ever see Amber after Mimi went away?"

"A coupla times. I tried to get her to tell me where my Mimi'd gone. Last time I went down to where she was staying, turned out she was gone too."

"You went down to the Kensingtons and they told you Amber had left town." Sarah wondered if this was a story that Neil had planned to use for years in case any ever caught up with him.

155

"Yeah, Wanda told me." His eyes grew distant with memory and an eerie grin crossed his face.

"What's so funny?"

"Nothin'. Just remembering somethin'."

"Oh, come on. Share the joke."

"I was just thinking about how everyone thought – nah, I can't tell you this."

Sarah moved her chair closer to the table and leaned in towards him. Trying not to breathe in the overpowering smell of alcohol that his pores were emitting, she said in a low, confidential and (she had to admit) sexy voice, "You can tell me. We're friends. Who would I tell?"

"It's not that. It's just –"

"It's just what?"

He sat up straight suddenly and replied, "It's just that I know from experience it's a stupid idea to tell a woman you're trying to get friendly with about other women you've laid in your lifetime. I'm right, aren't I?"

Sarah sat stunned for a second, trying to assemble all the information he was giving her. "Well, what you did twenty years ago isn't necessarily going to change my feelings about you today," she said stalling. "So, are you trying to tell me you and Amber were lovers?"

He snickered and upended his beer. "'Lovers' is a girl's word for it. Amber and I were never in love."

"All right, you had sex with her."

He snickered again. "Yeah, me and plenty of other guys. There was nothing very secret about that."

"Then what are we talking about here? Somebody else you had sex with?"

Her frank way of speaking stopped him cold for a moment and she was afraid she had lost him. Gently she tried again. "We were talking about when Wanda told you Amber was gone. What did she tell you that was funny?"

Neil signaled the bartender that he wanted another round before he answered her. "It wasn't anything she told me. At first I thought she was lying so she brought me in and showed me Amber's empty room. Even the sheets were gone from the bed. I remember it was Halloween and the doorbell kept ringing with kids looking for candy. We went back upstairs because she had to answer the door. She gave me a beer and then somehow we ended up in her bed, fucking our brains out."

"You weren't worried about her husband coming home?" Sarah took a sip of her own beer, which was warm and flat by now.

"She said he had been called out to a fire and that he probably wouldn't be back till dawn. She was a real surprise to me I'll tell you. For such a dowdy bitch, she fucked me with a vengeance." He looked at Sarah out of the corner of his eye. "Does this bother you, me talking like this?" When she shook her head, he smiled and lowered his eyelids. "Or does it turn you on?"

With a sick feeling in her stomach, she returned his smile but said nothing.

"She kept me at it until I passed out in her bed. She kicked me out some time before daylight. When I got home, the police were waiting for me. Said they'd had an anonymous tip that I was the one who started the fire."

Things were falling into place. "Is this the Cherry Lodge fire we're talking about?"

"That's right. Wanda was my alibi and that's why they never made me go to court. Didn't want to drag her into it. I guess there were even a few kids who remembered seeing me there." He shook his head and laughed before downing a fresh shot of whiskey. "A few years later, she tried to get me to do it with her again when Lou was out at a fire but I must've been feeling rational or something because I told her I didn't think I needed a replay of that scene. I heard she fucked Bob Boxer that night instead of me. Guess she was hot."

"Back to Amber, when do you think she brought her boxes to your house?"

He shrugged. "Must've been when I was at work or something. Like I told you, I didn't even find them for a few years. I always thought maybe she'd come back for them, and I could corner her into telling me where my Mimi was. But she never did."

"Somebody must have helped her move them," Sarah mused thoughtfully.

"Huh?"

"She didn't have a car, so somebody must have lent her one or helped her move those boxes. Somebody must remember."

"Who cares?" Neil reached across the table and grabbed her wrist roughly. "I like a chick I can talk dirty to. This is turning me on. You want me to tell you about someone else I've balled?"

Sarah tried not to shudder and glanced discreetly at her watch. She had to manage this for another fifteen minutes. "How about Mimi? What was she like in bed?"

His face darkened and his features slumped into a frown. "I don't talk about her to anybody," he said. "If she'd stuck around, I wouldn't have needed to go out looking for it. I'd be a happily married man with a wife waiting for me at home with open legs."

"She's the one you really loved, huh? I guess you were really mad at her after she left."

"Mad is too mild a word for what I felt."

"She was probably afraid to come back if she knew how angry you were. Maybe she was afraid you would hurt her."

His grip on her wrist became painfully tight. "I would never have hurt her." His voice was a hoarse whisper. "Teaching someone a lesson is one thing, hurting them is another. I know the difference."

"Did Mimi ever have to be taught a lesson?" Sarah lowered her voice to a whisper also.

"My Mimi was good, it was Amber who was the bad influence on her. And there was nothing you could do to change her. Mimi knew how to be sorry and apologize, but not Amber."

"You really disliked Amber, didn't you?"

When he looked at her, his eyes had glazed over with an unidentifiable emotion. "I hated her. But I enjoyed watching her get down on her knees and suck my cock. She acted like she couldn't get enough of—"

"Are you Sarah Scupper?"

Both Sarah and Neil jumped nervously, startled by the intrusion of the bartender. He was holding a portable phone out to Sarah. "You have a call."

"Thank you." She took the phone from him, trying not to look at the red mark Neil's grip had left on her wrist. "Hello?"

"Sarah, it's Tyler. Is it time to come home?"

"Yes. Oh, yes. I'll be right there."

"Everything okay?

"Fine. See you soon."

She stood up and picked up her purse. "I've got to go. The bartender at the inn just threw up all over himself and the bar, and the place is packed. I guess my night off is over."

"What? You're leaving? But I got a hard–on a mile long."

She smiled and shrugged. "Sorry. See you another time, I guess."

"How about I come by when you get off work?" Neil staggered unsteadily to his feet. "I don't have to be at work until seven in the morning."

"That's sweet," she said heading for the door. "Why don't you give me a call soon. Don't forget to pay our tab. And make sure you leave that bartender a good tip." She winked at him.

As soon as she had slipped out the door, she sprinted for the car. Despite the wealth of information she had seduced out of Neil, she could not put enough miles between herself and him. She wondered how she would ever get out of this unsavory deception now. Well, that could be dealt with later. First she had to get home and tell Tyler what she had learned.

CHAPTER TEN

Sarah slipped in the back door of the inn and headed immediately upstairs to take a shower. She knew it was only a token gesture, but she felt that she needed to scrub herself clean after her repulsive conversation with Neil.

Tyler was nowhere to be seen and she figured he must be downstairs in the bar. She dropped the ivory knit outfit in the hamper; she wasn't sure she'd ever be able to wear it again. As the hot water pounded against her back and her scalp, she was able to relax and distance herself from the situation at hand.

It seemed like years since she had asked Tyler to help her prove Reed's innocence. She had never expected it to turn into a puzzle of this dimension, involving fires that had been set and extinguished nearly twenty years ago.

Wearing her most favorite, worn–in jeans and softest, most comfortable t–shirt, she put her wet hair up in a ponytail and went down to the bar to find Tyler. The Night Heron lounge was nearly empty. Tyler was sitting on the couch in front of the fireplace with his ankle up on one of the padded armrests.

"Hey, Sarah, look who's back." Tyler waved his arm towards Reed who was leaning against the mantle, drinking a beer. He smiled at her, his Baltic blue eyes full of questions. Sarah felt her face grow warm as she remembered all the unresolved issues between them. "We've been doing a little talking," Tyler went on, pretending not to notice the dynamics between the two of them. "And I've invited somebody over that I thought Reed would like to meet."

"I think he's setting me up on a blind date. Do you know anything about this, Sarah?"

Sarah shook her head, not knowing what to say. She was surprised that Tyler had worked so fast.

"I think this may be the prescription that cures all of our illnesses," Tyler remarked with an enigmatic grin. "Speaking of dates, how was yours, Sarah?"

Sarah shuddered. "He's such a slimeball. I had to let him think that it turned me on to hear him talk about his sexual escapades with other women. But I learned some information that you will find fascinating and more than coincidental."

"Like what?" Tyler patted the couch cushion beside him and Sarah sat down.

"Well, I found out who the woman was that kept Neil out of court for the Cherry Lodge fire." She paused, relishing the drama of the moment.

"Well, who?"

"Wanda."

"Wanda! Shit, the plot does thicken, doesn't it?"

"Now here's the part that I've been trying to put together. Cherry Lodge burned on Halloween, right? And what I didn't realize until tonight is that it was the same Halloween that Amber's going away party was happening at the Darby Mountain House."

Reed leaned forward, his interest piqued by the mention of Amber's name. Tyler held up his hand suddenly at the sound of the door opening and closing. "Hold on a second. I believe our mystery guest has arrived."

They all turned to look. Arden stood in the doorway. The soft lighting made her look—much younger than her nineteen years and her attire added to that illusion. Under a denim jacket she wore a short dress made of sheer crinkled fabric in a swirling paisley pattern of green and purple. Her legs were bare except for green socks and purple high–top sneakers. But when she caught sight of Tyler, the look in her eyes added years of experience and the little girl image melted away as she came towards them.

"Excuse me for not getting up," Tyler said, extending his hand to her. "I had a biking accident a few days ago, but let's not talk about that now. You found a ride, I see."

"Yeah, a friend brought me over." Her eyes focused for the first time on Sarah and suddenly there were worry lines wrinkling her smooth forehead. "What's up?" She moved away from Tyler and rested her leather backpack on a wooden chair nearby. It was clear she thought that maybe a showdown was at hand.

"I wanted to introduce you to Reed here. I don't believe you've met."

Still frowning, Arden looked curiously at Reed and then a flash of recognition crossed her face. "I know who you are. You came into the restaurant that time with Tyler, and Russell Bedwin told me you were the guy the cops thought started the Centennial fire."

"Reed, this is Arden Kensington. She's Amber St. Pierre's daughter."

For a second, Reed and Arden both stared in astonishment at Tyler. To Sarah and Tyler sitting on the couch, the look on their faces bore more than a passing resemblance. Tyler reached for Sarah's hand and squeezed it excitedly as Reed and Arden turned back to stare at each other. In profile their cheekbones took on the same structure and the tilt of their noses was identical.

"Did you know my mother?" Arden asked.

Reed nodded, tilting his head slightly as he assessed Arden's looks from head to toe. "It was a long time ago," he replied finally, an odd grin playing on his lips. "Before you were born. How is your mother?"

Arden turned to Tyler in confusion who purposely kept his face a blank. Turning slowly back to Reed she said, "I never knew my mother. She moved to Hawaii when I was a year and a half old and never came back."

"Oh." Uncomfortable now, Reed shifted his weight from foot to foot. "I'm sorry. I didn't realize—"

"Were you lovers?"

Arden's candid question caught them all short.

162

Reed laughed. "For a few short months that seemed like a lifetime in those days. How old are you?"

"Nineteen."

Reed closed his eyes and sighed briefly. "Older than your mother was when I knew her. Hard to believe, isn't it?"

Sensing that Reed was about to take the plunge again into the Peter Pan pond of memories that never–grow–up, Tyler quickly spoke up. "When exactly is your birthday, Arden?"

"January 30th, 1973."

"And if we count back nine months, or to be more precise, thirty–nine weeks, you were conceived somewhere around the end of April, 1972."

"So what's your point?" Arden looked slightly annoyed. "Is there something particularly cosmic about that time of history?"

Tyler looked up at Reed. "Oh, I don't know. Maybe Reed can tell us about what was going on at Carlisle College in April of 1972."

Reed laughed lazily and leaned back on the mantel again. "What do you want me to say? The moon was in the 7th house and Jupiter aligned with Mars? April 1972. I should be able to remember, I left here a few months later. End of April would have been spring break. Let's see, I must have gone somewhere off campus for a week...Oh, that must be when Amber and I took that trip to Nova Scotia. I remember it looked like such a short distance on the map but it must have taken us nearly twenty hours to drive there."

"So you and Amber were still hanging out together."

"Yeah, I remember it was like a week after we got back that I walked in on her during that orgy I told you about. Oh, sorry, I–" Reed blushed deeply as he realized what he was saying about Amber in front of Arden.

Arden did not react as if she had heard him. She was staring at him with a strange, enraptured look on her face.

Tyler cleared his throat and reached for the white envelope in his shirt pocket. "Arden, this is a letter that, uh, we found that your mother had written and never mailed before she left for Hawaii. It was to Mimi. Why don't you read that second page there and then pass it on to Reed."

"A letter that my mother actually wrote?" Arden's hand trembled as she reached for it. "How did you find it? What does it say?"

"I'll explain all that in a minute. But I think the contents of this letter will explain why you're here."

As she scanned the limp page of lined notebook paper, Arden slowly sat down on the edge of a chair only to pop up a moment later. Her eyes shining, she threw her arms around Tyler's neck, still clutching the old letter. "Thank you, thank you, thank you! How did you manage it so quickly?"

"Actually, you'll have to thank Sarah for that. But first, let's share the news with Reed."

In her usual spirited manner, Arden bounced back to standing and handed Amber's letter to Reed who had been watching her curiously with a slight grin on his face. She waited by his shoulder expectantly as he quickly read the paragraph of importance. His inquisitive expression change to wonder as he lowered the paper and stared in disbelief at each one of them in turn, his gaze finally coming to rest on Arden and her intense excitement.

He shook his head and went back to the letter, starting it at the beginning and reading it through to the signature. He looked up at Tyler who handed him the envelope which he also studied intently. "It was never mailed. Where did you get this?"

"In a box of Amber's possessions that we, uh, found stored in an old barn," Sarah explained gently. "It's for real, Reed. And we think it explains why Mimi wanted to meet with you."

"Arden sent Mimi a letter several years ago, when she was twelve," Tyler went on. "Mimi never answered it, possibly because she had lost track of Amber by then. She may have wanted to meet with you to see if Amber had ever contacted you, or maybe just to let you know the truth about Arden."

Reed's eyes suddenly sparkled with tears as he turned to face Arden. "And I always thought that when I became a father I would have to change diapers and help with midnight feedings. Why, I bet you can already ride a two–wheeler without training wheels."

She reached for his hands and squeezed them. "When Tyler said he would help me find my mother, the last thing I expected was a guy like you."

Reed cautiously reached out a finger and caught the tiny crescent moon with turquoise blue inlay that dangled from her ear. "Your mother used to wear things like this. She loved to wear jewelry, nothing expensive just interesting or symbolic. She especially liked to wear amber, you can guess why. I remember I bought her a necklace of amber beads once."

"I made this earring out of a necklace of hers. It's the only thing of hers I have. Tell me about her, will you? No, tell me about you first."

"No, you tell me about yourself first."

Sarah and Tyler slipped quietly away, leaving the couch and the fireplace to Reed and Arden who had eyes only for each other.

"You certainly tied that one up neatly with string. Pretty slick, Tiger," Sarah whispered to him as they headed up the stairs. Her own throat was tight with the emotion of it all.

"I think everybody got what they wanted. Including me." He stopped in mid–crutch swing and blew a kiss to her over his shoulder.

"Meaning you've got me all to yourself? Well, Scarecrow, your heart's desire was always in your own backyard, you just have to pay some attention to it."

"Damn these crutches." Tyler tossed them into a corner of the upstairs hall and limped into the living room. "Well, it's happy, but it's not an ending. We're still no closer to finding out who killed Mimi or whatever happened to Amber. And those two down there know less than we do."

"I think Neil is one hell of a good suspect. Now let me tell you what I learned tonight."

"In bed."

"What?"

"Tell me in bed. And tell me naked."

When Sarah went downstairs the next morning to make some coffee, she found Reed stretched out on the couch in front of the fireplace. His eyes were wide open and he stared dreamily at her.

"Reed! Didn't you go to bed?"

"When I came back after dropping Arden off, I was too wound up to sleep. Sarah, it's so exciting. I think I'm in love. With my daughter. I never knew how much I wanted a relationship like this."

Although it loomed in the forefront of her mind, Sarah did not want to remind him that he was not yet off the hook for murder and arson. She and Tyler had spent a few hours last night discussing their lack of positive proof.

"She's going to come over to the farm with me next weekend so we can spend some serious time getting to know each other. By Jesus, I should call my mother and father in Minnesota and tell them! What time is it?" He looked at his watch.

"Look, Reed, the barn can wait a few days if you want to hang out with Arden for a while. You don't have to start construction this week."

"No, no, I need something to keep me occupied. She has to work anyway, she says she's not ready to tell Lou and Wanda just yet, she's afraid they'll throw a fit. And now we're both really anxious to find out where Amber is and at least talk to her about this. How could she have abandoned Arden like that? I just can't understand it."

Reed followed her into the kitchen and continued to talk nonstop as she made coffee and toast. She was relieved

166

when, after gulping down a cup of coffee, he finally went out to the barn to begin work.

"Tyler, you've got to try getting through to Hawaii again today," she said as she lowered the breakfast tray onto the upstairs coffee table. "Not only should we try to confirm why Mimi wanted to see Reed, but we've got to find out if her husband knows where Amber ended up."

"I've left a couple of messages on their answering machine. Maybe I should see if Diana Stellano can convince him to call me back." Tyler was flexing his injured ankle and practicing put weight on it. Most of the swelling had subsided, but it remained a spectacular display of green and purple bruises.

"Well, just don't forget that Hawaii is six hours behind us. It's two in the morning there right now."

"But it's eight in Connecticut. I'm sure Mrs. Stellano is up." He took a few steps and winced. "Shit. I've got to start using this foot, it's driving me crazy being laid up like this."

"Really? I've been kind of enjoying it. I don't ever have to worry about where you are or why you're late." Sarah disappeared into the bedroom and emerged with a heaping basket of dirty laundry. "You have any clothes that need washing?"

Tyler limped past her and emerged with an armful of clothing. "At least let me do the laundry, Sarah. I should be able to manage that."

"Two flights down into the cellar? I don't think so, bub. Why don't you go relax on the porch swing with the portable phone and make your calls? If you want to be useful later on, you can prep dinner for me tonight. It's my night to cook."

Disgruntled, Tyler shoved his notes, his laptop computer and the telephone into a canvas tote bag and then carefully made his way down the stairs, trying to use his foot normally. By the time he reached the front porch, it was already throbbing painfully again.

With a sigh of frustration, he sat down heavily on the flowered cushion. The sky was clear, the air was fresh.

Even the sound of Reed's solitary hammer driving nails into new wood had a cheerful ring to it. Tyler wished he could hop on his bike and ride it over the mountain to Carlisle. He wanted a chance to poke through Neil's barn on his own, he wanted to find the real estate office and interview the ex–bartender of the Darby Mountain House. But his bike was still at the repair shop, where Sarah had dropped it for him on Saturday. It probably wouldn't be ready for days.

Still wallowing in self–pity, he pulled the phone out of the canvas carry–all. He punched in the number for New Hampshire information. "Yes. Cyrus Parker in Manchester?"

The operator had nothing under that name or under the initial C. So much for tracking down Amber's father. Sighing again, he put his call through to Diana Stellano in Connecticut.

It was close to three in the afternoon when the call from Hawaii finally came in. Tyler was perched on a stool next to the large work island in the kitchen, chopping mushrooms for shrimp stuffing. Sarah brought him the telephone.

"It's Steve Farrell," she whispered meaningfully.

"Steve. Hi, Tyler Mackenzie here. Thanks for calling."

"No problem. I didn't realize my mother–in–law had hired you or I would have called sooner. I haven't responded to any messages from people I don't know. Too many ambulance chasers out there."

"Well, I wasn't sure if Mrs. Stellano wanted you to know I was working on this for her. Look, I'm really sorry to bother you, I know you probably don't want to talk about it, but you seem to be the only guy who can answer a few of the questions that have come up."

"Like what?"

"For starters, do you have any idea why your wife made the trip up to Carlisle?" While he talked, Tyler looked around desperately for a pen and paper.

168

"Not specifically. Something had been bugging her, she hadn't been sleeping well. Mimi told me she had some old demons from her past to put to rest and that she wanted to visit her mother and then travel up to Vermont and that she would rather go alone. Now, of course, I wish I had insisted on going with her." Steve's voice caught slightly in his throat.

"You shouldn't blame yourself," Tyler assured him sympathetically. "You couldn't have known. Did she ever mention an old college friend named Reed Anderson?"

Sarah came through the kitchen door and left Tyler's notebook and pen on the counter within his reach. "I'm going to get the clothes out of the dryer," she mouthed. "I'll be back in a minute."

"Reed Anderson..."

"She sent him a letter, asking him to meet her here at the West Jordan Inn. They hadn't seen each other in twenty years."

"She didn't like to talk about her college days. When I met her she'd already been on Maui for six or seven years."

"Did you ever meet her friend Amber?"

"Amber? No, but I've got to tell you I'm pretty bad with names. What did she look like?"

Their conversation continued on in the same vein for several minutes, making little or no headway. Tyler told him about the letter they had found that Amber had written to Mimi. Steve didn't remember Mimi receiving any letters from twelve–year–old Arden nor had he ever heard of Neil Richelieu. He did have a vague memory of Mimi talking about a wild girlfriend of hers who she went to college with, but that was all. Finally Tyler mentioned the health food store in Lahaina that Mimi had written about in her letter to Amber.

"Oh, sure, Jason. I'd forgotten Mimi lived with him when she was younger. Hard to picture her being attracted to Jason, but I hear he used to weigh about 150 pounds less than he does now. Let me get the phone book, I'll give you his number."

As Tyler scrawled down the address and phone number that Steve gave him, Sarah came through the swinging doors, examining something in the palm of her hand.

"Thanks, Steve, this should be very helpful. Listen, if you come across any old letters, or pictures, or anything that you think might shed some light on who might have harbored a grudge against Mimi, give me a call."

"So what you're telling me is that you think her murder was premeditated?" Steve had trouble getting the words out.

"Not necessarily premeditated, but there's a good chance it was done purposefully. I'll let you know if I ever find out any more."

"Well, what about this Anderson fellow she was supposed to meet? Isn't it possible he did it?"

"He is actually the prime suspect in the case. However we don't think the news Mimi was going to give him would have given him cause to uh, kill her."

"How do you know what she was going to tell him? It might have been something other than the fact that she thought this twelve–year–old girl was his daughter."

"You're absolutely right there. I'll have to get back to you on that one. Thanks for your help." Tyler broke the connection and sat staring at the phone in his hand.

Steve was right. What if it wasn't quite as black and white as they'd made it out to be? Maybe she was going to tell Reed he was a father, but maybe she was also going to tell him something else, something that he wouldn't like. Or hadn't liked when she did tell him that night.

"Tyler?"

Sarah was looking at him questioningly. "You find out anything?"

"Not much. I've got another call to make anyway – to Jason of the health food store. What are you looking at?"

"I found this in the washing machine. Do you have any idea what it is?" On the counter, she set a tarnished earring inlaid with a yellow stone.

170

"Shit, I forgot all about that. Something I picked up out of the dirt when they found that skeleton at the Cherry Lodge excavation. Must have belonged to the corpse. I don't think it's very valuable but I suppose I should turn it into the police. They probably have the mate. Unless you want it," he added teasingly.

"Why would I want it? I'm not a Taurus."

"What?"

"My sign of the zodiac is Pisces not Taurus. That's what this symbol stands for." She traced the outline of the bull's head and horns with her fingertip.

"Really." Tyler was irritated that he had not figured that out himself. "Then this is probably a significant clue as to the birthday of that skeleton. And what kind of stone do you think this is?"

"I'd guess it was amber."

There was the ghost of a pause before they looked at each other, wide–eyed and silent. The color drained from Sarah's cheeks as she gulped and whispered, "Do you know what month she was born in?"

"Her birth certificate is still upstairs, isn't it? Go get it."

Sarah was gone before he had finished speaking. Tyler stared at the earring, wondering why he hadn't made the connection before. It was obviously amber. Hadn't Reed mentioned that when he knew Amber she wore only jewelry made of the stone for which she was named?

Sarah was back, breathing heavily. She plunked the birth certificate down on the counter next to the pile of chopped mushrooms. "May 10th, 1954. She's Taurus. Oh my God, Tyler, it all makes perfect and horrible sense. Why she never showed up for her own going–away party. Why she left her purse behind..."

"Hold on, hold on. We don't know she didn't sell or give these earrings to somebody else. Remember Reed said she only wore amber jewelry when he knew her, but two years later she was into silver and turquoise and blue moons."

"Well, what else was that skeleton wearing for jewelry?"

171

"I don't know. I didn't take an inventory. It seemed like there were a lot of necklaces, but it was hard to tell with the dirt and all." Abruptly he picked up the phone again and began dialing.

"Who are you calling?"

"Jason of Lahaina Health Foods. He can tell us if Amber ever got to Maui."

Sarah paced the length of the narrow kitchen, nervously wiping counters and putting things away. Her mind was racing as she began to empty the dishwasher, trying to remember the details of Neil's description of that Halloween night so long ago. When Tyler finally put the phone down, one look at his face told her the answer.

"She never got there, did she?"

He shook his head and then shook it again more violently, this time to clear the image of lively and wild Amber as a decaying bunch of bones surrounded by a crowd of curious townspeople. And then he remembered Lou's reaction when he had been called down. "Like he'd seen a ghost," he murmured.

"What?"

"Lou Kensington. He was there at the Cherry Lodge excavation that day. He nearly passed out when he looked at the body. I thought he was just a sensitive guy. But I think he recognized her. He knew right away it was Amber."

"His former lover."

"Right."

After another awed silence, Sarah suddenly pounded her fist on the edge of the sink. "So why didn't he say anything? Why didn't he tell anybody who it was? He should have been outraged and horrified. He should have wanted to see justice done!"

"I don't know." Tyler leaned on the counter and rested his forehead in his hands. "This changes everything, don't you see?" He sat up as quickly as he'd gone down. "It gives us a motive for Mimi's murder."

"Because she knew that Amber never got to Hawaii."

"Right. And because she'd received a letter from Arden saying that she'd been told her mother had left her as an infant and moved to Hawaii."

"But who could have known that besides Arden?"

"The person who gave her the address. Lou Kensington."

Once again their eyes met. "You don't think—"

"I don't know what to think! I need to sit down with all my notes and rework everything now." Tyler began limping to the door, apparently abandoning the stuffed shrimp for the moment.

"Tyler, let's not say anything to Reed and Arden about this yet, okay? They're so happy, it would only ruin it for them." Sarah felt sick just thinking about it.

"Of course. And don't give Arden any of those letters just yet, like you said you were going to. I need to go over them again."

Sarah could hear his uneven progress up the stairs, as she sat down heavily on a wooden stool. The amber earring on the counter seemed to be staring at her like a macabre cat's eye. Sweeping it into her pocket, she tried to steady her shaking hands as she reached for the cutting knife.

CHAPTER ELEVEN

"So let's start with the list of suspects."

Tyler set up his laptop computer on the coffee table, sat down on the floor and began to type.

"Suspects for what?" Sarah kicked off her shoes and stretched out on the couch behind him. Sipping a margarita, she peered over his shoulder at the blue screen.

Tyler shot her a withering look and replied, "For who killed JFK, what do you think?"

"No, I mean, are we trying to figure out who killed Mimi, who killed Amber, who set the fires, or did all of it?"

"Let's just list anybody we're suspicious of and then we'll check their motives. Number one is Neil, of course."

"Well, let's set up the events as we know them. We know that Amber was planning to leave for Hawaii, when, November 4th, was it? And we know she wrote a letter to Mimi on October 29th that never got mailed. We know that a going–away party was planned for her on Halloween night that she never made it to. And we know that Cherry Lodge burned down on Halloween with her in it, but she may have already been dead."

Tyler was typing as fast as she talked. "I'm impressed, Sarah. Go on."

"So we pretty much know she was must've disappeared somewhere in the twenty–four hours preceding Halloween or someone would have missed her. We also know that somebody did a damn good job of setting it up to look like she left town early." She sat up and drained the rest of her margarita in one gulp. "Now you tell me how you think Neil could be the one who did it."

"Okay. He follows Amber home from work and tries to get her to tell him where Mimi is. When she won't tell him, he gets violent, knocks her around a little too much, maybe kills her by accident. Packs up all her stuff, stores it in his barn, and hides her body in the cellar of the deserted Cherry Lodge. Comes back on Halloween and pretends he doesn't know she's gone."

Sarah gazed at him in silence for a second. "Okay, except for one major thing. Two major things really. One, why would he tell us that those boxes are in his attic after all these years?"

"Maybe because he thought I was going to give him some money for them."

"Well, why didn't he get rid of them in the first place? And two, why did Wanda lie to him about where Amber was when he came looking for her on Halloween?"

"Don't forget that's what HE told you. He might have forced Amber to write a note saying she was leaving for Hawaii early or something."

Sarah shook her head. "I can't believe he would have packed up those boxes as neatly or as completely as he did."

"My guess is that Amber packed up those things herself. It may even be true that she moved some of them there before she was killed. Maybe he just added to the collection with the stuff she had been planning to take to Hawaii."

"But it wasn't sorted out that way. In my mind she hadn't really packed for the trip yet. Well, let's go on. Who's suspect number two?"

"Lou Kensington, obviously." The name appeared on the screen with a star next to it. Tyler sat back, thoughtfully contemplating what he knew about Lou. "If you could only have seen how he reacted to that skeleton."

"What I don't understand is why he didn't identify it as Amber if he recognized her by some of that jewelry she was wearing."

"Maybe he wasn't sure."

"Oh, come on, the guy was intimate with her. You would think for that reason alone he would want to give

175

her a decent burial. Which, of course, leads me to believe that he may be the one who put her there."

"Maybe he didn't identify the remains because he wanted to spare Arden the ugly reality of it. The same as we do."

They were both quiet for a while after that.

"Okay," Sarah said finally. "Let me paint you a new scenario. Suppose Lou and Amber had some sort of lover's quarrel, remember in her letter she suggests he's getting hard to take. Maybe she threatens to tell Wanda about them."

"You think Wanda's in the same house and never caught on?"

"It's possible. We know she's wrapped up with baby Arden and probably hasn't been giving her husband the sexual gratification that he needs which has made him seek it elsewhere. So anyway, suppose they have a fight and it gets rough and he kills her by accident?"

"I guess that could happen," Tyler conceded begrudgingly. "Go on."

"So we're talking about the town fire chief here. Who else would know better how to burn down a building quickly and efficiently? Who else would know the best place to put a body in that building so that it might never be found? Who else would be able to have some control over the investigation into how the fire started?"

"God, I hate when you come up with the right answers. Or questions, in this case."

"Not only that, Lou obviously had access to Amber's room any time of day or night. He could easily have packed up her things and planted them at Neil's as evidence. He could just as easily have made up the story of her leaving for Hawaii early. And years later he covers his guilt even more by giving Arden an address on Maui where she can write to Mimi about her mother. And of course she never gets an answer."

"Okay, but there is still one wrinkle in your story."

"Which is?" Sarah had a challenging gleam in her eye.

176

"If Wanda isn't interested in sex, then why does she sleep with Neil on the night of the fire?"

"Damn." Sarah played with the ice in the bottom of her glass.

"Because that ends up giving Neil an alibi and keeping the whole thing out of court."

"Yes, but isn't that convenient for Lou? Even though he's set Neil up, something could go wrong. Besides, who would ever suspect the fire chief of starting fires in his own town?"

Tyler chuckled mirthlessly. "Job security."

"I'll say. Look at all the fires in that town. What if..."

But Tyler was already shuffling through his notes. "Yes, I think we should take another look at all the fires in Carlisle."

Sarah and Tyler did not have a chance to talk again until the following evening. It was a busy night at the inn and Sarah was back behind the bar, juggling her time between serving drinks and seating people in the dining room. Tyler's ankle was well enough to push a gas pedal again and he had spent the day in Jordan Center. Several hours in the newspaper archives and a few at the library had given him dozens of details. What he really needed now was a friendly fireman.

When Arden breezed in looking for Reed, he picked her brain for a few minutes.

"Why don't you just ask Lou?" was her immediate response. "He knows the most. He's always there at every fire."

"Somehow I don't think your adopted dad is a good choice for me to talk to right now. Isn't there anyone else you can think of?"

"Well, Ray Polifax loves to talk and he's had his eye on my dad's, I mean Lou's, job for years, waiting for Lou to retire. He's the math teacher over at the high school." She caught sight of Reed in the front hall and gave him a wave. "You know, Wanda thinks I've been coming over here to see you. She keeps railing on me about it; she doesn't seem to like you much anymore."

"Yeah, just wait until she finds out I've reunited you with your natural father. Then she's really going to love me. Do me a favor and don't mention it for a while yet." Tyler took a big swig of his St. Pauli Girl beer, trying not to imagine the consequences of that confession.

"Well, I'm going to have to tell her soon enough. I haven't figured what story to give her when I go off to Reed's this weekend."

"You're nineteen! Why do you have to tell her anything?" Tyler thought back to his own escapades at that age; telling his parents never even entered the picture.

"Because she's so nosy and overprotective. She's always afraid something's going to happen to me." She was leaning on the edge of the bar, the full sleeves of her sheer white shirt trailing precariously near a few spots of melted butter. Her red velvet vest was open enough to reveal that she wore nothing beneath the shirt. Arden did seem like an accident waiting to happen as she stood there, fidgeting impatiently.

"You should move out."

"I'm thinking about it. Well, I'll see you later." And before she stained her shirt or vest, she was gone, headed out through the front hall to meet Reed.

"So what's the skinny, sailor?"

Tyler turned back to see Sarah sitting on the stool next to him, her back resting against the polished wood of the bar. There were only a couple of regular customers left in the lounge, the rest had taken their drinks and moved into the dining room.

"About what?"

"Tell me what you found out in your research today. Was our man in attendance every time?" Her eyes were bright with curiosity; Tyler could not remember her ever taking such an interest in his work before.

178

"Looks that way. Here's an outline I made up of just the facts, ma'am. Hotel, owner, date it burned, was it insured, who put it out, how it started, who was charged."

"Not much in that last column."

"No, but notice the pattern here." He ran his finger down the dates. "Look how many of these fires occurred at the end of the month."

Sarah could see he was right. The thirtieth and thirty-first showed up more times than any other date listed.

"So what do you think that means?"

"I'm not sure. Notice that the pattern doesn't start until Cherry Lodge; it burned on the thirty–first. So did Darby Mountain House. The Centennial didn't though. That was on the fifth."

They gazed at the list together. The fires in the earlier part of the century seemed to be completely random as far as date and year. "Look, they actually went seven years without a fire in the forties. But every two or three years since 1974 there's a fire on the thirtieth or thirty–first. Too weird."

"It might be just a coincidence, you know, the full moon or something bringing out the crazies. And there's no repetition here – several different methods of arson were used. Look, gasoline–soaked rags, suspected electrical fire, cause unknown, stray cigarette butt, gas stove explosion."

"Hmmm." Out of the corner of her eye, Sarah caught one of the diners in the next room signaling her and she got up, leaving Tyler to contemplate his outline alone again. Lost in thought, he did not even hear the outside door open and close, or notice that someone had sat down next to him.

"Hey. Thought you were going to look me up, man."

Neil's voice jolted Tyler back to the moment and he turned to look at him. But looking at Neil was not nearly as revealing as smelling him.

The man reeked of alcohol as only a true drinker can. The smell mingled with his strong body odor as well as the fumes of motor oil and grease. Tyler fought the urge to get up and move down a few seats.

"Hey, Neil. I've been kind of laid up for a few days but I'll be by soon. But I'm glad you came over. I wanted to ask you a few questions."

"Really." Neil's tone indicated his lack of interest in anything Tyler had to say. "I actually came by looking for that foxy bartender. We've sort of got a thing going, she and I." He hefted his belt buckle with a significant gesture.

"Really." It was Tyler's turn to sound disinterested.

"Yeah. Nice piece of ass, don't you think? And she ain't dumb either, I like that. She's working tonight, isn't she?"

"Oh, she's working tonight, all right." Tyler wondered what Sarah's reaction would be when she saw Neil. "Here, let me get you a beer. This one's on me." He moved around to the other side of the bar and filled a frosted mug with Budweiser on tap.

"You allowed to do that? Help yourself, I mean."

"Well, I've helping out since I've been staying here for so long now." Tyler's excuse sounded lame but he didn't think it mattered. "Let me ask you something about Amber while we're sitting around. I keep running into dead ends in my search to find her–" no pun intended, he added silently – "And I wondered if you remembered any enemies she might have made."

"You mean people that might have wanted to do her in?" Neil's eyes narrowed and glistened at the same time. "Hell, she worked in that sleazy–assed joint turning tricks. You never know what kind of weirdoes she might have fucked."

"The Blue Moon? I thought I heard she and Mimi both worked there." Tyler found himself cowering instinctively from an expected blow.

"Yeah, well, Mimi didn't do THAT kind of work there, I made sure of that. It was bad enough her prancing around serving drinks in those little skirts that barely covered her ass. I let her know what would happen to her if I found out that anybody else was getting a piece of it. I made sure she got the message too." Neil had already finished the beer Tyler had given him only moments before.

180

"And how'd you do that?" Tyler was behind the bar, refilling the empty glass before Neil had time to consider the casually–phrased question.

"Hey, women will always pay attention if you let 'em know you're stronger than they are."

"Smack them around a little, is that what you mean?"

Neil stiffened, suddenly on guard. "You're trying to trick me into saying I beat on her, aren't you, you bastard?"

"Relax, Neil. Nobody's gonna bust you for something you did twenty years ago to a woman who's dead now." The last phrase slipped out of his mouth before he could stop himself.

Neil stared at him for a second and then his stiff posture disappeared and he slumped over his beer like a marionette without strings.

"Well, let me ask you this then, Neil. Can you think of anybody back in those days who might have wanted to do Mimi in?" Tyler stayed on the opposite side of the bar, he felt safer there.

Neil shook his head morosely. "There was only one person I can remember who was mad at Mimi all the time."

"And who was that?"

"Her mother."

Her mother. Tyler leaned heavily on the sink as, for a moment, the picture twisted itself into a new and very bizarre line of reasoning. Was it possible that Diana Stellano –

His thought process was interrupted as Sarah came whizzing into the lounge carrying a tray of empty glasses from the dining room. "Oh, as long as you're right there, Tyler, would you mind dealing with these?" She set the tray on the stainless steel counter next to the sink. "Let's see, I need two Seven and Sevens, a Captain Morgan and Coke, a gin and tonic and a glass of chardonnay."

She had all the glasses lined up with ice in them before she noticed Neil watching her with gleaming eyes and a goofy grin. "Hey, beautiful."

"Oh, uh, hi, Neil." Sarah concentrated on mixing drinks, uncomfortably aware of his gaze.

"How soon do you get off?" he asked.

"Not for a few hours. But we need to talk. Tyler, would you give Neil another beer on me? I'll be back in a minute." She gave Tyler a desperate look as she swept passed him, holding the fresh drinks above her head.

Neil drained his current mug as though he were drinking water and reached for the new one that Tyler put in front of him. Neil had been loaded when he arrived; Tyler wondered how many beers it would take before he passed out.

A few minutes later Sarah seated herself on the stool next to him, self–consciously crossing her legs and tugging at the short black skirt she was wearing. Her long braid rested over the shoulder of her red, short–sleeved sweater, its darkness contrasting with the bright color of the top. As Neil reached out to put a hand on one of her bare knees, she stood up as quickly as she had sat down.

"There's something I've got to tell you. Things have changed since the last time we talked." Nervously she picked at the scalloped edge of a cardboard coaster. Without out moving her head, she rolled her eyes up to see where Tyler was. Still behind the bar, he had moved to the far end and appeared to be deep in conversation with a couple of customers although she knew he had one eye and one ear on her.

"Like what could happen in two days?"

"Well, I found out I'm pregnant and I've decided to get married and have the baby."

"You what?"

Over his shoulder, Tyler gave her a quick, wide–eyed look that was a mixture of surprise and amusement.

"I'm sorry if it comes as such a shock to you but I'm not getting any younger and I figure if I want to have any children I'm going to have to go through with this. But we can still be friends." As she flashed him a shy smile, she saw that his face had taken on a ruddy flush bordering on purple. She touched his hand. "Right?"

"Who's the lucky guy?" he spat out bitterly.

"I – I'd rather not say right now. You seem kind of mad. I wouldn't want you to do anything irrational."

"Well, shit. You could still blow him off and hang out with me. I don't care if you're knocked up. I've had girlfriends before with kids by other men. That don't bother me."

"It's too late. We've already set the date."

Neil slammed his fist on the bar. "Damn! And you are such a hot chick! I know we could have had a wicked good time in the sack together. My fucking luck. It's the way everything goes for me."

A bell rang in the kitchen. "Oh, gotta go. Don't be angry," Sarah called over her shoulder as she flew off through the swinging doors. "Have another beer on me."

"Yeah, I'd like to have another beer on you, baby," Neil muttered. "I'd like to be sitting on your naked body drinking my Bud with my cock inside you, you slut. I'd like to–"

"Bad news?" Tyler sauntered over casually and took the seat that Sarah had been in.

"I'd say so. Here I am horny as hell, waiting for that lady to give me the green light, and she tells me she's having some other guy's fucking baby and doesn't want to get involved. Shit." He pushed his empty mug across the bar. "I feel like puking now."

"You want me to drive you home?"

"Home? Hell, no, I'm headed over to Samuel's in Jordan Center. Now I really need to score me some pussy tonight." Neil staggered to the door. "Hey, you still want to look through that stuff in my barn?"

"Sure, I'll call you."

"Hey, you're welcome to join me up to Samuel's. We can shoot some pool, pick us up some girls..." Neil leaned against the doorframe unsteadily.

"No, thanks. I promised to stay here and help out."

"Okay. Shit, I gotta get outside and take a whiz." He fumbled with the door handle for a second and then he was gone.

Tyler closed his eyes and breathed a sigh of relief.

"Did he leave?" Sarah materialized at his shoulder.

"Yeah, he's going out to 'pick up some pussy'." Tyler wrapped his arm around Sarah's waist and pulled her close. "Now tell me, whose baby are you having?"

"Yours, of course. Some day. When you grow up and settle down."

Tyler awoke at three thirty to find the bed next to him empty. Through the bedroom door he could see that the hall light was on, illuminating the stairs.

When Sarah did not return after ten minutes, he became slightly anxious. Grabbing a pair of shorts, he headed down the stairs. He was surprised to see a patch of light falling across the floor from the open door leading to the cellar.

"Sarah?" he called softly.

His ankle had stiffened up while he slept and he had some difficulty negotiating the steep staircase. It was dimly lit by bare bulbs that hung from the ancient floor joists running across the ceiling of the cellar.

His audible exclamation of pain brought a startled Sarah to her feet. She had been kneeling on the dirt floor by an old box of books. Her short silk robe was loosely tied, exposing a strip of her bare torso and a patch of dark pubic hair as well as her very dirty knees.

"What are you doing down here at this time of night?" Tyler sounded exceptionally cranky.

"You didn't have to come looking for me. Why don't you go back to bed? I'll be up in a few minutes."

Instead Tyler limped over to where she was standing and picked up the book she had dropped. "Don't tell me. You had a sudden urge in the middle of the night to read a Farmer's Almanac from March of 1980."

184

She snatched it away from him and, tightening the belt of her robe, knelt down at the box again. "I've got an idea that I'm working on. It might be crazy so I'm not going to tell you until I'm sure of it. Now just leave me alone and I'll be up soon."

"Fine." He started up the steep wooden steps again.

"Tyler."

"What?"

"Do you remember what date Arden said her birthday was?"

"Arden's birthday? What does that – I think she said January 30th. Why?"

"Yeah, that's what I thought too. Shit. I wonder what time the library opens." Heaving another stack of Farmer's Almanacs onto the floor, she consulted a folded piece of paper that she pulled out of the pocket of her robe.

"I could probably help you if you'd tell me what you were doing," Tyler called loudly over his shoulder as he headed back upstairs. When Sarah did not respond, he stormed back to bed. He was angry that she'd disturbed his sleep, but he was more upset that she wouldn't tell him what her hunch was.

Tyler was even more surprised when he woke up in the morning to find that Sarah had never come back to bed. Seeing her robe thrown across the back of a chair, he surmised that she was probably already up and dressed. But a sudden premonition made him look out the bedroom window.

"Damn. Where could she have gone at this hour?" Sarah was never up and about earlier than he was. The late hours that she kept had turned her into a confirmed mid–morning sleeper, with a few concessions to Tyler's habits when he was around.

The only thing that kept him from being entirely pissed off was that his ankle felt nearly all better. Probably his middle of the night stroll had taken the edge off its usual morning stiffness.

He wondered if Sarah remembered that he had wanted to go pick up his mountain bike at the repair shop this morning. Probably not. Wandering into the kitchen, he found Reed trying to figure out which switch turned the coffee maker on.

"Hi, Tyler. I know this looks stupid but–"

"It's already on. You just have to pour the water through and flick this switch. You seen Sarah this morning?"

"I heard her car take off a little while ago. Kind of early for her to be up, isn't it?"

"Yeah, she's onto something she won't tell me about. I found her down in the basement looking through old Farmer's Almanacs in the middle of the night."

As they waited for the coffee to brew, they chatted idly about Arden. "I can't wait to take her over to my place tonight. I've got this fantasy that she's really going to love it and that she'll want to come and live with me. Do you think that's weird, a middle–aged man wanting his grown–up daughter to live with him? I mean, people will probably talk and think the wrong things–"

"Who cares what people think? The only person I'd worry about is Wanda. She's spent the last nineteen years making Arden her own."

By the end of their conversation, Tyler had convinced Reed to let him borrow his pickup if Sarah did not return in the next hour. Reed said Tyler could use it all day if he wanted, he wouldn't be needing it until late afternoon.

Tyler made a quick list of the people he wanted to talk to; unfortunately most of them worked during the day. He wondered if Ray Polifax, the math teacher and volunteer fireman, would have any time free during the school day and then decided it made more sense to meet him for a drink in the evening if possible. He would at least stop at the high school while he was in Jordan Center to see if he could arrange it.

He still could not believe that Sarah had just taken off this morning without leaving a note or saying goodbye. She

186

was starting to act just like him and Tyler realized that he didn't like it.

"Sarah Scupper! I can't believe it. You're actually coming to ask me some questions about astrology? I never thought I'd see this day!" Ruby Craven got up from the blue velvet Victorian settee to greet Sarah. The old floorboards of her tiny house shook under her ample weight as she crossed the floor.

"I know, cynical, old disbelieving me, having to humble myself at your feet." Sarah looked around the cluttered living room for a place to sit. Old lace curtains hung not only from the windows but were also tacked decoratively from ceiling to wall in several places. Colorful silk shawls were thrown over the backs of chairs while overstuffed embroidered and patchwork pillows filled most of their seats. There was an ornate standing lamp with a fringed shade and another similar one trimmed with hanging crystals. Neither looked to have been dusted for some time.

"Well, make yourself at home, my dear. I'll put the kettle on." Ruby passed through a plastic bead curtain into a closet–like kitchen. "It's good to see you, no matter what excuse brought you here. Now that I don't teach my astrology class on Thursday nights, I never get in to the inn anymore."

Leaning over a rocking chair, Sarah removed a long–haired gray cat which she had mistaken for a fur pillow and sat down to watch Ruby bustle about in her picturesque kitchen. Ruby's salt–and–pepper hair still hung to her waist, although these days, the gray seemed to be overtaking the black. She was dressed in a never–gone-out–of–style outfit from twenty years before – an Indian print skirt that swept the floor and a tie–dyed t–shirt.

"I'm not really here to have you do my horoscope, Ruby," Sarah admitted as she admired the view from the enormous picture window that filled one entire wall of the little living room. Ruby lived on top of a mountain at the end of a steep, rocky driveway that had to be negotiated by foot when the ground was covered with snow. Most people thought she was more than a little crazy to live where she did, but Sarah thought the view alone made it worth the effort. She could also see Ruby's yard, which was a terraced extravaganza of fruit trees, berry bushes and perennial beds as well as herb and vegetable gardens.

"Really? That's a shame because I'd already done your chart years ago just to satisfy my own curiosity. You sure you don't want me to share it with you?" Ruby poked her head through the bead curtain so that Sarah could appreciate the mischievous grin that her full lips had curved into.

"No, actually what I need is for you to look up some dates in your Ephemeris." Sarah stumbled over the unfamiliar word, but was pleased at herself for remembering the name of the book that Ruby used for plotting where the sun, moon and planets were at any given time in the last century.

"Very good! I wouldn't expect you to remember the Ephemeris. I didn't think you paid that much attention to the things I told you. I bet you're really a closet astrologer, aren't you, Sarah?"

The good–natured teasing went on for another few minutes while Ruby prepared the tea. Finally she settled herself comfortably on the Victorian sofa again, with an orange tabby cat in her lap and a cup of tea in her hand.

"Now, my dear, what exactly is it you need to know about these particular dates?"

CHAPTER TWELVE

Tyler felt a well–remembered uneasiness as he sat in Reed's truck in the high school parking lot waiting for the school day to end. It didn't matter how many decades he had been out of high school, whenever he visited one he still felt as though he was breaking the rules by not being in class at the proper time. He could easily recall a similar occasion some twenty years earlier. He had been waiting in his brother's car in the parking lot after skipping school for the day with his girlfriend, hoping that his brother would take his time getting out the door so that it would appear that Tyler had merely arrived there before him after the bell rang.

Finally, like a river of lava erupting from a volcano, teenage humanity burst through the doors and spread out in every direction. Tyler made his way against the flow of traffic and into the main hallway. After asking a few questions of the right pair of girls, he found himself being eagerly escorted to the door of Mr. Polifax's algebra class.

"Are you that new math teacher everyone's been talking about?" one of them asked between giggles.

"No, math was not my best subject in school." Tyler laughed at the idea of himself teaching plane geometry to anybody.

"Are you one of Mr. Polifax's old students?" the other girl asked innocently as they stopped outside the classroom.

Tyler had to laugh again as he got a good look at Ray Polifax erasing equations from his blackboard. Slightly built with bushy red hair, his round–cheeked baby face and pale blue eyes made him look younger than the forty years that Tyler suspected he was.

"I don't think that would be possible," he answered. "Thanks for the directions." He knocked on the open door before walking in.

A few minutes later he was back in the truck, headed for West Jordan. Ray Polifax was already committed to an after–school conference, but when he heard Tyler was doing a story on the hotel fires in Carlisle, he agreed to stop in at the inn on his way home. He said he could give Tyler about an hour of his time but that his wife would want him home for dinner by six thirty.

Reed was looking a little anxious by the time Tyler drove into the parking lot at the inn. "I told you I'd be back in plenty of time," Tyler said defensively as he lifted his repaired mountain bike out of the back.

"Yeah, well, I've noticed that your idea of 'on time' and my idea are a little different. Besides, Arden called a little while ago and she sounded very upset. She wanted me to come by and get her right away. When I told her you had my truck, she said she would get a ride over here somehow. She said she couldn't stay at home any longer."

"Hmmm. Wondered what happened. Sarah's back, isn't she?" Tyler nodded towards her car.

"Yeah, but she said she was going to be sleeping. Left me with the phone." He pulled it out of his tool belt and tossed it to Tyler. "Your turn to manage the inn, friend. I've got to batten down the hatches here for a while. She's looking pretty good, isn't she?"

Tyler looked at the new frame of the barn that Reed had erected in the last few days. He was a swift and efficient builder and Tyler knew that it was his sterling reputation for hard work and honesty that had kept the Carlisle police from being able to officially arrest him on the murder and arson charges.

"Yeah, looking good, Reed, looking good." Tyler shoved the portable phone in his back pocket and walked his bike across the yard. He had another hour until Ray arrived. Maybe he would take the bike for a short spin, see how his ankle held up.

He had barely straddled the seat when a beat–up Ford Corsica without a muffler pulled into the parking lot. Arden got out of the passenger seat, dragging a backpack and a cloth satchel out after her. She blew a kiss to the rugged–looking driver who honked the horn and gave her a grin that displayed several missing teeth. Then, burning another layer of rubber off his tires, he squealed back onto the main road.

But when she turned around to greet Tyler, he could see her puffy cheeks and red–rimmed eyes. Leaning his bike against the porch rail, he came forward to help her with her bag.

"What's the matter?" he asked, already suspecting what her answer might be.

"Oh, I had a fight with my mother, with Wanda, I mean, and the shit hit the fan." Arden heaved her pack onto the porch and sunk down on the top step.

Tyler sat down next to her and leaned his back against a post. "What happened?" he asked nonchalantly.

"Oh, she still treats me like a baby and I'm just sick of it. I told her I was going to spend a few days with a friend who lived in Vermont. She wanted a phone number where she could reach me. I told her she didn't need to reach me, I'd be back soon enough. Then she accused me of having an affair with you – for some reason she thinks you're married– you're not, are you?"

Tyler's face reddened slightly as he shook his head. "Go on. What'd you tell her when she said that?"

"Well, I didn't deny it." It was Arden's turn to blush. "I just told her it was none of her business where I was going and who I spent my time with. And then all of the sudden we're just yelling all kinds of stupid things at each other and she says something about how upset my father will be with me and, well, I just wasn't thinking. I was so mad and I yell at her that he's not my real father anyway and that I know who my real father is and that maybe I'd just go live with him and never come back."

"Holy shit!" Tyler smacked his forehead and sat up, his sham of nonchalance gone. "What did she say to that?"

"Actually she shut up for a while, she went kind of white, and then she called me a liar and said there was no way I could know who my real father was, that nobody knew." Arden paused and twisted her hands nervously.

"And?"

"I'm sorry, but I told her you had found out and that it was true, we had proof. She wanted to know what kind of proof and I wouldn't tell her. She called me a liar again, saying that the whole thing was a twisted fantasy that I had made up. I hadn't seen her that mad since the day I asked her where my real mother was. Then I told her I had decided to move out, that her behavior was suffocating me."

"She must have loved hearing that."

"So then she switches completely, stops yelling and starts crying, telling me what an ungrateful child I am, how she raised me from a baby, how she gave up everything for me, that she needed me to stay and help her run the restaurant. When I told her to stuff it, she –she–" Arden raised a hand to her cheek and her own eyes filled with tears. "She slapped me across the face. It was the first time in my whole life I can ever remember her hitting me. I don't get it. Why can't she just let me go like other mothers do with their grown–up daughters?"

Tyler put a comforting arm around her shoulder. "Probably because she loves you so much. I think you meant everything to her when you were small. Sometimes mothers get a feeling that their lives are meaningless after their children leave home."

"But it's not like we hang out together! She has her life and I have mine. We work together at the cafe and we share the same house. That's it." Arden sniffled a few more times and then blew her nose in a ragged tissue, seemingly in control again.

"So was that the end of it?"

"No, but the rest is just a blur, it got even uglier. She called me a whore, I called her a whore–"

192

"You called your mother a whore?"

"Well, she's not really, but I do know for a fact that she's cheated on Lou a few times."

"Really? How do you know that?" Tyler hoped she wouldn't notice his diverting of the subject.

"A couple of times when I was younger, I know she had men over when my dad was out for the night. You know, how you wake up and hear a stranger's voice and you sneak out to see who it is and it turns out it's coming from the closed door to your mom's room and then the bed springs start squeaking..." Arden shrugged. "I remember mentioning it to her once the next day and she laughed at me and said I was dreaming. But I know I wasn't. One of the times I even recognized the guy's voice."

"Who was it?"

She looked at him suspiciously. "Why do you care?"

"Just testing your memory, that's all. I don't really care."

"Well, it was this guy who had been painting our house, Bobby Boxer. I knew it was him because I'd been listening to his voice outside my window every morning and he had a really distinctive laugh."

"Bobby Boxer." He knew the name from all the research he had done in the last few days. "He's the one who was suspected of starting the Darby Mountain House fire, wasn't he?"

Arden squinted at him cryptically. "Yeah, I guess he might have been. You do your homework, don't you?"

"So what do you think Lou is going to say when Wanda tells him you're leaving home?"

"Oh, he'll support me in whatever I decide to do. He's always been more open–minded than her." She stood up and brushed off the backside of her cut–off shorts. "I'm guess I'd better go tell Reed what went down." She headed across the parking lot to the open frame structure where Reed was sweeping up sawdust and nails with a long–handled broom.

193

Watching her walk away with a little of the usual bounce back in her step, Tyler still felt a twinge of something – lust, longing, emotion, or just the pain of being too old and wise to give in to the fantasy of an affair that would lead to nowhere.

Tyler went inside, wondering whether either Wanda or Lou would ever speak to him again about anything. He fixed himself a turkey sandwich in the kitchen where Clive was already prepping for dinner. He was contemplating whether or not he ought to make sure Sarah was awake when he saw someone ride into the yard on a Kawasaki 500. When the driver removed his helmet and unzipped his leather jacket, Tyler was surprised to see that it was Ray Polifax.

A few minutes later they were settled in a pair of white wicker rocking chairs on the porch with a couple of tall glasses of beer. Tyler quickly explained about the article he was writing on the hotel fires of Carlisle.

"I've learned so much I'm considering turning it into a short book," he remarked half–jokingly. "I've been trying to get the fireman's perspective, but Lou Kensington is pretty close–mouthed about the heroics of the fire department."

"I'd hardly call it heroics. We've never arrived in time to save any of the old hotels. We do much a better job on small houses and cats caught in trees." Ray's eyes twinkled over the rim of his glass.

"Well, let's put it this way. Lou is a pretty modest guy and he doesn't like to talk about himself much. How long has he been chief?"

"Oh, about twenty–five years I'd say. He was already chief when I joined the department back in 1974."

1974. There was that year again. "So were you there when Cherry Lodge burned down?"

"Yeah, that was my first big hotel fire. It was pretty exciting for a young guy like me. We thought we did a damn good job of containing it. Never would've thought somebody was trapped inside." Ray looked up. "You know about that?"

Tyler nodded. "Any word yet on who the corpse might be?"

"Well, they're thinking it's one of the college students just because of the kind of jewelry she had on. But then again, it was Halloween so you never know."

"So do any of the hotel fires you fought stand out in your mind for any reason?"

"Tyler, they all stand out in my mind. You don't easily forget the sight of an enormous building lit from the inside by a furnace of flames or the heat of a fire that size. The shame of it is that most of them could have been stopped if we'd caught them in time. Granted, those old wooden hotels might as well be built out of matchsticks, they go up so easily. But for some reason we never seem to get there until it's too late."

"So how do you get called to a fire?"

Ray tapped a small black beeper on his belt. "Someone calls the fire station to report a fire. If no one's there to answer the phone, the call relays to Lou's home number and then to the police station. In either case, the rest of us volunteers get beeped to report to the fire station."

"So is someone usually there at the fire station?"

"Well, Lou's there a good bit of the time. He's the only one of us who gets paid and even though it's not much, he spends quite a lot of each day there, servicing the trucks and what not. Wanda and he live a pretty simple life so they seem to get by on what little he makes and what the cafe brings in. They're lucky – they own their house outright, inherited it from Wanda's grandmother, and they have a few rental properties as that Lou takes care of."

"So basically Lou is the one who alerts the others as soon as a fire is called in." Alarm bells of a different sort were dinging in Tyler's head.

"Basically. He does a great job too. You should have seen how fast we arrived at the Marshall's house last week when their kitchen caught fire. Somebody had laid a newspaper on the counter too close to the gas stove and their two year old turned on a burner. Let me tell you, they were damn lucky to still have a house."

"But you never manage to get to the abandoned hotels on time." Because maybe Lou takes his time getting the word out, he finished silently.

"Abandoned is the key word there. Nobody around to see what's happening, no telephone nearby to call from once someone does see it. I'm sure more than a few of them were insurance fires. We always suspected Ed Keeler of having the Darby Mountain House burned down for that reason." Ray put down his empty glass and leaned forward earnestly. "But you have to understand, Tyler, it's better to let these places just burn to the ground once they get started. Look at the Centennial. It would have been a lot easier if it had burned all the way down than having to deal with the ruined remnants of a four story building. And a lot safer."

"I'm sure that's true. I read somewhere that Lou got an award for doing such a great job of keeping the in-town fires from spreading to other houses."

Ray nodded emphatically. "The man knows his stuff. I don't know anybody who knows as much about fires as he does. Carlisle might be a ghost town if it wasn't for him." He looked at his watch. "I'm going to have to get going soon. I guess I haven't really told you very much. Maybe we could get together again on the weekend?"

Tyler stood up. "Actually you've been incredibly helpful. Let me ask you this, do you remember Amber St. Pierre who used to live with the Kensingtons back around the time of the Cherry Lodge fire?"

To his surprise, Ray's already rosy cheeks deepened in color. "Yes, I do remember her. She worked over at the Blue Moon, a nightspot of notorious repute. I spent more than a few nights hanging out there the summer between my freshman and sophomore years of college. I've always been slightly amazed that Lou and Wanda let her stay with them."

"Why is that?" Tyler feigned innocence.

"Because she was so, well, wild and they are fairly conservative, church–going types."

"Did you know her well?"

Ray's blush expanded so that even his ears were red. "Yeah, me and half the other guys in Carlisle. Look, my number's in the book if you have any more burning questions about the department." Ray grinned at his own pun as he shook hands with Tyler.

"Actually there is one more thing." Tyler fell in step with Ray as he walked back to the parking lot. "Has anyone ever speculated on why so many of those hotels caught fire on the last day of the month?"

Ray shrugged. "Sure I guess so. But we also speculate why lots of fires happen when the moon is full too. And the simple answer is always that it brings out the crazies. If you think we've got some kind of serial arsonist here, think again." Ray zipped up his jacket and straddled his motorcycle. "There's almost no two of those hotel arson cases that started alike."

"I know that," Tyler said aloud to the roar of the Kawasaki's engine as Ray rode away from the inn. "Tell me something I don't know."

Looking around, he realized that the parking lot was now half full of customers' cars which meant Sarah must be tending the bar. He hurried back inside to find her.

"Hi, sweetheart." He leaned over the bar and gave her a kiss. "When can we talk?"

"Soon. Soon as all these people get their drinks." She looked especially lean and willowy tonight, dressed in a sleeveless black jumpsuit with a wide leather belt. A few strands of her long hair were held away from her face by a mother–of–pearl barrette. Sarah always managed to achieve simple elegance with little or no effort.

A few minutes later, she brought her glass of water over to the quiet end of the bar where he was waiting. "So where'd you run off to this morning without so much as a kiss?" he asked, cutting right to the chase.

"I went to see an old friend of mine who's an astrologer. She lives about an hour away from here, on top of a mountain."

Tyler held back all of the smart retorts he could easily have come back with. "And?"

The corners of her mouth twitched with a triumphant smile. "I just had this weird feeling about the dates of those fires and Ruby was the only person I knew who could quickly confirm it. She has this book she uses to do people's horoscopes that can tell you exactly where the sun, the moon and all the planets were at any specific time on any given day of any year."

"And?"

"Well, not only did nearly all those hotels burn down on the night of a full moon. They all burned down on the second full moon of the month!"

Tyler looked at her uncomprehendingly for a moment, not realizing the importance of what she was saying. She was too excited to wait for it to sink in.

"The blue moon. They all burned down on a blue moon!" She squeezed his arm and their eyes met.

"On a blue moon," he repeated slowly. "My God, what do you think it means?"

"I kept remembering how Edwin Keeler mentioned the Blue Moon Halloween party that was supposed to be Amber's going–away party and how Amber had a thing about blue moons." Sarah lowered her voice. "Instead Amber died in a fire that night."

"But I don't get it." Tyler shook his head in confusion. "If Amber was the one into blue moons, why did all these fires happen after she died?"

"I don't know. But you've got to admit, it's more than coincidental. And wait until you hear this." Sarah's eyes sparkled in that way they had been doing lately. "Ruby told me that, once, a long time ago, another person had come to see her who was interested in the dates of blue moons. A young girl with a baby."

"Amber."

Sarah nodded. "She came to have the baby's horoscope done. Ruby told her that the baby was born on the second full moon in January of 1973."

"Arden was born on a blue moon? Arden?" Tyler stared into space for a second. Then he leaped out of his seat and started pacing the room. "She couldn't have done it. She was only a small child when the Wallaby Hotel and the Darby Mountain House burned down."

"Sarah, can we can get another round down here when you get a minute?"

"Sure, coming right up." She caught Tyler by the arm as she passed him. "Just wait a second. There's more."

Tyler waited impatiently until Sarah finished serving the drinks.

"Okay, so here's the irony of it," she continued. "Turns out that Ruby realized afterwards she'd given Amber wrong information. She'd been looking up 1972, not 1973. There was no blue moon in January of '73. The whole horoscope was wrong. But she never got a chance to tell her of the mistake."

"So Amber's whole blue moon obsession started because of misinformation from a novice astrologist?"

Sarah nodded grimly. "And somehow it triggered a whole chain of events for decades afterwards." A bell rang in the kitchen and Sarah disappeared through the swinging doors.

Tyler stared blindly after her for a few seconds and then abruptly left the lounge.

The sun was low in the sky, about to disappear behind the western mountains. Reed's truck was gone; apparently Arden and Reed had already left for the "weekend" at his farm. It was just as well, he needed to think things through before he confronted Arden with any questions.

A short spin on his bike might help to clear his head. It would still be light for another hour or so.

His ankle felt stiff at first, but after a few minutes it seemed to loosen up with the rhythm of his peddling. He stayed in the valley that the village of West Jordan nestled in, not attempting any of the steep hills or mountains that surrounded the town. He didn't notice how quickly the air cooled after the sun dropped behind the trees. His mind was spinning faster than the wheels propelled by his legs.

Was it all connected to Amber or did it all start with Arden? Or was it really about both of them? Who knew about Amber's obsession with blue moons? Edwin Keeler for one. Reed had claimed ignorance – he had said Amber was into amber when he knew her. Mimi probably had known. Arden had never mentioned it, she seemed to know so little about her mother. Because no one had ever told her. But her parents must have known about it. After Arden had pestered her incessantly, Wanda had given her Amber's blue moon pendant that Arden now wore as an earring. And Lou had been Amber's lover. Who knows what they talked about in her bed?

But in that last letter to Mimi, she had written that she was tired of him, that she couldn't wait to get away. Did she finally tell him the truth in the end?

Tyler rolled to a stop by the river, breathing a little heavily from the swift ride. Mist was beginning to rise from the water. By morning it would have thickened to a fog that would hang over the whole valley until it burned off in the sun.

What if she had told Lou it was over and in a fit of enormous pain and despair, he had killed her and then set the Cherry Lodge fire to erase all traces of his crime and his passion. And what if blue moon after blue moon, for years to come, he burned down one hotel after another in a sort of demented memorial to his lost lover?

As Tyler shuddered at the weird logic of it all, he realized how cool the night was becoming. Before his ankle stiffened up again, he pedaled back to the inn. It all made unfortunate and perfect sense. Even Mimi's murder. She could have blown Lou's whole arrangement by letting Arden know that her mom never made it to Hawaii at all. That, as far as she knew, Amber had never left Vermont.

The hard part was going to be proving any of it. He wondered if Sarah knew when the next blue moon was due to happen.

CHAPTER THIRTEEN

"What do you mean am I insane? Of course, I'm insane. But it's a beautiful morning and I've got to get back in shape again." Tyler put his backpack on and adjusted the straps of his biking gloves. Straddling the seat, he added, "Don't worry. I'm not going to stay out until sunset and I'll come back over the mountain road and not the highway. Nobody would dare try that trick again anyway."

"You're such a lunatic. Well, be careful. You've made some enemies in Carlisle now." Sarah did not look at him; instead she concentrated on digging out the root of a stubborn dandelion that was growing on top of a delphinium.

"Look. I'm going to talk to a realtor who may or may not remember anything about a girl who worked at a place where he tended bar twenty years ago. Does that sound like a threatening situation?"

Sarah shrugged and wiped a stray hair out her eyes with the back of her arm. "Just don't do anything stupid that might let Lou Kensington know we're on to him. Carlisle is a very small town, you know, and Lou has a lot more friends there than you do."

"Sarah. Please. Have a little faith. I'll see you later."

"Hey, Tyler!"

He stopped at the end of the driveway and looked back at her impatiently.

"Bring me back some of those lupines that grow in the field at the top of the mountain. They should be in bloom right now."

"Sure thing."

He didn't stop to rest until he reached the field she had mentioned. An ancient cow pasture surrounded by overgrown stone walls, it was in its full glory at this time of year when it became a tapestry of wild lupines in a mixture of deep purple, periwinkle, pink and white. Its memorable beauty remained with him as he rode on and he reassured himself that he would not forget to pick Sarah a bouquet on the way home.

The temperature was into the eighties by the time he reached Carlisle and it brought to mind that very first day he had ridden his mountain bike into town. He wondered if he could remember the way to Arden's swimming hole at the river. The water would certainly have warmed up by now.

The realty office was just across the street from the cafe. He was surprised he hadn't noticed it before, but then again, he hadn't been looking for real estate. It was a small storefront office with just two desks for the agents and one by the entrance for their secretary/receptionist. She was a square–bodied woman with tightly curled hair and an acne–scarred complexion that was not enhanced by the bright paisley print of her silky polyester dress.

"Can I help you?" she inquired politely.

"I was hoping to talk to Mr. Sims." The empty office seemed to indicate he was not around.

"He should be back in a minute, he just ran down to the store for a newspaper. But he's supposed to meet a client at noon. Do you have an appointment?" She looked at the open appointment book on her desk, knowing full well that he did not.

"No, but this won't take long. I'll wait." Before she could object, Tyler sat down in a green leather chair and began to study the real estate listings and photographs on the bulletin board behind his head. Within a few minutes of quick study he not only knew what was for sale in Carlisle, but that Richard P. Sims and his partner Jefferson K. Whitehall had been licensed to sell real estate in both Vermont and New Hampshire since 1983 and that they had won an award in 1990 from the Small Business Association of the Northeast Kingdom.

The jingle of bells over the door brought him to his feet. "Tyler Mackenzie," he said, extending his hand to the tall thin man who entered. Behind aviator glasses with thick lenses, his inquisitive green eyes did a quick once–over on Tyler. As he moved to sit behind his desk, Tyler noticed that his graying hair was pulled into a ponytail that was tucked neatly into the collar of his suit jacket.

"Rick Sims. What can I do for you today?"

"Well, actually, Rick, I'm not here about buying any property. I wanted to probe your memory a little bit about someone you used to know back when you tended bar at the Blue Moon."

He could feel the invisible curtain come down between them as Rick straightened up in his seat. "Who exactly are you with?"

"I'm a private insurance investigator retained by a company down state and I've been trying to locate the whereabouts of an Amber St. Pierre. She stands to inherit a large sum of money if I can find her. But unfortunately the last place she was seen was in this town about nineteen years ago."

He could see Rick's shoulders relax visibly during his answer. Raising his arms behind his head, he leaned back in his desk chair, a distant smile playing on his lips. "Amber St. Pierre. Now there's a name I haven't heard in a long, long time."

Tyler exhaled and sat down. "So you do remember her?"

"Remember Amber? Who could forget her? She turned a job that I was growing sick of into something rather interesting for a few years there. But I thought she left here for the Bahamas, or Hawaii, that's it, Hawaii. She was going to join that girlfriend of hers..."

"Mimi."

"Right! Mimi." Rick shook his head, still smiling. "What a pair. I bet Mimi would know where she was."

Tyler restrained a remark about them being in heaven together now and then quickly explained to Rick about Mimi being the woman who died in the Centennial fire.

"Oh, that's right. I think someone mentioned that to me but it didn't click. Well, damn, fire away." He grimaced sheepishly at his own pun. "I can't imagine what kind of help I can be to you, but I can spare you a few minutes of reminiscing about Amber." He looked at his watch. "Actually, what do you say we go over to the cafe and catch an early lunch? I've got to show a couple of houses at noon." He stood up. "Besides, if anybody would know about where Amber ended up, Wanda would and she runs the cafe."

Tyler shifted uncomfortably in his seat. "Well, actually, I do know Wanda and she hasn't been very helpful." But he was afraid of not getting another chance to talk to Rick today. And Wanda usually didn't come out of the kitchen much during the lunch hours. "But, sure. Let's go grab a bite to eat."

As they stepped out together into the sunshine, Tyler remembered his bicycle. "Mind if I stick my bike inside behind your door?"

"Suit yourself. I'm sure where you come from you might have to worry about theft, but this is Carlisle. We're still fairly crime free."

Except for arson and murder, Tyler responded silently. Aloud he said, "That sounds like a real estate sales pitch to me."

"Well, it is one of our major selling points." The two tall, thin men crossed Main Street and opened the door to the cafe. A cool blast of air–conditioned air rolled out towards them, mingling with the smell of home–style cooking.

Tyler chose a table against the back wall that could not be seen through the swinging doors to the kitchen. A colorless teenage girl whom he'd never seen before took their order.

"Arden's not around today?" Rick asked the waitress.

The girl shook her head. "She took a few days off."

"Have you met Arden?" Rick asked when they were alone again. Tyler nodded. "Then you know she's Amber's illegitimate daughter? She'd stand to inherit anything you have for Amber if you couldn't find her, you know."

"Does everyone in town know that Arden is adopted?"

"Well, not everyone, of course, but anyone who's been around twenty years probably remembers. Lou and Wanda didn't make a big deal of it or anything, in fact they tried to keep it kind of quiet." Rick lowered his voice. "I mean, essentially Arden was abandoned. Amber went off to Hawaii and just never came back. It's not the kind of thing you want a small child to find out about. I have to admit, it did surprise me though."

"Why's that?"

Rick waited until the waitress had delivered their coffee before continuing. "Well, I knew Amber pretty well by the time she left here."

"A lot of people seem to have known Amber in the few years she was here." Tyler wondered if Rick would admit to an intimate relationship with her as well.

"Well, look what she did for a living. But I knew her in a way other people didn't. She talked to me. I was the bartender. Everyone spilled their guts to me at one point or another."

Tyler leaned forward intently. "So she talked to you about problems she might be having with people."

"All the time. And she had plenty of them. The girl thought with her body, not her mind. More like a lot of guys I've known."

"She talk to you about Lou Kensington?" Tyler asked the question so softly that Rick would not have caught it if he hadn't been looking directly at him.

Rick's eyes became veiled again. "How did you find out about that all these years later?"

Tyler shrugged. "I'm a private investigator. So she did talk to you about their relationship."

"You're not going to repeat any of what I say to you, are you?" Tyler shook his head. "And you're telling me that me talking about this old thing with Lou might help you find her?"

"In a manner of speaking. I know that it was one of the driving forces that spurred her towards leaving Carlisle."

Rick stirred his coffee for a moment and stared at a spot on the wall. "He was driving her crazy," he said finally. "As I recall, she hated going home after work because he was always waiting for her. She admitted that it had been her own fault for encouraging it at first, but by the end she felt trapped there. She couldn't afford to move out, because then she would have to pay for rent and a babysitter. And he didn't want her to go away. From what I remember her telling me, he was begging her to stay, saying he loved her, all the tricks in the book. I think that's why she sneaked off the way she did without saying goodbye to anybody." He laughed. "Old man Keeler was rip–shit. He'd planned this big going away party for her on Halloween. But it was the only easy way she could go."

"Do you think he was physically abusive to her?"

Rick's eyes narrowed again. "No, but what does that have to do with anything?"

"I'm just trying to recreate the scene, trying to figure out where she might have gone next. I mean, if she had been physically abused, she might have gone to a battered women's shelter or something."

"I doubt it. I used to try to convince her to take the baby and go live some place like that. But she was afraid she'd have to give up her Blue Moon job and she was probably right. Those places are like nunneries. She was also afraid they would say she was an unfit mother and take Arden away from her."

"Hmmm. That's interesting. From what I've gathered, she didn't really want to be a mother anyway."

The conversation stopped for a moment as the waitress returned with their sandwiches. "You know," Rick commented thoughtfully as he spread mustard on his roast beef, "That's the only part of it all that has never made sense to me."

"What's that?"

"Well, right before she left, Amber became paranoid about leaving Arden with Lou and Wanda. She didn't want to have to deal with Lou every time she wanted to find out how her daughter was doing. From what I can recall she never really planned on leaving her with them forever."

Tyler nodded. He could understand that line of reasoning.

"Anyway, I can clearly remember her saying she had decided to take Arden with her to Hawaii. I think she was afraid to confront Wanda, so she was just going to spring it on her at the last minute."

Tyler stopped chewing.

"I have to admit, I was more than surprised when I discovered a month or so after she left, that Arden was still with the Kensingtons. I remember seeing her riding around in a shopping cart at the supermarket with Wanda. They were inseparable, those two. So I guess Amber thought better of her decision. I must say, I'm still surprised that she never contacted them again after all these years."

"Inseparable."

"Huh?"

"I imagine Wanda must have put up quite a fight when she got wind of Amber's idea of taking the baby away. Don't you?"

Rick chuckled wryly. "Yeah, I've heard she has quite a fiery temper." He dipped a French fry into some ketchup and popped it in his mouth. "Maybe Amber changed her name. Maybe that's why you can't find her."

"Yeah, maybe." Tyler's mind was like a great slide puzzle. The shifting pieces were suddenly clicking into place, creating a new picture he hadn't seen before.

"I hate to say it, but it's also possible she got into something really bad when she left here and died young. She certainly had the potential."

"What about Mimi?" Tyler changed the subject abruptly. "Did she ever make any enemies in this town?"

"You mean who might have murdered her when she came back? I can't imagine. She was sweet, pretty, voluptuous, didn't go looking for trouble like Amber. Mimi had enough of it just dealing with Neil Richelieu. He's the only person comes to my mind." Rick's eyes were focused on the outside window. "I see my noon appointment parking across the street. I'm going to have to run."

He started to pull his wallet out of his pocket but Tyler held out a restraining hand. "Forget it. It's on me. I'm going to stay for another cup of coffee anyway."

"I'm sorry I couldn't tell you anything more useful."

Actually you've been more helpful than you could ever imagine, Tyler replied silently. Aloud he said, "It's been very interesting. You've given me some food for thought anyway."

Through the window, he watched Rick lope back across to his office. Then he settled back in his seat trying to figure out how to make his next, inevitable move. When the waitress dropped off the check, he asked her to tell Wanda that Tyler wanted to talk to her for a moment.

Almost immediately Wanda's head appeared around the edge of the swinging door, her eyes fixed in a hard and hateful stare, and then retreated back into the kitchen. Tyler asked for a refill on his coffee and sat back to wait, mulling over the things Rick had told him. He discreetly checked inside his backpack to make sure his voice activated tape recorder had a fresh tape in it.

He was on his second refill when Wanda finally came out to confront him. He wasn't sure if she'd use the time to calm herself down or to work herself up. "I don't know what else you want from me, you bastard," was her opening remark. "You've ruined my life enough already. I hope you realize that you're not welcome in this establishment any longer."

"Look, Wanda, I don't know what went down between you and Arden, but I don't think it really has a lot to do with you and me." It was a totally ambiguous statement and it confused Wanda enough that she lost her train of thought.

"You and me? What the hell are you talking about?"

"The work we were doing together. I've got one last hotel I want to see this afternoon and then my article will

209

be done. The old Charlemain, the one you told me about on the edge of the reservoir, the one with the turrets."

Wanda laughed in disbelief. "You actually think after what you did –" She stopped suddenly, realizing the entire restaurant had quieted down to listen to what she was about to say.

"Why don't you meet me out there after you're done here and you can say what you have to say to me then?" Tyler suggested softly.

Wanda crossed her arms over her stained white apron and contemplated him angrily. He tried to keep his expression as pleasant and open as possible, hoping he didn't come across as a sleazy snake.

"Okay. Two thirty at the Charlemain." Picking up his half full cup, she turned abruptly and went back into the kitchen.

Obviously she didn't want him hanging around until two thirty, so Tyler paid his check and sauntered outside. He strolled across the street to the real estate office to retrieve his bicycle, noting that the temperature felt like it was into the nineties by now.

"How do I get to the old Charlemain Hotel from here?" he asked the receptionist.

"Oh, it's not far." She described the route, which was less than a mile going south out of town. "It's an interesting place but it's all boarded up now. Don't think about going inside, the floors are rotted out in some places."

He assured her he wouldn't, knowing full well that Wanda would know some easy way to break in. He still had a couple of hours to kill and a dip in Arden's swimming hole sounded like the perfect answer.

Swimming and sunning left him feeling almost too relaxed as he approached the Charlemain, his tires nearly silent on the grass–covered road. He leaned his bicycle against a tree and then, on second thought, he hid it behind a hedge. Wanda didn't know how he was traveling and it might be interesting to watch her for a few moments if she thought she had arrived first.

He circled the old wooden structure, admiring the turn–of–the–century gingerbread ornamentation and the decorative shingles of the turrets on each of the four corners of the building. Next to the hotel was the entrance to a wildly overgrown garden and he settled himself inside the trellised archway that had once led the way to what had probably been formal, manicured flowerbeds. Wild roses still grew up the latticework of the archway, providing a dense and fragrant hideaway as well as offering some well–deserved shade.

Seconds later he heard a car engine shutting off and then the slamming of a door. He could see Wanda moving uncertainly towards the building. There were dark circles showing beneath the armpits of her blouse, but he had a feeling the beads of sweat running down the side of her face were not caused by the heat.

"Tyler?" she called softly. She stood perfectly still for a moment and when he did not respond, she headed purposefully around the side of the building. He heard her strike or kick something a few times. Soundlessly he left his hiding place and crossed to where he could view her.

Wanda was not to be seen, but an open cellar hatchway indicated where she had gone. Most women would hesitate before entering the old dirt–floored cellar of an abandoned building, but Wanda was obviously not the squeamish type. He himself paused, wondering if he should follow her. He had not brought a flashlight and decided to wait around the corner for her to come back out.

A squeaking of hinges on the other side of the hotel indicated she had found another exit. She obviously knew her way around. Tyler made sure his tape recorder was on, and then taking a deep breath, shouted her name.

"Oh, there you are!" He came around the corner to the less attractive, back side of the hotel where she was standing very still.

"I didn't hear you drive in," she remarked eyeing him oddly.

"Have you already been inside?" he asked, ignoring her comment.

"No, I was just checking to see if the back door might be open. And lucky for us – it is!" He was not sure if she was aware of how forced her gay tone sounded. She flashed him a dimpled smile and extended her hand. "I'm sorry I was so rude to you back at the cafe. But I've been pretty upset since Arden left."

Her apology was completely false, but Tyler pretended he was taken in by it. She had some cards up her sleeve and he wanted to give her the opportunity to play them.

"How'd you know this back door would be open?" he asked innocently. "Have you been out here lately?"

"It's been open for twenty–five years. High school lovers use this as a place to meet and, you know." She blushed and pulled her hand away. "There are a few old mattresses still left in the rooms upstairs."

She stepped inside the doorway and Tyler followed her.

"Unfortunately the place has been really trashed by kids over the years and there's not much of the old grandeur left."

As Tyler's eyes grew accustomed to the dim light, he could see she was right. The place was in complete disrepair. Old wallpaper hung off the walls in tattered ribbons, floor boards had been pulled up, light fixtures ripped out of the ceilings. As a final touch, four letter words and unsightly graffiti were scrawled here and there.

"I fucked Susan Connors," read one legend to be rejoined by another, "So did I!"

"Well, this is too bad," he said, making his way gingerly towards the front of the hotel. "I'm surprised it hasn't been torn down."

"It serves a purpose. It was always a more interesting building from the outside than the inside anyway." Wanda stopped at the foot of a grand staircase and peered upward.

"Can you still get up into the turrets?"

"I think so. Would you like to try?" Her pleasant compliance was beginning to make him a little nervous.

"I'll follow you," he deferred.

They made their way slowly up the wide staircase, careful to avoid the missing steps and rails. The windows of the upper floors were not boarded up and even the long, narrow hallway was much lighter than downstairs had been. Wanda indicated a few of the rooms with mattresses as they walked by them.

"Maybe we'll stop on the way back down," she murmured suggestively and it occurred to Tyler suddenly that maybe that was what she'd had in mind the whole time, maybe that was why she was being so nice to him. He tried to dismiss the disturbing image and concentrated on keeping his wits about him as they began to climb a circular stairway at the end of the hall. The air on the second floor had been rather cool but as they ascended to the tower it seemed to get stuffier and when they finally reached the windowed cupola on top, it seemed oppressively hot.

Wanda struggled to open a window and with Tyler's help, managed to force the ancient sash to work, although it would not stay up on its own. Tyler sat on the peeling sill and held the window up with his shoulder as they rested and admired the view.

"So you probably want to know how I found out who Arden's father was, don't you?" Tyler threw the question out in a casual way that he knew would catch Wanda off guard.

Startled for just a second, Wanda recovered her composure quickly. "How could YOU possibly know?" she sneered. "I doubt that her birth mother even knew. I certainly never had a clue."

"But Amber did know." Tyler's use of her given name made Wanda's eyes widen slightly. "And so did her best friend Mimi. The one who died in the Centennial fire."

"Well, if she died in the fire, when did you get a chance to talk to her?" Wanda crossed her arms, a defiant smirk on her face.

Tyler was silent for a moment, trying to decide how to play his own hand. He didn't want to put words in her mouth, he wanted to trap her into telling the truth.

"Amber wrote to her," he said finally. "I've seen some of their old letters."

"Oh, really? And where did you find those?" They were baiting each other now.

"In Neil Richelieu's barn. Amber left some boxes of her possessions there. As a matter of fact, I think Amber left ALL her worldly possessions there."

There was an odd gleam in Wanda's eye as she leaned back against her own windowsill and said, "And what exactly do you mean by that?"

Tyler's shoulder was beginning to ache. He stood up and the window he had been supporting came crashing down. "I mean that I don't think Amber ever went to Hawaii." He started to descend the stairs, knowing that Wanda would follow.

"Then where did she go?"

"I don't know, you tell me. Does a person like that go to heaven or hell?"

"So you think she's dead? With all her possessions stored in Neil Richelieu's barn? The old dirtbag that never got convicted of the Cherry Lodge fire? Well, that makes it look like he had something to do with her disappearing, doesn't it?"

"It certainly does. There's only one problem." He stopped at the bottom of the circular staircase and turned to confront her. "He had no reason to kill her."

"He wouldn't need a reason. He's certifiably insane." Wanda met his gaze unflinchingly.

"Maybe. But I also think he's too smart to hide a mountain of evidence on his own property. Or offer to show it to someone eighteen years later."

214

"Then what do you think happened to Amber? Let me just remind you that she was a low–life whore, who abandoned her child and never once came back to see how she was doing. Someone like that usually ends up overdosing in a crack house some place where she's been trading blow jobs for a fix. Who would care what happened to scum like that?" Wanda's voice trembled a little as she allowed herself to feel the hatred she'd kept pent up for years.

"Maybe someone who cared about her more than he had a right to. Maybe someone who envisioned Amber's life turning into something like you described and tried to stop her from leaving. Maybe someone who thought his life would be completely empty without her."

Wanda sneered again. "Which one of her tricks are you talking about?"

"The one she came home to every night. The one who loved her more than she could ever love him. The one who accidentally got violent when she insisted she was leaving him. Your husband."

There was a split second of deafening silence in the long empty hallway before Wanda threw back her head and laughed loudly. "Lou? LOU?" She walked past him down the hall, stopping in front of an open doorway. "You think Lou killed her?" She laughed again uncontrollably this time. "That's a new one. How could you possibly prove that?"

Tyler's palms were beginning to get sweaty as he followed her. "Plenty of people knew about their affair. You knew too, didn't you?"

"You're out of your mind! You're trying to tell me that my own husband was sleeping with another woman in my own house without me knowing?" She shook her head. "Come in here, Tyler. This room has a special feature I think you'll be interested in." She disappeared into a room on the left.

"But you did know, didn't you? You encouraged Amber to leave for Hawaii as soon as possible so that she would be out of your life." He looked around trying to pick out what she thought was so interesting about a plain hotel bedroom.

"I'm sure I did." With a couple of long strides she crossed the room to a narrow door made of natural wood stained to a dark walnut color. "Now, this probably looks like an ordinary closet to you—"

"You know what else I think, Wanda? I think Lou is responsible for burning down all the old hotels in this town." Tyler was speaking very quickly now. "I mean, who else would know how to do it so well and never get caught?"

Wanda shook her head, still smiling. "You have a wild imagination, Tyler. You'll love what I'm going to show you next." She opened the closet door. "This may look like an ordinary closet to you, but it is actually the entrance to a secret passage to the cellar. You see that row of hooks across the back? Why don't you pull that third hook from the left and see what happens?"

A secret passage. Tyler lost his train of thought for a moment, wondering if that was why she had opened the cellar door when she first arrived. He crossed the room to where she was standing. "Just like the wardrobe in the Narnia books, huh? Before we go in there, let me ask you just one more thing."

He looked at her waiting there, so complacent, so obviously enjoying the ideas he had just thrown out at her. And he knew he was right.

"Do you know what June 30th, 1996 is?"

The self–satisfied smirk seemed to freeze on her lips. "Let me guess," she replied sarcastically. "Your fortieth birthday?"

"It's the next blue moon."

She stared at him expressionless. "So?"

"But you knew that already, didn't you?" He walked past her and reached for the third hook on the back wall of the closet. Giving it a sharp tug, he said over his shoulder, "Tell me, do you have any special hotel in mind?"

Her response to his question was not what he had expected. Before he realized what was happening, the closet door had been slammed shut, leaving him in a total and stifling darkness. The next sound he heard was the scraping of a key and the clicking of an iron lock.

CHAPTER FOURTEEN

By one o'clock Sarah could take no more of the heat and humidity. She threw her gardening tools into a bucket and hosed the dirt from her feet, knees and lower legs. A shower and a nap seemed to supersede anything else she might have had on her agenda for the afternoon.

But as she toweled her hair dry, she noticed the message light blinking on the answering machine. She contemplated pretending to herself that she didn't see it and waiting until after her nap to play the messages back. But she knew she probably wouldn't be able to sleep at all if she did that. She grabbed a wide–toothed comb, pressed the rewind button, and proceeded to comb the snarls out of her hair as she listened to the message tape.

The first one was for Tyler from someone named Jim. "If I don't have your Myanmar piece on my desk by five o'clock today, you can start looking for someone else to work for. In other words, you're fired!"

That sounded pretty serious. She knew Tyler hadn't worked on that article in weeks and she wondered if she should try to get in touch with him. But it probably wouldn't get him back home any sooner even if she did.

The second message was for Tyler also. "Tyler, it's Steve Farrell on Maui. Hey, I was going through Mimi's computer files yesterday and came across something I think is significant. Give me a call – never mind, I'm going to be out all day. Anyway, the gist of it is that I found a letter that Mimi sent to Wanda Kensington a couple of months ago. She asked if Wanda could meet with her during the three days she had planned to be in Carlisle. She said she also wanted to meet with Arden if Wanda thought it would be okay. If you want a copy of it I'll fax it to you. Give me a call."

There were no other messages. Sarah leaned against the edge of the kitchen, picking at her wet hair with the comb, thinking about just exactly what Steve's message implied. It meant that Wanda knew Mimi was coming back to Carlisle for a visit. Possibly Wanda was the only person in town who knew what days Mimi would be there.

So what would Wanda have done if Mimi had been given the chance to tell her that Amber had never made it to Hawaii all those years ago?

But somebody had killed Mimi before she had the opportunity to meet with Wanda.

Or had they?

The first place Mimi had gone in Carlisle after she checked into her motel was to the cafe for lunch. Chances were she didn't know that Wanda ran the cafe. But did that matter? She hadn't met anybody she knew at the restaurant and apparently nobody recognized her either. And nobody remembered seeing her again after she left the restaurant that day.

But if Wanda had come out of the kitchen during lunch, she might have recognized her.

And Mimi was the only one who could tell Arden that Amber had never made it to Hawaii. That Amber had never meant to abandon her as an infant. That Amber had been running from a perverse living arrangement with Arden's adoptive parents.

Sarah's fingers trembled as she tried to find the R's in the yellow pages of the telephone book. There was only one realtor in Carlisle.

"Tyler Mackenzie? Oh, the guy on the bicycle. Yes, he did meet with Mr. Sims, they had lunch over at the cafe. When he came back for his bike he asked me how to get to the old Charlemain Hotel."

"How long ago was that?"

"A couple of hours ago. He might still be there. But they don't have any phone you can call him on." She laughed at her own joke.

"Thanks. Thanks a lot. Where is the Charlemain anyway?"

The secretary at the realty office repeated the same directions she had given Tyler. Sarah put on her underwear while she listened and looked around for something quick to dress in. The floral rayon dress she had laid out to wear to work later did not seem appropriate for traipsing around old hotels, but it was the nearest thing at hand and slipped easily over her head. As she ran down the stairs, she grabbed the wet hair hanging down her back and swept it up in a big barrette.

She was not sure why she felt such urgency to find him. Surely she could wait until this evening to tell him that they'd figured it all wrong. But the woman on the phone had said Tyler had gone to the cafe and then come back looking for the Charlemain. And he never went to those old hotels alone. He always went with Wanda. Wanda who was ripshit mad at him for alienating her baby, Arden. Wanda who'd committed murder less than a month ago to keep the truth from surfacing. About the murder she'd committed twenty years ago so she could keep that baby.

Sarah made a right turn at the corner in the village. Putting the car into four wheel drive, she started up the Darby Mountain road.

"Okay, very funny, Wanda." Tyler could feel the blood pounding and rushing in his ears. "So now I'm supposed to figure out which hook really opens up the secret passage so I can get out of here, right?"

There was no response except for the sound of Wanda's footsteps walking out of the room. A faint strip of light showed under the bottom of the closet door. Despite the warm stuffiness of the closet, Tyler was suddenly cold and shivering. He felt around for the inside handle of the closet door but he couldn't seem to find it. After a moment of desperate groping, he knew that there was no inside handle.

He could hear Wanda returning, dragging something big behind her. She let it go with a soft thud on the floor of the room.

"Wanda! Talk to me! What's going on here?"

Wanda laughed unpleasantly. "If you didn't know what was going on here, I obviously wouldn't be doing what I'm doing." As she walked away again, he tried to calm himself by breathing deeply but his chest was constricted with fear. He had to keep talking to her; he could talk his way out of anything.

She was back again dragging something else.

"Wanda! What are you doing out there?"

"Piling mattresses on the floor. Save your breath, Tyler. You're going to need it."

"Wanda, listen to me! I'm on your side! I want to help you!" He hoped he didn't sound as desperate as he felt.

"You're the one who needs the help now, Tyler."

"What I'm saying is, I understand how you must have felt. It must have been awful for you when you found out Amber was screwing your husband. And then when she wanted to take the baby away to Hawaii with her – well, that was unthinkable, wasn't it? She was unfit to be a mother. She couldn't possibly take care of little Arden who you loved so dearly, who had become the focus of your life."

He stopped to catch his breath and to see if she would respond. There was no sound. He had to believe she was just standing there listening to him in shocked silence.

"It was probably an accident, right? You didn't mean to kill her, but you were just so upset that you became physically violent. You couldn't believe what you had done, but you realized that if you got rid of the body nobody would miss her. You could just say she left a few days early. Hiding her body in the basement of the Cherry Lodge and then burning down the hotel was a stroke of genius, Wanda. And when Neil came by looking for her that night, you gave yourself an alibi that would serve your husband right if the story ever came out. As well as a scapegoat for the whole cri– affair."

A cry of rage and the sound of her fists pounding on the closet door made his hair stand on end. "You can't know my life like that! You made it up! You have no proof!" Her body slumped against the wooden door between them as she sobbed angrily.

"Let me out, Wanda, so I can help you. Nobody else knows about this but you and me. I won't tell anybody. I'll get you some professional medical help. You're really brilliant, Wanda, a true genius. No one has pinned a single fire on you yet. Nobody's made the connection. No one knows about Amber and the blue moons."

"Lou knows," she sniffed. "We never talk about it, but he knows. I won't ever let him forget what he did. Every time he goes out to fight a fire on a blue moon, I make sure he knows that I remember how he betrayed my trust with that whore while I was upstairs taking care of the baby he could never give me. In my own house. In my own house!"

By this time Tyler had fished his tape recorder out of his backpack and pressed it up against the crack beneath the door. "Wanda, I'm so sorry for everything that has happened to you. You certainly have made the best of a messy life. Now, please, unlock the door. I want to call Arden and tell her to come home to you. You need her."

He was sure he had convinced her now. Then, just as suddenly as she had broken down, she turned against him. He heard her stand up and then turn and rage at him, "She doesn't need me anymore! She's grown up! She has her own life! After all these years, it makes my whole existence seem pointless. Working towards nothing. And to top it off, you introduce her to some jerk who claims to be her real father... I'm not letting you out of there, Tyler. You deserve the fate you're about to meet."

"Wanda! I'm sorry! Please believe me!" The crack of light he was talking to began to disappear. There was a dull thud against the door and the sound of Wanda's movements became muffled. With sinking hopes, Tyler realized she had shoved one of the mattresses up against the door.

She knelt on the floor and lifted one corner of it to speak to him. "Nobody's going to hear you call for help now, Tyler. So save your breath. It will all be over pretty quickly. The straw in these old mattresses is as dry as kiln–dried kindling."

"Wanda, I lied to you. There are plenty of people who know what you did now. I sent your whole story to my editor in New York before I came by today. You can't get away with killing another person."

"It doesn't hurt to try. I've always had luck on my side. Besides, nobody would believe you anyway." She dropped the mattress back down and pushed it firmly into place.

"Wanda, people know we were meeting here. Customers in the restaurant probably overheard us. I told that woman in the real estate office when I went back for my bicycle. I called Sarah and left a message on the answering machine." Through the floorboards he could sense the vibrations her feet made as she walked away.

She was right. He'd better save his breath now. Getting air was his first priority. Getting out was a close second.

Sarah turned off the highway onto the road leading to the Charlemain Hotel. The afternoon air was hot and still and the bright sunshine seemed to be mocking her instinct that Tyler might be in trouble.

As she pulled up to the old hotel there was no sign of life but some of the long grass in the overgrown driveway was flattened down as though someone had recently driven over it.

"Tyler!" She shouted his name before she was even out of the car. A quick look around did not reveal his bicycle anywhere. Maybe he was already gone.

She circled the building looking for an obvious way in, but it seemed to be tightly boarded up. "Tyler!" she called again. "Are you here?"

Maybe he was in the gardens looking around. Or maybe he had come and gone in Wanda's car and wasn't here at all. But if he had been on his way home, she would have passed him on the mountain road.

Suddenly she felt stupid and reactionary. She gave a half–hearted look through an archway of wild roses. The old perennial garden hadn't been cared for in years but there were some hearty varieties that had apparently managed to bloom on their own, summer after summer on the sunny, south–facing slope. Giant foxgloves and columbines and some white delphiniums – she might as well pick a bouquet to take home with her.

With a huge armload of flowers, she started to make her way back up the hill. She stopped for a moment, just to enjoy the view, trying to imagine what it had once been like, the big old hotel looming grandly over a luxurious hillside of well–tended plantings. It was then she noticed two things almost simultaneously.

Tyler's bike was leaning against an old boxwood hedge near the entrance to the garden.

And a thin wisp of black smoke was drifting out of one of the upstairs windows of the Charlemain.

His only tool was his Swiss army knife. After several very unsuccessful attempts at prying the lock through the crack in the door, he began banging on the walls and floor of the closet, trying to see which boards had the most give to them or seemed the thinnest. When he realized that the walls were plaster, he gave a war cry and shoved the knife with all his might into the rear wall. He could feel the old plaster crumbling away beneath his fingers. Stabbing and picking at it again and again, he had managed in a few minutes to open a hole almost large enough to fit his hand through.

More importantly, he could feel the air. He stuck his nose up to the hole and breathed in. Musty and smelling of old mouse turds, it was still fresher than the air of his confinement. He put one eye to the hole but the darkness was as complete as his own. He must have reached the space between the walls where the electric wires and water pipes were hidden.

He scraped away at the hole, stopping at times to pry and tug at the plaster with his fingers. He was finally rewarded as a huge chunk came loose in his hands, setting off a cloud of dust that made him cough and choke on his precious air supply.

When his breath returned to normal he caught the first faint, but unmistakable, odor of smoke.

Drenched with sweat now, he pulled off his shirt and tied it around his head. It would keep the drips running down his forehead from falling into his eyes. Even though he couldn't see anything, it annoyed him just the same. He started to shove his arm through the hole but his fingers immediately came in contact with another wall barely six inches away.

He felt for his knife where he had placed it at his feet but his hand was so slippery with sweat that he could not hold on to it. He dried his palms on his shorts and then dried the handle of the knife as well. He had to hold on to it. If it slipped through his fingers between the walls, all hope would be lost.

Praying that he was still dealing with dry old plaster, he began prodding and scraping at the new, unfamiliar surface.

Sarah raced up the hill toward the building, trying to decide what to do next. She didn't know enough about fires to be sure. She thought if she broke a window to get in, it might provide the flames with the oxygen they would need to expand and grow. As she ran around the hotel again, this time she noticed the bulkhead doors to the cellar. If the fire was on the second floor, she might be able to get in through the basement.

But as she grabbed hold of the metal handle and pulled, she realized that she was crazy to go alone into a burning building. The fire department knew how to deal with rescuing people better than she did.

Before she got into her car, she turned and shouted one more time. "Tyler! Answer me! Are you in there? Tyler!"

Tears were streaming down her face as she gunned the engine and took off down the road, looking for the nearest inhabited house.

The first house she came to was a small white cape with no cars in the driveway. She banged on the back door and when no one answered, she tried the doorknob. Just like many small town dwellers, the inhabitants of this house did not feel the need to lock it. The kitchen phone was easy to locate; making a sound come out of her mouth after dialing 911 was much harder.

"The Charlemain Hotel in Carlisle is on fire. Hurry!" Her throat muscles were so tense, she could barely get out a croaking whisper.

By the time she had raced back to the hotel, she could hear sirens in the distance. She was relieved to see that the fire did not seem much bigger than when she had left it. Within in a minute, the first fire truck appeared on the scene. Her apprehension grew when Lou Kensington leaped out of the driver's door. Without stopping to look at her, he moved toward the back of the truck and began to put on his protective gear.

As she approached him, another fire truck pulled up in front of her, blocking her view of Lou. Two small pick-up trucks were close on its heels. Before she could open her mouth, she was being firmly told to stand back.

"If you're not on the fire department, we'd prefer it if you'd leave."

"Listen to me, somebody! I think my boyfriend is trapped inside that building."

Two men turned to stare at her. "What do you mean, you 'think'?"

"He said he was coming here and I found his bicycle over in the bushes there. I don't know where else he could be." As she spoke, Sarah had an awful sensation that maybe she was over-reacting. There were a hundred other places that Tyler could be.

"You the one who called this fire in?"

She nodded, unable to overcome the self–doubt she was suddenly experiencing. One of the men beckoned to Lou. "This lady says she thinks her boyfriend might be inside."

Lou stared grimly at her for a second.

"Look, this can't be just a maybe situation here. We don't just send a team into a burning building unless there is a strong reason to."

The sound of rushing water made all their heads turn. A yellow–suited volunteer was hosing down the grass and bushes around the hotel.

"You see what he's doing? You know why? Because a rundown building like this isn't worth saving. It's safer to let it burn to the ground than leave a dangerous ruin standing. I wasn't planning on sending anybody inside. What makes you think he's in there?"

"I came looking for him and I found his bicycle in the bushes over there." What would happen if she told Lou in front of the other firemen that she thought his wife was responsible for this fire?

"Bicycle? What's his name?"

"Tyler Mackenzie. He's been doing research on the old hotels of Carlisle."

"Oh, he's the guy your wife's been giving tours to, isn't he, Lou?" Someone called down from the top of the truck.

"He doesn't usually come out to these hotels alone." Sarah moved her face closer, forcing Lou to meet her gaze. The look in his eyes was unreadable, but she sensed his fear of the truth.

"All right." He turned his back on her. "We'll do a quick sweep of the rooms outside of the burning area but nobody goes into a danger zone unless there is just cause." He called to two men who were unwinding the hose on the other truck.

"Duchamp! Polifax! Get your oxygen on!" He walked away to explain the situation to them. One of them turned his head to stare hard at Sarah while Lou was talking.

227

Her eyes filled with tears again and her trembling legs felt as though they would not hold her up. She leaned against the open door on the driver's side of the fire truck. Maybe she was crazy. What if one these guys lost his life inside the building looking for Tyler and then it turned out he hadn't even been in there?

Her eyes fell on the cellular phone resting on the leather seat of the truck. There was a list of emergency numbers in a laminated plastic holder next to it. Ambulance, Hospital, Towing...Suddenly she knew what she needed to do and who could help her.

"Highway Auto Body."

"Neil? It's Sarah Scupper. I need your help right away."

"Sarah Scupper? From the West Jordan Inn? Hey, how the hell..."

"Neil. I'm talking life and death here. And I need your help. Meet me at Wanda Kensington's house in five minutes or sooner. Please." Her voice broke on the last word.

"Baby, I don't know what you're talking about, but I'm on my way."

At the same time, in the dark closet, Tyler's eyes were also filling with tears. He had finally managed to hack through the far wall of the other room. A small circle of daylight was his reward.

His heart had leaped with hope when he had heard the sirens a few moments before. But he'd done enough research now to know how they fought the fires of old, uninsured hotels. They tried to contain the fire, but they never put it out until the building was a heap of innocuous ashes and rubble on the ground.

He had begun shouting for help but the rasping sounds coming out of his parched throat came back at him as muffled echoes of the closed space around him. He redoubled his efforts at the wall and a few minutes later a small hole was his prize.

As his eyes continued to water, he realized it was not just the emotion of the moment that was making him cry. The acrid smoke was beginning to seep into his dark cubbyhole.

With all his remaining strength he ripped with his hands and shoved with his shoulders against the plaster wall that was restraining him in the closet. To enlarge the circle of light on the far side, he had to be able to get more than just his arm into the crawl space between the walls.

He yelped angrily as he punctured his thumb with a nail and again a few seconds later when the same nail ripped open the flesh on his forearm as he shoved his upper body into the narrow musty space between the rooms. Exhausted and bleeding, he collapsed onto his knees, which were still on the closet floor. Some rational part of his brain was reminding him that he would need to get a tetanus shot now.

The blood was pounding so loudly in his head that he missed the opening words that were being shouted into a bullhorn outside the building. But he was close enough now to stick his ear against the hole in the wall.

"...in the building, please stay where you are but yell so we can find you! Tyler Mackenzie! Or anyone else who is in the building! I repeat! We have two men in the building right now! If you are there, please shout so they can find you!"

Somebody knew he was in here. Had Wanda confessed? If she had, they would know where to look for him. And they wouldn't have said, "If you are there..."

What was wrong with him? He was drifting and thinking, not shouting for help. Putting his mouth to the hole, he shouted, "HELP! HELP! I'M OVER HERE! STUCK BEHIND THE WALL!"

But he could not seem to make much noise come out of his sore, dry throat. He called and called until he began to cough and sputter. Putting his eye to the hole, he saw that smoke was beginning to seep in under the door of the room on the other side of the wall.

Neil came squealing to a halt in front of the Kensingtons' house just as Sarah was getting out of her car. Racing over to his truck, she greeted him with the words, "Bring that thing along too." She pointed to the shotgun on the rack behind his head.

"It ain't loaded." He reached for it with a grease—blackened hand. He had obviously dropped whatever he was working on and come running when she called without bothering to clean up.

"Doesn't matter. We don't want to kill anybody. Just scare them. Come on, let's go."

He grabbed her by the forearm roughly and pulled her back to face him. "Mind telling me what's going on here, baby? You look like twenty miles of bad road."

"What's going on is that I found out who framed you for that fire all those years ago. And who set all the others since. And now I believe she's set fire to the Charlemain with Tyler locked up inside. And we're going to make her tell us where he is."

"Who? Wanda?" Neil followed her up the sidewalk to the front porch. "You shittin' me? The fire chief's wife's been torching all the hotels in town all these years?"

"Ssshh!"

He lowered his voice. "That sure as hell is the most perverted job security scam I've ever heard about. So what are we doing here?"

"We've got to make her tell us where Tyler is as fast as we can. That's what I need you for. I don't care what you have to do. Tyler is not going to burn to death for her crimes!" The last word came out as a sniffle. Sarah swallowed hard and straightened her shoulders. "Okay. Here we go."

She banged loudly on the door. "Wanda? Are you home?"

Without waiting for a response, she opened the door and the two of them boldly walked in. "Wanda! Where are you? We need to talk to you!" She tried to force the desperation out of her voice.

They tromped through a pristine living room with a shiny hardwood floor. The neatly arranged scatter rugs and knick–knack shelves seemed the perfect foil for the insanity of the woman who they searched for. From the back of the house came the sound of a toilet flushing. Wordlessly, Sarah led the way.

"The bedroom is back here," Neil mouthed into her ear. Pushing past her, he kicked open the door, brandishing his shotgun.

Wanda was standing on the other side of the bed, stripping the sheets off. Her jaw gaped when she saw who her visitor was. The sheer white negligee and matching robe she wore, suggested that he was not who she was expecting.

"What are you doing in my house?" she gasped. "Get out!"

"Who are you expecting this time, Wanda?" Neil sneered at her. "Who's your newest victim to fuck while your husband fights fires?"

"If you don't leave immediately I'm calling the police!" As Wanda reached for the phone, Sarah put a restraining hand on Neil's elbow.

"Let her call," she whispered from behind his back. "We'll need them here when we're done."

"Rosalind! It's Wanda. Listen, send a squad car over to my house right away. Neil Richelieu is here threatening me with a shotgun." She slammed down the phone. "You're not going to get away with this, Neil."

"No, you're the one who's not going to get away with this, Wanda." Sarah edged around Neil's large frame to confront her. "And if you don't tell me now where Tyler is in that burning hotel, Neil's going to make you tell."

It took Wanda only a few seconds to recover from the initial shock of seeing Sarah there. "I don't know what you're talking about," she replied as she continued to pull the sheets off the bed. "But if you know what's good for you

you'll leave before the police arrest you as Neil's accomplice."

"Wanda." Sarah spoke in a small, very controlled voice. "I know everything that Tyler knows about you. Now if you don't tell me where he is, in five seconds Neil is going to cross this room and break your arm."

The two women stared at each other over the unmade bed. Above the lace bodice of her negligee Wanda's chest was beginning to move up and down a little faster.

"Very well. Neil?"

Before Sarah even saw him move, Neil had crossed the room to where Wanda stood. In one swift movement, he grabbed her right arm and twisted it behind her back, still juggling the shotgun with his other arm.

Wanda shrieked with pain.

"I haven't even broken it yet, bitch. Tell us where Mackenzie is or the pleasure will be mine to enjoy."

Sarah's stomach turned when she saw how Neil's eyes glistened at the idea of inflicting pain and injury, but right now she didn't even care. The clock was ticking for Tyler; she had to save him.

Wanda was still screaming and trying to squirm out of Neil's grasp. "Let me go, you bastard! You're both out of your minds!"

A cracking noise made Sarah gasp and Wanda begin to sob.

"You son of a bitch!"

"Just tell us where he is, Wanda."

"Never!"

Sarah realized that Wanda was inadvertently admitting that she knew where Tyler was. She had to push her further. "Wanda, I talked to Mimi's husband today. He has a copy of the letter she sent you asking you to meet her that afternoon she died. I know you killed Mimi and I know why. Now just tell me —"

Neil's cry of rage cut her words off. "You killed my Mimi!" He flung Wanda to the floor and before Sarah could stop him he began pummeling her with the end of the

232

shotgun, punctuating each blow with the same words. "You killed my Mimi!"

"Neil! Stop!" Sarah threw herself at him, knocking him off balance. The shotgun flew out of his hands. When it hit the floor it went off with a explosive blast that left them all silent for a second.

Sarah came to her senses first. She quickly turned to Wanda, who lay dazed and beaten on the floor. Blood was running out of her nose, a huge lump was rising on her forehead and her arm lay at an impossible angle to her body. But her eyes were open and filled with pain.

Sarah leaned over and spoke quietly into her face. "Wanda, please, just tell me where Tyler is. I promise I won't let Neil kill you. But I love Tyler. And I don't want him to die."

Looking into Sarah's face, Wanda's eyes clouded over with tears before she closed them. "Locked in a closet. Second floor. Third bedroom on the right."

"Was he – alive?"

"Yes."

As she finished whispering, the wail of a police siren could be heard approaching. Sarah reached for the bedside telephone and punched in the number she had hastily scrawled on the back of her hand.

"Lou Kensington here."

"I know where Tyler is. He's on the second floor, in a closet of the third bedroom on the right."

"In a closet? What the hell? Who is this? How do you know where he is?"

"Your wife told me. Wanda!" Sarah held the receiver up to her mouth. "Tell him it's true!"

"It's true." Wanda repeated in a tiny voice not opening her eyes.

"Wanda–"

"I'm sorry, Lou."

Sarah spoke into the phone again. "Now, please! You have to save him!" Sarah tried not to break down at the sound of her own desperate voice. "The police are here. I have to go."

She looked over at Neil. He still sat on the floor with his head in his hands, sobbing and repeating to himself, "She killed my Mimi. She killed my Mimi."

"Sargent Boyce, Carlisle Police. What's going on here?" A tall man in a blue uniform crossed the room to Neil and got out his handcuffs, while Sargent Boyce knelt beside Wanda. "My God, Wanda. Are you all right?" He looked up at Sarah. "Call an ambulance."

"Wait, you've got it wrong here. She's the one you should be handcuffing." Sarah felt suddenly exhausted but she knew she had to explain what had happened. "She started the fire at the Charlemain. She locked my boyfriend in a closet there and tried to kill him. Not only that but she burned down the Centennial and a host of other hotels all the way back to the Cherry Lodge."

"Who? Wanda? I'd have to be out of my mind to believe that." He yanked the phone out of her hand. "I'll call for the ambulance myself."

Sarah sat down on the edge of the mattress, unable to hold herself up any longer. "Call Lou Kensington. He'll tell you it's true."

Boyce stared at her in disbelief and then turned to his partner. "Craig, help me get these two into the car and then you wait here with Wanda for the ambulance." He grabbed Sarah firmly by the arm. "Come on. We're going to take a ride over to the Charlemain and clear this up right now."

Worried sick now as to whether Tyler was still alive, Sarah did not say how relieved she was that she would not have to drive herself back to the fire.

Someone was shouting into the bullhorn again. "Duchamp! Polifax! Return for new instructions now! Tyler! If you can hear me, just hang in there! We're going to try to get you out!"

234

They knew he was in here, somehow they knew. Maybe they just couldn't find him, or maybe they just couldn't get to him. But if they came into the room next door, would they even notice the hole in the wall?

His lungs were starting to ache, and with a sinking feeling he realized that smoke was seeping into his closet from the space between the walls. And then the sound of a mechanical click suddenly reminded him of who he was and why he was there. The tape in his handheld recorder had come to an end and needed to be flipped over. Even if they never found him, maybe they could at least find his tape recorder with Wanda's confession on it.

He put his eye up to the hole again. At a right angle to the wall he was peering through was the outside wall of the bedroom with two windows in it. The window nearest to him was barely five feet away. If he had something heavy enough he might be able to heave it through that window and let them know where he was.

First he made sure he was able to get his whole arm through the hole right up to the shoulder. He flexed it a few times to make sure he had enough mobility. Then he withdrew it and quickly felt around in his backpack to see what he might have that would work. The only thing that had a remote chance of being solid enough to break the window was the tape recorder itself.

His lungs and throat felt like they were on fire now and his eyes stung fiercely. He decided to try a practice shot with something else to make sure he could hit the window. Grabbing one of his sneakers, he slipped it through the hole in his hand and then winged it to the left.

It bounced off the window with a resounding rattle of glass and landed on the floor in the middle of the room.

There was no time to waste. He gave his tape recorder a kiss for good luck. Closing his eyes, he flung it with all his might in the right direction. His raw arm scraped against the ragged plaster; his shoulder slammed painfully up against a two by four. But the wonderful sound of splintering glass made it all worth it.

He was having difficulty breathing now, so he rested where he was. He left his right arm hanging down the side of the wall in the room with the broken window, hoping that if somebody came they would notice it. He tried to picture what it must look like – the misplaced limb of a dismembered Barbie doll or one of those fake bloody arms that people hang out of their trunks.

He began to cough uncontrollably as he felt himself slipping helplessly into a state of unconsciousness.

He did not feel the hand that felt for a pulse in his wrist or the pickaxes that grazed his body as they pried the wall away. He recovered consciousness for a second but all he saw were a pair of steel blue eyes staring at him through a plastic shield. He was not aware of being draped over Ray Polifax's shoulders and carried out of the burning building. He did not know how quickly the EMTs had him into the life squad van or how swiftly they forced his lungs to breath oxygen again. And he never saw Sarah sobbing with relief in the back of a police car when she was told he was still alive. But only just.

CHAPTER FIFTEEN

"Is this it?"

"It must be. There's his truck over by the barn." Sarah pointed out Reed's pickup parked near a natural wood structure that appeared fairly new in comparison with the classic white farmhouse across the yard.

"If you can call that a barn. It looks more like a studio or workshop to me. A handy piece of architecture from the handyman himself." Tyler climbed stiffly out of the passenger side of the car. "Wow. This place has quite a view. Maybe it was a mistake bringing you here, Sarah. You might decide you want to have a go at it with this guy after all."

"Excuse me, but I was the one who drove you here," Sarah reminded him teasingly. She joined him on the other side of the car to admire the sight of the gently rolling green hills that surrounded the farm on all four sides. "The countryside is less extreme than around West Jordan. You couldn't really call these hills mountains."

They were silent for a moment, letting the peaceful beauty of the early evening settle in around them. "You're right, I could live here," Sarah commented after a few moments.

"Well, I couldn't. Not for very long, anyhow."

She squeezed his hand. "You could learn. You're not getting any younger, you might think about settling down one of these days."

Before he could reply, the sound of a screen door slamming announced that their arrival had been noticed. "Wow, what a great surprise! Reed! Tyler and Sarah are here!" Arden leaped over the three steps of the back porch and ran down the lawn to greet them, her fair curls bouncing, her gossamer skirt billowing in the evening breeze.

She looked like she belonged there, as though she had sprung fully grown from the green grass beneath her bare feet; like a wood sprite or dryad that would never age, but would always be her same fresh, beautiful, bouncing self. Still aching from his ordeal, Tyler felt infinitely older than her now. Someday she too would come to earth and feel her bones creak and her step grow heavier. For some reason that realization was more painful to him than anything he had gone through in the last few days.

"We saw you on TV! How are you?" Arden threw her arms around his neck and kissed him on the cheek. "I can't believe she tried to kill you! What a witch she's turned out to be!" Arden released him and stepped back, shaking her head. "I'm so glad she's not my real mother. I can't believe I used to wish she was."

Sarah had been watching Arden in amazement, wondering how she could be so lighthearted in regard to the truth about Wanda. But she only knew part of the story, there was plenty that they still had not disclosed to the TV reporters and newspapermen.

"Sarah. Welcome!"

She had not seen Reed approaching; he must have come from the barn or the other side of the house. In his own way, he also looked as much a part of the landscape as Arden did. He was wiping his hands on his jeans, on which circles of fresh earth still clung to the knees. "I'd give you a hug but my hands are filthy. I was just weeding the beans out back."

"Reed's been teaching me all about gardening. And about carpentry too. I've been helping him build a mud room off Mr. Johnson's porch."

Reed grinned. "She's actually got quite a knack for it. I'm going to see if I can hook her up with a crew of women carpenters that I know." He turned to Tyler. "I'm surprised to see you out and about so soon, Tyler. Sounds like you had quite a brush with death there."

"Well, you know I always wanted the inside story on the Carlisle hotel fires. And you couldn't have been more inside than I was."

They all laughed at his black humor and then trooped en masse up to the farmhouse. The conversation steered itself towards lighter subjects, away from the real issues at hand. Reed brought out some homemade beer and they sat on the porch, swatting at black flies and mosquitoes and talking about what life was like in this particular neck of Vermont.

Inside the house the telephone rang and Arden hopped up to answer it. "It's probably for her anyway. She's only been here a week, but all the single guys in town have got her number." Reed shook his head. "So while she's in there, give me the low down. How much do they have on Wanda?"

"Enough to put her away for life, I'd say. My guess is she's going to try to cop an insanity plea. And she'll probably get it. There's no question in my mind that she's insane." Tyler smacked a mosquito that was chewing on his knee.

"Hopefully they'll be able to prove that she killed Mimi," Sarah remarked. "How many of the blue moon fires they'll be able to pin on her is another thing. Some of them happened so long ago and she was really good at covering up her tracks."

"And of course she tried to kill me. I got a really good confession from her on tape before she set fire to the Charlemain."

"So it must have been Wanda who set fire to the barn at the inn," Reed mused.

"Yes, she was definitely trying to incriminate you and scare me away at the same time. And it was Wanda who ran my bike off the road also. She's been trying to warn me off ever since I started on this case."

Reed frowned. "Now explain to me again why Wanda needed to kill Mimi. And this blue moon thing. I don't really get that either."

239

The screen door slammed again as Arden rejoined them. "That was Teddy Ballard. Wants me to go with him on Sunday to the stock car races."

"The stock car races?" Reed made a face. "So are you going?"

"I don't think so. He's a real hunk but he doesn't have too much upstairs."

Sarah stood up. "Come on, Reed. Let's take a walk and I'll croon to you about the moon in June."

"You're too corny, Sarah," Tyler said squeezing her ankle.

"Not for me. I'll show you my woodworking studio."

"That sounds suspiciously like showing her your etchings!" Tyler called after them.

Arden settled down next to him on the ragged old couch that served as comfortably worn–in porch furniture. As she brushed against the bandage on his left arm, he winced audibly.

"Sorry. What happened there?"

"Fifty–seven stitches. Tore the skin wide open on a nail inside the Charlemain."

"Oh." Unusually tongue–tied, Arden played with the beaded drawstring of her skirt. After a moment, Tyler reached over and took her hand. "Arden, we need to talk about what happened and what's going to happen. They're probably going to ask you to testify in court and you need to be ready for that."

Even in the gathering dusk he could see her blue eyes widened. "Testify? You mean against Wanda?"

"For or against. Most likely for. The defense will probably use you as a character witness on Wanda's behalf."

"But what will I say?"

"You'll tell the truth, that she was a good mother, that she loved you very much and that you were never aware of any wrongdoing when you were growing up."

"Oh." She was silent again for a moment. "What about Lou? What will happen to him? Is he in trouble too?"

"I don't know. My guess is he'll probably be forced to retire from the fire department, but I don't think he'll have to go to jail. But I do know one thing."

"What's that?"

"When the initial shock and excitement dies down, it would probably help him to have your support." With his good arm Tyler killed a mosquito that had landed on her knee. "These bugs are a pain. Let's go inside."

Sarah perched on the edge of a workbench and Reed sat on a sawhorse. "Sorry, I don't entertain out here much. Now would you please start at the beginning and explain to me how you guys figured out all this stuff about Wanda."

Sarah sighed thoughtfully. "Well, somehow we've managed to keep the nitty–gritty beginning of this story away from the media but it's bound to come out in a few days, as soon as the forensic team compares dental records and what not. And Tyler and I both think it would probably be best if the truth came to Arden from you rather than from the local six o'clock news."

"What truth? And what are you saying about a forensic team?"

For an answer, she unbuttoned the breast pocket of the vest she was wearing and fished out a small object which she handed to him.

"It's an earring," she said. The stone is amber."

He turned it over in his palm a couple of times. "Where'd you get this? In one of Amber's boxes in Neil's attic?"

"No, actually Tyler picked it up off the ground at the Cherry Lodge excavation. It was lying a few feet from the skeleton they discovered there."

His eyes met hers, widening in disbelief. He swallowed a couple of times and then he closed his eyes as a visible shudder went through his whole body.

In a quiet voice, Sarah explained to him about the Cherry Lodge fire being the first of the "Blue Moon Fires" as they were coming to be known and about how Amber was supposed to have left suddenly for Hawaii that day. She told him about what Rick Sims had said to Tyler about Amber wanting to take baby Arden with her because she didn't want to ever have to come back to face Lou, whose attentions had been driving her crazy.

"By putting all of Amber's stuff in Neil's barn, Wanda tried to set it up to look like Neil was using her as an alibi for the fire when really it was the other way around."

Reed shook his head in amazement and waited for her to continue.

"We really don't think Lou ever knew that Amber was in the cellar of that burning building. Wanda must have led him to believe that Amber left on her trip early because of him. But we do know that Wanda never wanted to let Lou forget how he had betrayed their marriage under her own roof. A blue moon only comes once every few years, but she planned a fire and a sexual rendezvous of her own each time one occurred just to torment Lou.

"She was very clever. After all, she was a fireman's wife. Who knew better how many different ways to burn down a building? And no one ever suspected. A model citizen, a pillar of the community. The only threat to her existence was that someday her daughter might try to find her real mother."

"And discover that Wanda, her adopted mother had lied to her," Reed finished the thought for her, understanding where the story was going now. "And that's where Mimi fits in."

Sarah nodded. "Exactly. Mimi was the only wrinkle in a very smoothly made bed. Seven or eight years ago, Mimi got a letter from Arden asking about her mother. At the time, she was a working mother of two small toddlers, and had no interest in opening up anything to do with her own rather sordid time in Carlisle. But over the years, the guilt began to eat away at her, and finally, when she knew that Arden would finally be an adult and able to make her own decisions about her life, she decided to come back to Carlisle and set the record straight. She wanted you to know that Arden was yours and she wanted to talk to Wanda about letting Arden know that Amber had never showed up in Hawaii all those years ago."

"And so Wanda took care of Mimi the way she knew best. Even if it wasn't a blue moon. What a sick woman."

"It is scary to think of the weapons people will use in the name of love." Looking out the window, Sarah saw that it was totally dark now. Through the trees, the lights of the farmhouse glowed a warm yellow color.

"So it was very convenient for her that I came along as a scapegoat for Mimi's death."

"And very inconvenient for her that Tyler came up to investigate it."

"AND very inconvenient for me."

She turned away from the window to find him looking at her wistfully. "Reed—"

"You don't have to say anything, Sarah. It's obvious that even though you are the salt and Tyler is the pepper, you're a matched set of shakers that belong on the same table. But if you ever decide that it's over..."

"Thank you, Reed." She slid off the corner of the workbench and gave him a quick hug.

"Don't thank me. You and Tyler saved my ass. And besides, you gave me Arden. My life is pretty full right now." He turned off the light and they moved outside into the soft darkness.

"It's really fortunate that she was here when all this happened," Sarah went on.

"That's one way of looking at it. But Wanda might not have gone after Tyler if Arden hadn't left home."

"What I mean is that Carlisle is a circus right now. The TV and newspaper people would give anything to know where Arden is hiding out."

"She's not hiding out," Reed admonished her. "She lives here now."

Arden looked at Tyler across the wooden kitchen table. "Tyler, are you sorry about what happened between us?"

"Sorry? Well, a little bit. It made things pretty rough between Sarah and I for a few days. I guess mostly I just feel sorry that I'm not as young and footloose as you. It's hard for me to accept that fact."

"Well, I'm not sorry about it. I just feel like we're closer because of it."

"Maybe." The silence that followed was both comfortable and uncomfortable.

"Tyler? What about my real mother? Did you ever come up with any ideas of where she might be?"

Looking into her trusting eyes, Tyler had to bite his lip to keep from telling her. The time was not right yet. She still needed to come to terms with everything she had learned about her adoptive mother in the last few days.

"I'm sure we'll find her," he replied evasively. "But I wouldn't get your hopes up. Chances are if she hasn't contacted you for so many years, she may not still be alive."

"I know that. But I'd still just like to know."

They could hear Reed and Sarah coming up onto the porch. "Hey, what about Neil? Did he get off?" they heard Reed ask.

"Well, no. He's got a couple of counts of aggravated assault against him but considering the circumstances I think the judge will probably be lenient on him. I knew I was taking a risk involving him, but hey –" She looked through the screen door. The tiny holes of the screen gave a soft, hazy quality to the image of Tyler and Arden seated at the kitchen table beneath an old–fashioned hanging fixture. "It was worth it."

Neither of them said much on the drive back to West Jordan. The visit had left them both with a sense of closure that was satisfying yet strangely exhausting.

"I guess it's time for me to get back to the Myanmar article," Tyler remarked after a while. "I'm surprised Jim hasn't been on my case about it. I'll give New York a call in the morning."

"Oh." Sarah swallowed guiltily. "There's, uh, something I forgot to tell you."

"Like what?"

"The same day that Steve from Hawaii left the message about Wanda —"

"The same day you rescued me from the jaws of death."

"Yes, that very same day. Jim left you a message."

"Why do you sound so guilty? What's the big deal?"

"Well, he said that unless you faxed him the Myanmar story by five o'clock that day you would be, well, fired." She shrank down in her seat as far she possibly could while driving.

"Fired? That son of a — how many days ago was that?"

"I don't know. Three, four, five. You have to understand it was the farthest thing from my mind after the whole scene at the Charlemain. I'm really sorry, Tyler."

"It's not your fault. I couldn't have turned anything in by five that day anyway even if I hadn't been otherwise engaged. I've barely worked on that copy at all. Damn."

A heavy silence hung over them for the next few minutes. Finally Tyler said, "Well, Diana Stellano said she was sending me a hefty check. That should hold me over for a while."

"Actually, I'd like to hold you over for a while." Sarah reached over and laid a hand on his knee.

"You would, would you?" He laid his hand on top of hers.

"Why don't you stay here and help me run the inn for the summer? I could use a gourmet cook."

She nearly held her breath waiting for his reply.

"So how many times has Jim called that you haven't told me about?" he asked at last.

"Only the once. I swear it. On your knee, I swear it."

"You haven't been waiting to spring this idea on me?"

"Only for about five years. But really, the thought just occurred to me. Let's try it, Tyler. You could freelance from here. Besides, you're getting good at this missing persons thing. Maybe you should do a little advertising."

"You mean WE'RE getting good at it." He squeezed her hand. "What the hell, I'll give it a try. I don't have much else on the horizon. Except maybe a book about the Blue Moon Fires."

"And dinner in Key West."

"What? Oh, right." He'd forgotten about his promise to her in the hospital.

Sarah turned into the parking lot. The headlights illuminated the open framework of the barn; Reed had promised to come back and finish it before the summer was out. She looked over at the lighted windows of the inn. The task of managing it had seemed so defeating before; suddenly it did not seem quite so insurmountable.

"I'm beat. I think it's early to bed for this invalid," Tyler announced.

"Not so fast, sweetie. You've got to plan tomorrow's menu first," Sarah laughed.

"Oh, yeah. Well, guess who's your midnight snack?"

Leaning on each other, they went inside.

ABOUT THE AUTHOR

A lifelong lover of travel, mysteries and creative expression, Marilinne Cooper has always enjoyed the escapist pleasure of combining her passions in a good story. She lives in the White Mountains of New Hampshire and is also a freelance copywriting professional. To learn more, visit marilinnecooper.com.

ALSO BY MARILINNE COOPER

Night Heron

Butterfly Tattoo

Blue Moon

Double Phoenix

Dead Reckoning

Jamaican Draw

Made in the USA
Columbia, SC
09 August 2018